EDWARD MARSTON was born and brought up in South Wales. A full-time writer for over forty years, he has worked in radio, film, television and theatre and is a former chairman of the Crime Writers' Association. Prolific and highly successful, he is equally at home writing children's books or literary criticism, plays or biographies.

www.edwardmarston.com

a&b

INSPECTOR COLBECK'S CASEBOOK:

THIRTEEN TALES FROM THE RAILWAY DETECTIVE

EDWARD MARSTON

Allison & Busby Limited
12 Fitzroy Mews
London W1T 6DW
www.allisonandbusby.com

First published in Great Britain by Allison & Busby in 2014.
This paperback edition published by Allison & Busby in 2014.

A CIP catalogue record for this book is available from
the British Library.

10 9 8 7 6 5 4 3 2 1

ISBN 978-0-7490-1618-0

Typeset in 11/16 pt Sabon by
Allison & Busby Ltd.

The paper used for this Allison & Busby publication
has been produced from trees that have been legally sourced
from well-managed and credibly certified forests.

Printed and bound by
CPI Group (UK) Ltd, Croydon, CR0 4YY

To train-lovers everywhere

PREFACE

Detective Inspector Robert Colbeck first came into existence in 2003. An American publisher, Crippen and Landru, invited me to put eighteen of my stories together in an anthology, *Murder Ancient and Modern*. A nineteenth story was to be published separately and given to everyone who bought the anthology. At that point in time, *The Railway Detective*, the first book in the series, had been commissioned. A short story seemed like an ideal opportunity to give Colbeck a trial run on the page. It was called 'The End of the Line' and is the last story in the present anthology. Readers of the series will see how much Colbeck has matured in every way since his first outing.

I grew up with steam locomotives. My father and my uncle were engine drivers and other members of the wider family worked on the railway in some capacity. Since I was born and brought up on the corner of Railway Street, I heard – day and night – trains of every description steaming to and from Cardiff

General station. Whenever we went to coastal resorts like Penarth, Barry Island or Porthcawl, we travelled by rail from the much smaller Queen Street station. Steam trains were dirty, smelly, noisy, cramped, uncomfortable and frequently late but we loved them.

It was no surprise, therefore, that the first radio play I sold to the BBC was set largely on a train. When I later adapted it for television, British Rail supplied a carriage with the side cut away. We put it on rollers so that it could be rocked and used back projection to give the impression of speed and movement. The railway also featured heavily in *Bright's Boffins*, a children's TV comedy series I created and helped to write. In fact, one thirteen-part series was set in a disused railway station. The climax in the last episode was a high-speed chase of one steam engine by another. What the viewers didn't realise was that we only had the use of one engine so – thanks to a bit of televisual trickery – it was actually chasing itself.

I'd always wanted to celebrate the early years of steam and The Railway Detective series has given me the chance to do so. Railways were the defining phenomenon of the Victorian age, transforming lives in a way that was unimaginable beforehand. They had a profound effect on the nature of crime, enabling the villains to flee the scene very quickly and, by the same token, giving the police increased mobility. Crimes on the railway itself grew steadily in number. There is thus no shortage of work for the Detective Department at Scotland Yard. Robert Colbeck, Victor Leeming and Edward Tallis will always have their hands full.

My sincere thanks go to my literary agent, Jane Conway-Gordon, for her enthusiastic support of the series and to Susie Dunlop of Allison & Busby for introducing Colbeck to an ever-widening audience. My wife, Judith, deserves a special mention because she made me read each of these stories aloud to her so that I could hear the infelicities in a first draft. For any errors that sneaked through, I hang my head.

EDWARD MARSTON

CONTENTS

WETTING THE COAL

Dawn was breaking when the locomotive backed slowly but noisily towards the coal stage. Tall, brick-built and topped by a massive water tank, it was a ghostly shape looming above them. As they came to an abrupt halt beneath the chutes, Ezekiel Ryde, the fireman, urinated over the dwindling stock of coal in the tender.

'Always keep it wet,' he said, cheerfully. 'It burns better that way.'

'Then make sure you use the hose when you're up there,' said the driver.

'I will, Perce.'

Percy Denton waited patiently until Ryde had finished relieving himself and adjusted his trousers. The driver looked into the tender.

'We need two tub loads.'

'Are you sure, Perce?'

'There's less than half a hundredweight so we can manage a full ton.'

'Right.'

Ryde was a stocky man in his late twenties who thrived on the physical demands of his job. Jumping down from the footplate, he crossed to the ladder that rose vertically against the wall of the coal stage. It took him seconds to climb up the metal rungs and step into the cavern above. Ryde had expected to shovel coal from the bunker into the two small wheeled tubs but, to his surprise, both had already been filled. He switched on the tap and used a hose to give both piles of coal a thorough soaking. Bending down, he then gave the first tub a firm shove and sent it rolling along the ramp towards the chute where it was tipped up so that its load cascaded down into the tender. The thunderous noise was accompanied by clouds of coal dust, rising up at him out of the gloom.

When he pulled the empty tub back to its original position, he addressed the full one and was puzzled by its weight. Although it seemed to have the requisite half-ton of coal, it felt lighter than its predecessor. Ryde heaved it forward and tipped it down the chute, causing another small avalanche. But this one was very different. As the second load hit the tender, Percy Denton let out a cry of alarm.

'What's wrong?' asked Ryde, mystified.

'*He* is,' replied the driver, pointing at the tender.

'Who are you talking about?'

'Can't you *see*, man?'

Ezekiel Ryde narrowed his eyelids and peered down. In the poor light he could just make out the shape of a human body sprawled lifelessly across the pile of coal.

'This will annoy my father-in-law,' said Colbeck with amusement.

'It annoys *me*, sir,' complained Leeming.

'Because he works for a rival company, he hates it when we travel on the Great Western Railway. He loathes Brunel.'

'I loathe *anyone* who builds railways.'

'But they've been such a boon to us, Victor,' argued Colbeck. 'Even you must admit that. Look at this latest case. News of the murder was sent to us by telegraph as soon as the body was discovered. The station is over fifty miles from London. Think how long it would take us by stagecoach. The train will get us there in a fraction of the time.'

'That doesn't mean I have to *enjoy* the journey, sir.'

Leeming folded his arms and looked disconsolately out of the window. He had a rooted objection to rail travel. When they arrived at their destination, however, he would forget the discomfort and throw himself into the investigation with alacrity. For that reason, Colbeck did not try to reconcile him to a railway system that had revolutionised the lives of the whole nation. Instead, he speculated on the nature of the crime they'd been engaged to solve. The telegraph's scant details had been enough to rouse his interest and set his mind racing. Didcot was a tiny Berkshire village that had grown steadily since the station was opened there. As a junction, it saw rail traffic going in different directions. Any killer wishing to flee the scene of the crime would have a choice of exits.

Colbeck wondered which one he might have taken.

Percy Denton and Ezekiel Ryde were at once reassured and intimidated by the arrival of two detectives from Scotland Yard. Though both were strong men, they'd been badly shaken by the discovery at the coal stage. Denton had almost fainted and Ryde had promptly emptied the contents of his stomach. As Colbeck and Leeming interviewed them in the stationmaster's office, the murder took on more definition. The victim, it transpired, was Jake Harnett, a porter in his early twenties. What he was doing in the coal stage, nobody knew. A single man who lived locally, Harnett hailed from Bristol. Colbeck made a mental note to arrange for his family to be informed of his death. Passing on the bad news to Harnett's landlady was a task he reserved for himself.

Inevitably, the versions given by the two men were jumbled, repetitive and even contradictory at times. Colbeck sought to make them relax.

'I see that your locomotive is one of the Iron Duke class,' he said.

'Yes,' said Denton in amazement. 'You recognised it?'

'Well, it is very distinctive. Was it built in Swindon?'

'Bolton.'

'Then it's one of the later batch,' said Colbeck. 'Built by Rothwell and Co.'

As he talked knowledgeably about the locomotive's salient features, he could see that he had a calming effect on both men. He was speaking their language. As a result, the rest of the interview was more productive.

Having dispatched Leeming to ask the station staff about their dead colleague, Colbeck made his way up the rising mound to the rear of the coal stage. Open to the elements at the front and the back, it was a cold, unwelcoming place with a coal bunker, two tubs, a large shovel and a hose attached to a tap in one wall. There was no sign of blood or any other evidence of a violent assault. What interested him was the size of the tubs. They were quite compact. To cram the body of a grown man into one of them would not have been easy. Jake Harnett would have been bent double before being covered with coal. It explained why one truck was lighter than the other.

Colbeck walked over to the storage hut to which the body had been moved. The railway policeman on guard stood respectfully to attention when Detective Inspector Robert Colbeck introduced himself. Harnett lay on his back, covered by a rough piece of sacking. When he drew it back, Colbeck solved two mysteries. The victim was short and slight enough to be concealed in a tub and the cause of death was apparent. Harnett was wearing a suit and Colbeck, the dandy of the Metropolitan Police, winced when he saw how badly it had been torn, scuffed and blackened. However, the coal dust could not hide the blood that had seeped through the man's waistcoat. He'd been stabbed in the chest.

When Leeming had finished talking to the staff, he met Colbeck on the station platform to compare notes. A clear portrait of

Jake Harnett had emerged. He was conscientious and popular with his colleagues and with passengers alike. Facial injuries sustained when he fell into the tender had made it impossible for Colbeck to notice how allegedly handsome he'd been.

'He had an eye for the ladies, sir,' said Leeming, disapprovingly.

'That shouldn't necessarily make him a target for murder.'

'Jealousy is a powerful motive.'

'Indeed, it is, Victor,' agreed Colbeck. 'What was the general feeling?'

'They didn't so much admit it as hint at it,' said Leeming, 'but they suspected that Harnett might have . . . taken liberties with the wrong person.'

'In other words, she was a married woman.'

'Yes, sir.'

'Were any names suggested?'

'Not at first but I could see that they all had suspicions. So I reminded the stationmaster that a murder would bring bad publicity to the GWR. If he knew anything, he *had* to tell us. I was blunt with him, sir.'

'Did your bluntness produce a result?'

Leeming nodded. 'Her name is Rose Brennan,' he explained. 'She's the wife of a local dairy farmer. Whenever she came with milk churns, Harnett was quick to help her and pay compliments. He was a charmer, by all accounts.'

'I fancy that Mrs Brennan's husband was immune to his charms.'

'Oh, he was, Inspector. According to the stationmaster, Edgar Brennan was enraged when he saw the attention his wife was getting. He took Harnett aside and threatened him. I think Brennan could be our man.'

'There's a huge difference between "could be" and "definitely is" so we mustn't rush to judgement. How far away is the Brennan farm?'

'It's less than a mile.'

'Good,' said Colbeck, 'we can discuss the possibilities on the walk there.'

Edgar Brennan was a big, brawny man in his early forties with a weather-beaten face. He looked startled when the detectives arrived to speak to him. He showed his visitors into the low-ceilinged parlour with a bare floor and sparse furniture. When Colbeck explained the reason for their visit, Brennan was impassive.

'Don't you have a comment to make, sir?' enquired Colbeck.

'No,' replied the other, gruffly.

'Yet you knew Mr Harnett.'

'I disliked the man.'

'You did more than that,' said Leeming. 'You were heard threatening him.'

Brennan stiffened. 'I'd every right to do so, Sergeant.'

'When did you last see him?'

'It was not after dark at the station, if that's what you mean. I haven't seen him for days so you can stop accusing me.'

'We're not accusing you, Mr Brennan,' said Colbeck. 'You happen to be an interested party, that's all. We came to break the sad news.'

'It's not sad news to me, Inspector.'

'I'm sorry you take that attitude.' He exchanged a glance with Leeming. 'Could we speak to your wife, please, Mr Brennan?'

'There's no need to talk to Rose.'

'I'm afraid that we must insist, sir.'

The farmer was aggressive. 'You can't come barging in here, telling me what I can and can't do.'

'You're obstructing the police in the exercise of their duties,' said Colbeck, meaningfully. 'That renders you liable to arrest. Why are you afraid to let us talk to Mrs Brennan?'

'That's none of your business.'

Leeming confronted him. 'We are making it our business, sir.'

There was a tense moment as the farmer squared up to him, fists bunched. In the event, the argument went no further because the door opened and Rose Brennan stepped into the room. She was taken aback at the sight of the two well-dressed visitors. For his part, Colbeck was momentarily stunned. Several years younger than her husband, the wife had the kind of arresting natural beauty that was unimpaired by her tousled hair and rough working clothes. She reminded Colbeck so much of his own wife, Madeleine, that he stared in wonder at her. It was left to Leeming to introduce them and to explain why they were there.

Rose gasped. 'Jake Harnett has been *murdered*?'

'We believe that you knew him, Mrs Brennan.'

'The man was a nuisance to my wife,' said the farmer, curtly. 'But Rose never really knew him.'

'Let Mrs Brennan speak for herself,' suggested Colbeck.

Rose glanced nervously up at her husband before shaking her head.

'What Edgar tells you is right,' she said, uneasily. 'I met Jake . . . Mr Harnett, that is, at the station a few times but I never really got to know him.'

'There you are, Inspector,' said Brennan, dismissively. 'We can't help you. If you're looking for people who warned Harnett, I'm not the only one, by any means. There's Tom Gilkes, for instance.'

Colbeck's eyebrow lifted. 'Who is he?'

'Tom is part of the family. His wife, Lizzie, is my sister-in-law. She had the same trouble with Harnett as Rose.'

'Where might we find Mr Gilkes?'

'He lives at Greenacres Farm. You came past it on your way here.'

'Then we'll bid you good day,' said Colbeck, looking from one to the other.

Brennan had a smirk of satisfaction on his face but Rose was patently upset and kept biting her lip. Colbeck opened the door to leave then turned round.

'We may be back,' he said, quietly.

On the walk to the other farm, Leeming's earlier prediction had hardened into fact.

'Brennan did it,' he said.

'I dispute that.'

'He's full of anger, sir. And he's more than strong enough to kill a man.'

'Granted,' said Colbeck, 'but you have to remember *how*

Harnett was killed. He was stabbed through the heart. That would be far too quick a death to appease Brennan. He'd have preferred to batter him to death with his fists. Then,' he added, 'there's his wife to consider.'

'She was young enough to be his daughter.'

'What happened when she heard about the murder?'

'She was very shocked.'

'And what would you do if your wife had a terrible shock?'

'I'd put my arms around Estelle to comfort her.' Leeming realised what he was being told. 'Brennan did nothing. He just stood there. Doesn't he care for his wife?'

'He cares enough to guard her jealously,' said Colbeck, 'and she's obviously afraid of him. But he's not our man. If he'd gone off somewhere last night, it would have shown in her face. Rose Brennan is not clever enough to hide her emotions. That look in her eye gave the game away.'

Leeming was confused. 'What game is that, sir?'

'Harnett wasn't a nuisance to her at all. She *enjoyed* his interest.'

Aided by a yapping dog, Lizzie Gilkes was rounding up the cows and driving them towards the milking parlour. She carried a stick and used it viciously on the rumps of any animals who tried to stray. Lizzie was an older version of her sister. Though she lacked Rose's beauty, she had the same shapely figure. When she saw the two men approaching her, she crossed over to them.

'Can I help you?' she asked, warily.

'I believe that you can,' said Colbeck. 'Are you Mrs Gilkes?'

'That's me – Lizzie Gilkes.'

Colbeck performed the introductions then told her why they were there. News of the murder made her step back in disbelief.

'Jake Harnett is *dead*?' she gulped. 'He can't be.'

'When did you last see him?'

'It was yesterday morning when I put our churns on the milk train.' She heaved a sigh. 'I can't believe it. Who would want to . . . ?' She broke off as a thought struck her. 'Someone's been gossiping, haven't they? That's why you're here. Someone told you about Tom.'

'Your husband was mentioned,' admitted Leeming.

'Well, he didn't do it,' said Lizzie with a touch of belligerence. 'I can swear to that. Tom works all hours during the day so he needs every ounce of sleep he can get. He was snoring beside me all night.'

'How do you know?'

'Are you married, Sergeant?'

'Yes, I am, as a matter of fact.'

'You'd know if your wife wasn't beside you in bed wouldn't you? Tom and me are two of a pair. We work till we drop then sleep like logs. Don't take my word for it,' she went on. 'Tom will say the same.'

When she hauled her husband out of the milk parlour, he ambled towards the detectives. Gilkes was a tall, rangy man in his late forties with a beard.

'What's this about Harnett?' he asked. 'Is it true?'

'I'm afraid that it is, Mr Gilkes,' said Colbeck.

'Then find the killer for me. I'd like to shake his hand.'

'Don't speak ill of the dead, sir,' said Leeming, reproachfully.

'You didn't know Harnett.'

'Did he bother your wife?'

'No, he didn't,' she said, sharply.

'But he bothered my sister-in-law, Rose,' said Gilkes. 'He cornered her one day and I had to rescue her. I gave the little bastard a flea in his ear. Edgar did the same – that's Rose's husband.'

'We've met Mr Brennan,' explained Colbeck. 'We had the feeling that he would not be sending a wreath to the funeral.' Gilkes gave a harsh laugh. 'It's not a laughing matter, sir. You are, after all, a suspect.'

'It was nothing to do with me!' protested Gilkes.

'I *told* you that, Inspector,' said Lizzie, hotly.

'Nevertheless,' said Colbeck, 'we're bound to take the threat made to Mr Harnett seriously. Your husband is like Mr Brennan. My guess is that neither of them minced their words.'

'You're quite right there,' agreed Gilkes. 'I told that slimy porter to . . .'

He was silenced when his wife put a hand on his arm. She took over.

'I can see how it looks to you, Inspector,' she said with a conciliatory nod, 'and I don't blame you. Tom and Edgar had to speak to Jake Harnett but that's all they did. Edgar is no killer and I'd swear on my mother's grave that Tom didn't murder Harnett. Yes, it's only fair that they're suspects, I suppose, but you'll have to look elsewhere for the person you want.'

'I accept that,' said Colbeck, graciously. 'One last question, if I may. Why did your sister marry a much older man?'

'Edgar's first wife died,' said Gilkes, sadly. 'She was trampled to death when she tried to stop a runaway horse. She was with child at the time. It was a tragedy.'

'That's why my sister did it,' said Lizzie. 'She took pity on him.'

May Tranter was a plump, grey-haired woman in her fifties with a local accent. When she heard that her lodger had been murdered, she was so overwhelmed with horror that she collapsed into Leeming's arms. He eased her into a chair. It was minutes before she was able to speak.

'What was Mr Harnett like?' prompted Colbeck.

'Oh, he was a delight to have around the house,' she said. 'We treated him like the son we never had. He always had a smile on his face.'

'Did he have any enemies, Mrs Tranter?'

'Dear me! No, he didn't! Who could dislike Jake?'

'Someone obviously did,' murmured Leeming.

'They teased him at the station but that was only because he was so handsome. I think they were all jealous. Jake was a good, kind, hard-working man. He was always ready to help us. My husband was a platelayer till someone was careless with his pickaxe,' she told them. 'He's never been able to walk proper since. Jake used to do the things that Eric just couldn't do any more.'

'He sounds like an ideal lodger,' said Colbeck.

'He was, Inspector – in every way.'

'Was there a young lady in his life?'

'There must have been. A man with such good looks is bound to make hearts flutter.' She gave a girlish laugh. 'I know that mine did. Not in an improper way,' she added, quickly. 'I just felt . . . motherly towards him.'

'Did he go out often?'

'Yes, he went for a walk most evenings.'

'Are you sure that it was only a walk?'

She frowned. 'It wasn't my place to pry, Inspector.'

'What time did he go out yesterday evening?' asked Leeming.

'It was quite late, Sergeant. Eric and I were just about to go to bed.'

'Did he tell you where he was going?'

'He was off on one of his walks. Jake looked so smart, especially when he was wearing his uniform at work. He always took pains with his appearance.' She grabbed Colbeck's shoulder to plead with him. 'You will catch the man who did this to him, won't you?'

'The killer will soon be arrested, Mrs Tranter,' said Colbeck, confidently. 'I can guarantee it.'

'Where are we going?' asked Leeming as they headed for the railway station.

'We're going to retrace Harnett's footsteps.'

'Are we off to the coal stage, then?'

'No,' said Colbeck, 'because that isn't where he went.'

'How do you know?'

'Put yourself in his position, Victor. You're a young man on his way to an assignation. When you're wearing your best clothes, you'd never go anywhere near dirt and dust. I've been to the coal stage,' Colbeck reminded him, 'and it is markedly deficient in romance. It would cool any man's ardour.'

'So where did Harnett go?'

'It was somewhere not too far away, I suspect.'

'Ah,' said Leeming, reading his mind. 'I realise what you mean now, sir. Harnett arranged a rendezvous with a young lady but her husband found out about it and came in her stead – or he simply followed her. Whichever way it happened, he killed Harnett and carried his body to that truck.'

'That's why it can't have been too far away.'

'Why not leave the body where it fell?'

'I think that someone resented that handsome face and that smart suit. They wanted to besmirch the immaculate porter. Squeezing him into a small tub was a final humiliation for him.'

When they reached the coal stage, Colbeck looked in all directions. His gaze settled on a stand of trees nearby. They'd offer protection from the wind and a degree of privacy. Leeming, meanwhile, was studying the bunker.

'Does the fireman have to shovel all that coal into the tubs?'

'Yes, Victor, it's dirty work. Would it interest you?'

'No job on the railways interests me, sir.'

Colbeck laughed. 'Not even being a detective?'

He walked towards the trees with Leeming at his heels. They split up to look for clues that might indicate a struggle had taken place. Colbeck searched for the place most suitable for an assignation. He found it at the very heart of the copse. It was a clearing overhung with branches that made it feel enclosed and secretive. Colbeck was certain that he'd found Jake Harnett's lair. Working systematically, he went from tree to tree, examining the ground beside each of them with care. It was slow, painstaking work but he was rewarded with the thrill of discovery.

'Victor!' he called out.

'I'm coming,' said the other, blundering through the undergrowth and into the clearing. Seeing what Colbeck held up, he was disappointed. 'It's only a piece of cloth.'

'Oh, I think it may turn out to be a useful clue.'

Leeming was baffled. 'Why are you grinning like that?'

They were not the only visitors to Greenacres Farm. Edgar and Rose Brennan had got there before them. They were in the parlour with Tom Gilkes. At the sight of the two detectives, the farmers became combative. Brennan took a step towards them.

'How many times must I tell you?' he demanded. 'I did not kill Harnett.'

'Neither did I,' said Gilkes, arms akimbo.

'Stop pestering us, Inspector.'

'Jake Harnett was a menace to women. He deserved what he got.'

Leeming wagged a finger. 'That's a very cruel thing to say.'

'Don't ask for an apology,' warned Brennan.

'What about you, Mrs Brennan?' asked Colbeck, turning to her. 'Do you take the same view as your husband and your brother-in-law?'

'No, I don't,' she whispered, lowering her head.

'Yes, you do, Rose,' scolded her husband.

'You were the one he pestered most,' said Gilkes.

Rose looked up. 'What happened to him was . . . very wrong.'

She burst into tears. Revealingly, it was Tom Gilkes who put a consoling arm around her. Edgar Brennan looked distantly embarrassed. Colbeck felt that he would take his wife to task when they were alone together. Leeming was eyeing the two men, trying to work out which of them had put an end to the porter's life. Colbeck's interest, however, had shifted to an entirely new suspect.

'Where's Mrs Gilkes?' he asked.

'She's feeding the chickens,' said Gilkes. 'Why do you need to bother her?'

'I just want to confirm something she said earlier, sir.'

'Haven't you asked her enough questions?'

'I won't keep her long.' As Gilkes moved towards the door, Colbeck raised a hand. 'Don't bother, sir. I'll find her.'

He went out, leaving Victor Leeming to face the hostile glares of the men.

Lizzie Gilkes had just finished feeding the chickens when Colbeck strode towards her. There was truculence in her tone.

'What are you doing here, Inspector?'

'I came to discuss your husband's sleeping habits.'

'I'm busy. I can't talk now.'

'And there's another reason I came,' said Colbeck, holding up the piece of cloth. 'I came to return this. It came off the dress you were wearing last night.'

She bridled. 'I don't know what you're talking about.'

'I'm talking about the rendezvous you had with Jake Harnett in that stand of trees near the coal stage. It's where I found the piece of cloth that he must have torn off your dress as you stabbed him in the chest.' Her face blanched. 'You were far too cool when we spoke earlier, Mrs Gilkes. You'd rehearsed what to say. But I saw you wielding that stick when you rounded up the cows. You're a strong and determined woman. You could easily drag the body of a slight man like Harnett to the coal stage from that clearing.'

'I was asleep all night behind my husband,' she said, voice rising.

'*He* was asleep but you were awake. When you were certain that he'd slumber for hours, you slipped out and made for the station. It's only ten minutes away. The sergeant and I timed the walk. You met Harnett, killed him, put the body in that truck, covered it with coal then came back here – all in well under half an hour.'

Lizzie backed slowly away towards the barn. Colbeck followed her.

'You and Mr Harnett were close friends, weren't you?'

'No,' she snarled. 'I despised him.'

'Then why did you agree to an assignation?'

'I didn't, Inspector. Jake wasn't expecting me. He never looked twice at me when Rose was around.' She was rancorous. 'I've had to put up with years of seeing my sister get all the praise and attention. I'm the plain one, she's the beauty. Jake took it too far.'

'Mrs Brennan was fond of him, wasn't she?'

'She liked him a lot more than she liked that oaf of a husband. Rose let him write to her. When she replied, she begged me to deliver the letter. Can you imagine how painful that was for me?' she wailed. 'I was just a go-between. It was all I was good for and Jake rubbed it in. So I lied to him.'

'Yes,' said Colbeck, recreating the scene, 'you told him that your sister would meet him last night but you went there instead. In the dark, he couldn't tell the difference between you – until it was too late.'

'I was doing it to save Rose,' she said with passion. 'Edgar would have beaten her black and blue if he'd realised what she was up to.'

'That's arrant nonsense. Don't pretend that you thought of anyone else but yourself. You were jealous, Mrs Gilkes, jealous of your sister to the point where you couldn't bear to see her enjoying a romance with a man nearer her age.' He moved towards her. 'Because *you* wanted Jake Harnett, you made sure that your sister would never have him.' He beckoned her. 'I shall have to place you under arrest.'

Lizzie was like a hunted animal, looking for a means of escape. Snatching up a hayfork leaning against the barn, she jabbed it at him. He stepped out of reach.

'You're ready to fight for your life,' said Colbeck with feigned admiration. 'I take my hat off to you, Mrs Gilkes.'

As he whisked the top hat from his head, he flung it in her face and distracted her long enough to duck under the fork and grapple with her. Colbeck twisted her wrist until she dropped her weapon then he tried to overpower her. But years of manual work had toughened her and she fought back hard, yelling obscenities and trying to bite him. It was no time for gentlemanly politeness. Lifting her bodily in one swift move, Colbeck carried her to the horse trough and dropped her into the water with a splash. Before she could begin to get out, he had the handcuffs on her.

* * *

When they caught the train back to Paddington, Lizzie Gilkes had been left in custody and her family had been left in a state of utter confusion. Victor Leeming was amazed that a woman had committed the murder and equally astounded at the way Colbeck had dropped her in the horse trough.

'It's not the sort of thing I'd expect you to do, sir,' he said.

'It worked, Victor. That's all that matters.'

'You should have called for me to help you.'

'I managed on my own,' said Colbeck. 'Lizzie Gilkes was a desperate woman with a fire blazing inside her. I put it out by wetting the coal.'

RAIN, STEAM AND SPEED

Light rain was falling as the train clanked into Berkhamsted station and came to a halt in a cloud of smoke and steam. Anxious to set off again, the locomotive seemed to be throbbing with irritation. No passengers alighted from any of the carriages but two sturdy figures stepped out of the brake van and waited until the guard passed them an object that was only inches in depth but a yard in height and some four feet wide. It was wrapped up well. Although it was quite heavy, one man carried it without much difficulty. His companion walked beside him.

When they left the station, they saw the carriage waiting for them as arranged. A short, stout, middle-aged man with his hat pulled down over his face was standing beside the vehicle, beckoning them over. The couriers went across to him and eased their precious cargo into the carriage. The short man climbed in after it and shut the door behind him.

One of the couriers banged hard on the door.

'Our orders are to see it delivered,' he protested.

'You've just done that,' said the passenger, brusquely.

'We must hand it over to Lord Stennard in person.'

'Your work is finished.'

To emphasise the point, he produced a revolver and aimed it at each man in turn. They backed away in alarm. The driver cracked the whip and the two horses surged into action. Before the couriers could even move, the carriage gathered speed and disappeared around a bend. Somewhere behind them, the train was also on the move, belching smoke and spitting steam as it left the station in its wake. The couriers looked at each other in dismay. There would be awkward questions to answer.

Just when Colbeck thought that he knew everything there was to know about Edward Tallis, the superintendent surprised him by revealing himself as an unlikely art lover. Seated behind his desk, Tallis told the inspector about the daring theft.

'We must get that painting back,' he insisted.

'I didn't realise that you were one of Turner's admirers, sir.'

'What I admire is British genius and Turner certainly had his share of that. I've no time for the fanciful daubing of foreign painters – especially those purveyors of French decadence – but I do enjoy looking at the work of our home-grown artists.'

'I appreciate good art from whatever country it comes,' said Colbeck.

'Then you need to be both more discriminating and more patriotic. However,' Tallis went on, 'we are wasting valuable time. Lord Stennard wants that stolen painting retrieved as soon as possible. Question the couriers.'

'Do you have an address for them, sir?'

'They're right here at Scotland Yard.'

'Good.'

'When you and the sergeant have interviewed them, make your way to Berkhamsted and try to pacify Lord Stennard.'

'We'll do our best.'

'A word of warning,' said Tallis.

'What is it, sir?'

'I've met the august gentleman. He's a peppery individual at the best of times, impatient, demanding and unpredictable. Handle him with great care or he's likely to explode in your face.'

Without realising it, Tallis had just described himself with great accuracy, so Colbeck had to suppress a smile. After long years of coping with the superintendent's hot temper, he felt that he was qualified to handle anybody. About to leave, he remembered something.

'It's rather ironic, isn't it, sir?'

'What is?'

'*Rain, Steam and Speed* was stolen outside one of the stations on the London and North Western Railway. Yet the painting depicts a train crossing the Thames by means of the bridge at Maidenhead and that's on the Great Western Railway. It would have been more appropriate if the crime had taken place on the GWR.'

'Enough of your drollery!' said Tallis, clicking his tongue. 'And, for heaven's sake, don't make that observation to Lord Stennard. He hates railways. That's why no tracks have ever been laid across his land.'

'If he hates railways,' said Colbeck, perplexed, 'why does he want a painting that features a train?'

'I wouldn't dare to ask him.'

Lord Stennard was a tall, slim, red-faced man in his sixties with a mane of white hair. He walked slowly down one side of his gallery, inspecting each painting in turn through the monocle held to his right eye. When he reached the end of the room, he crossed to the opposite wall to examine the exquisite portrait by Sir Joshua Reynolds before moving on to one of John Constable's landscapes. There were thirty paintings on display in the gallery. Some were owned by him but the majority were on loan for a limited period. It was less than a week before the great and the good of the county converged on Stennard Court to enjoy the private exhibition. Ostensibly, the collection was there for the benefit of his friends but, in reality, it was to satisfy his obsession with the work of great artists.

To have so many fine paintings under his roof at the same time was a source of inestimable pleasure to him and he walked up and down the gallery every day to savour the collection. This latest perambulation, however, did not yield the same excitement. When he pulled himself away from Constable, he was confronted by the yawning space reserved for one of Turner's masterpieces, *Rain, Steam and Speed*. Instead of arriving to complete the exhibition, it had been snatched away. The gap on the wall made him quiver with rage.

'Damn you, Inspector Colbeck!' he growled. 'Where the devil are you?'

* * *

When Colbeck and Leeming went into the room, the two couriers were seated. The younger of them, Stagg, stood to his feet but his companion, Richmore, remained in his chair. After performing the introductions, Colbeck told Stagg to sit down. The latter was dark-haired, bearded and in his thirties. But it was the surly Richmore who caught the inspector's attention. Running to fat, he was a broad-shouldered man in his forties with, impossibly, a face even uglier than that of Victor Leeming. When the questions began, it was Richmore who supplied most of the answers. It turned out that he'd once been a policeman.

'Why did you give the job up?' asked Leeming.

'Too much hard work and too little pay,' replied Richmore.

'There are other rewards than money.'

'I never noticed any.'

'Tell us exactly what happened from the moment you picked up the painting at the National Gallery,' said Colbeck. 'You start first, Mr Stagg.'

Stagg was quiet and hesitant but he had a good memory, even recalling the times of the departure from Euston and arrival at Berkhamsted. Richmore took over and gave a more embellished account, doing his best to shift the blame for the loss of the painting onto his colleague. He stressed that he'd had far more experience than Stagg and had an unblemished record since working at the National Gallery.

'Why did you take the painting by train?' asked Colbeck.

'I thought it would be quicker and safer,' said Richmore. 'We sat in the brake van and guarded it like two hens sitting on a clutch of eggs.'

'You say that the man in the carriage had a Colt revolver.'

'That's right, Inspector.'

'Had you ever seen one like it before?'

'Yes,' said Richmore. 'When the Great Exhibition was on, Samuel Colt was displaying his wares. I went along to see them. I wish I could have afforded to buy one. It would have been a lot more use than this.'

He pulled a weapon from inside his coat and Leeming instinctively drew back.

'That's an old five-shot pepperbox pistol,' said Colbeck. 'It's no match for a Colt. What about you, Mr Stagg? Were you armed?'

Stagg shook his head. 'We didn't expect trouble.'

'I did,' claimed Richmore. 'I'm always on guard.'

'Then why did you get robbed so easily?' asked Leeming.

'It wasn't my fault, Sergeant. I was distracted by Stagg.'

'That's not true,' said Stagg.

'You kept jabbering at me.'

'No, I didn't.'

'Right,' said Colbeck, taking charge, 'this crime only took place because someone knew that you'd be catching a particular train. How many people at the National Gallery were aware of your travel arrangements?'

'Very few,' said Stagg, 'and they're all above suspicion.'

'Did you tell anyone else where you were going today and at what time?'

'Not a soul, Inspector – I didn't even tell my wife or my son.'

'*Somebody* must have known,' insisted Leeming, turning to Richmore. 'What about you, sir? Did you mention it to your friends, perhaps, when you had a drink with them? It's very easy to let things slip out unintentionally.'

Richmore was adamant. 'I never speak to anyone about my work.'

It was not until they were on the train to Berkhamsted that the detectives had a moment to review at leisure what they'd been told. On one point, they were in complete agreement.

'Richmore was lying, sir,' said Leeming.

'I got the feeling that he's had plenty of practice at it.'

'He was full of himself. When a man like that has a few beers inside him, he can't resist boasting to his friends.'

'I fancy they'd be more likely to be acquaintances, Victor,' said Colbeck. 'Who'd want to have a braggart like Richmore as a friend? Would you?'

Leeming grimaced. 'I'd run a mile.'

'What did you make of Stagg?'

'I felt sorry for him. He got blamed for everything.'

'He's got a wife and child to support.'

'Yes – losing his job would be a big blow.'

'Stagg looked so unhappy.'

'So would I if I'd had to work alongside a bully like Richmore.'

Colbeck smiled. 'We both work alongside a bully named Tallis,' he pointed out. 'Did you know he was a devotee of British art?' He saw Leeming's eyes widen in astonishment. 'Yes, it was a shock to me as well. Despite evidence to the contrary, the superintendent has finer feelings, after all. Going back to the theft,' he said. 'If Richmore really *was* involved, he'd need an accomplice in Hertfordshire who could hire a carriage to make off with that painting.'

'What will the thief do with it, sir?'

'Well, he won't hang it up on his wall, I can assure you of that.'

'Then why bother to steal it?'

'I can see that you're not familiar with Turner's paintings. This particular one is famous and it's inspired many artists – my wife among them. Madeleine went to see *Rain, Steam and Speed* at least ten times at the National Gallery. Unfortunately,' said Colbeck, 'her own paintings of locomotives have nothing like the same value. As for the thief, I daresay that he might try to sell it back to Lord Stennard.'

'But Lord Stennard doesn't actually own it.'

'He'll feel responsible for its loss. After all, it was because of his request that it left the security of London and travelled to Berkhamsted.'

'What sort of man is he?'

'According to the superintendent,' warned Colbeck, 'he's inclined to rant and rave. Can you imagine how Mr Tallis would behave if unsolved crimes soared in the capital, newspapers pilloried him mercilessly and the commissioner threatened him with dismissal?'

Leeming was rueful. 'I can imagine it all too well, sir.'

'Then you've got a clear idea of what to expect from Lord Stennard.'

The blistering harangue went on for the best part of five minutes. Stennard upbraided the detectives for not getting to his house sooner, for making no apparent progress in the investigation and for not understanding the significant part that Turner would have played in the exhibition. It was only when he ran out of breath that the tirade finally abated. Leeming felt so uncomfortable that he ran a finger around the inside of his collar but Colbeck was unperturbed. He conjured up an emollient smile.

'When it comes to art, my lord,' he said, 'you are a man of impeccable taste.'

Stennard was taken aback. 'Oh . . . thank you, Inspector.'

'This gallery is a tribute to your skill in selecting the very best paintings.'

'Art is the nearest we mortals can get to the quintessence of beauty.'

'I don't see anything beautiful about a train crossing a bridge,' grumbled Leeming, 'for that's all that Mr Turner gave us, I'm told.'

'You must forgive the sergeant,' said Colbeck. 'He has yet to accept the railways as a vital part of our lives. In Turner's gifted hands, a locomotive became a thing of pure magic.'

'I might agree, Inspector,' observed Stennard, waspishly, 'if only the painting were actually here for me to enjoy it.' He indicated the stretch of blank wall. 'What will my guests think when they see that?'

'Hang a mirror there,' suggested Leeming before quailing under Stennard's basilisk stare. 'It's better than a bare space.'

'We have days to spare yet,' said Colbeck, 'so there's still a possibility that Turner will take his rightful place in the collection. As for our delay, my lord, do not ascribe it to idleness. It was occasioned by the fact that we had to talk to the station staff to see if any of them had witnessed the theft of the painting. Also, of course, we needed to speak to your coachman.'

Stennard blinked. 'Why on earth did you bother *him*?'

'It was because I couldn't understand why he was not at the station to meet the train as arranged and bring the painting here with the two couriers. His explanation was that he'd been held up because a cart had lost a wheel and overturned on the road, blocking his way. As a result of the accident,' Colbeck continued, 'it was over twenty minutes before he could continue on his way – except that it wasn't an accident, of course. It was a deliberate means of stopping him so that another vehicle could get to the station in his stead.'

'This is a conspiracy!' yelled Stennard.

'It was a well-devised plan.'

'The National Gallery will never forgive me.'

'I'm sure that they'll be mollified when you return the painting.'

'But I don't have it in order to send it back, man.'

'Oh, I suspect that it will be on that wall before too long,' said Colbeck, confidently. 'My guess is that the thieves stole it in order to sell it back to you – or back to the National Gallery.'

'The Gallery needn't be involved,' said Stennard, quickly. 'This is my problem and I'm ready to pay in order to make amends. Should I offer a reward for the safe return of the painting, Inspector? Will that lure them out of cover?'

'They'll need no encouragement, my lord. In all probability, they'll already have set a price. You must agree to hand over the money,' advised Colbeck. 'It's our best chance of making arrests.' The door opened at the far end of the gallery and the butler entered, carrying a letter on a silver salver. Colbeck beamed. 'Ah, it looks as if the demand has come sooner than I expected.'

Being married to the Railway Detective meant that Madeleine Colbeck shuttled between joy and loneliness. When her husband involved her in the investigative progress – albeit covertly – she was exhilarated. When a case took him hundreds of miles away from home, however, she felt as if she'd been cut adrift. On hearing the details of his latest investigation, she expressed horror.

'Someone *stole* my favourite painting?' she cried in despair.

'It was only for a short while, my love.'

'Laying rough hands on a work of art is sacrilege – like defacing a church.'

'Nothing will be damaged, Madeleine,' Colbeck promised her. 'If the painting is defaced in any way, it loses its value. They know that. It will be returned in good condition or they won't get a penny.'

'Is Lord Stennard really going to pay them what they demand?'

'He'll give the *appearance* of doing so. Victor and I will be on hand to ensure that we arrest the thieves and recover the money.'

'Will it really be as simple as that?'

'No,' he confessed. 'There may be unforeseen difficulties.'

'Take care, Robert,' she urged. 'One of them has a gun.'

'Victor will be armed. The superintendent agreed to that.'

'What about you?'

He smiled. 'I'll rely on my charm and affability.'

Seeing the protest hovering on her lips, he silenced it with a kiss. They were in the studio where Madeleine had been working all day. Her latest project was a painting of a locomotive that her father had driven when he worked for the LNWR. Unbeknown to Caleb Andrews, it was a present for his forthcoming birthday. Colbeck ran an eye over his wife's latest creation.

'Where locomotives are concerned, Turner couldn't hold a candle to you.'

She laughed. 'That's nonsense, Robert, and you know it.'

'His work is so opaque while yours has a bracing directness.'

'*Rain, Steam and Speed* is real art whereas my aspirations reach no higher than producing a passable photograph of my subject.'

'Don't underrate your talent,' he told her, studying the canvas. 'You bring a locomotive to life, Madeleine, and a lot of people agree with me. If all they wanted was a photograph, they wouldn't rush to buy your prints.'

'Tell me about this exhibition.'

Colbeck did so at length. During his visit to the gallery, he'd made a mental note of every painting on display so that he could tell his wife about the treasure trove of art. As the names of Old Masters rolled off his tongue, Madeleine listened with fascination. Each new painting elicited a fresh gasp of pleasure.

'Oh, Robert!' she sighed. 'I'd love to see the exhibition.'

'Then you shall,' he said, seriously. 'I'll make it a proviso. If the painting is returned to Lord Stennard, he *has* to let you have a private viewing of his gallery.'

Victor Leeming blenched when he saw the horse he had to ride. The animal had a fiery look in its eye and bucked as soon as he approached it. A reluctant rider, he doubted his ability to stay in the saddle. Colbeck patted the horse's neck to calm it down then helped the sergeant to mount.

'I don't feel safe up here,' complained Leeming.

'I asked for the most docile horse in the stable. Once he gets used to you, Victor, you'll have no trouble.' He indicated the carriage. 'You only have one horse to worry about. I have two.'

Dressed as a coachman, Colbeck's task was to drive Lord Stennard to the place appointed for the exchange of money and painting. Leeming was to follow at a discreet distance. Now that he was in the saddle, he felt that he might just be able to control the animal, whereas he would struggle badly to drive the coach. Stennard came out of the house with a small leather bag in his hand. Colbeck opened the door so that his passenger could get into the carriage. After closing it behind him, Colbeck climbed up onto the box seat and gathered up the reins. They set off.

The demand sent to the house had been well-written on crisp paper. The instructions were reinforced with a warning. If Stennard deviated in any way from what he was told to do, the painting would be destroyed. Colbeck knew that it was an empty threat. As the carriage rolled through the estate, he glanced over his shoulder to make sure that Leeming was keeping out of sight. The designated spot was on the open road about a mile away. When they finally reached it, they discovered that there was a change of plan. A long stick had been thrust into the soft ground beside the road. Fluttering at the top of it was a letter, held on by twine. Pulling the horses to a halt, Colbeck descended, picked up the letter and handed it to Lord Stennard who'd opened the door of the carriage.

'What's the problem, Inspector?'

'They're being very cautious, my lord,' replied Colbeck. 'We've been drawn out into the open so that they can have a good look at us. We'll be directed to a more sheltered location.'

Stennard read the letter. 'Take the left fork,' he ordered.

Colbeck resumed his role as the coachman. He flicked the reins and sent the horses off at a brisk trot. Leeming only knew the directions to the place they were just leaving. Colbeck was worried that he'd be unable to find them once they plunged into the woodland ahead but he had to obey orders. Taking the left fork, he drove on a winding road through trees so tall and close together that they blocked out most of the light. After half a mile, they came to a large clearing. As they emerged from the shadows, they found the sun dazzling. Colbeck brought the coach to a halt some twenty yards or more from a horse and cart. A thickset man in his fifties jumped down from the cart.

'Where's the money?' he demanded.

Stennard got out of the coach. 'Show me the painting first.'

The man lifted the painting off the back off the cart and walked across to them. Colbeck watched as the man removed the cloth so that Stennard could see *Rain, Steam and Speed*. He was so delighted that he handed over the leather bag at once. Before he released the painting, the man insisted on counting the money. Because he was poorly dressed and spoke roughly, Colbeck knew that he was merely a go-between and not one of the actual thieves. The inspector sensed that they were under surveillance from the trees ahead. That was where the real villains were lurking. Of Leeming's whereabouts, he was less certain. The sergeant might have lost their trail completely.

Having counted the money, the man turned round and signalled to someone concealed behind him. Then he gave the painting to Stennard, leapt up onto the cart with the leather bag and snapped the reins. The cart swung round before heading off at speed in the opposite direction. Stennard, meanwhile, was on his knees, holding the frame in his hands as if embracing a kidnapped child who'd been returned to him. Colbeck got down from the coach to look at Turner's work and felt a thrill of recognition. It was truly a masterpiece.

'Isn't it magnificent?' said Stennard. 'I'd have paid twice the money for it.'

'With luck, my lord, it won't have cost you anything.' Colbeck looked around. 'We'll just have to hope that Sergeant Leeming was able to stay on our tail.'

Leeming, in fact, was more concerned with staying in the saddle. Playful rather than mutinous, the horse kept bucking at unadvertised moments or going too close to bushes as if trying to brush off its rider. When the coach had reached its first location, Leeming had remained out of sight and watched through a telescope. Only when he saw the vehicle disappear into woodland did he come out of hiding and ride on. Pursuit was difficult but he eventually got within sound of the coach. He could hear its wheels rumbling over the road. When the noise stopped, however, he was lost. All that he could do was to wait patiently and listen.

Long, slow minutes rolled past. He kept his ears pricked but he heard nothing. The horse, however, became aware of a sound and sprang into life. Before he realised what was happening, Leeming was being carried through the undergrowth at a canter. He emerged from cover onto an open road and saw that he was chasing a horse and cart that was rattling along at full tilt. He dug his heels into his mount to urge it on and soon began to close on the fleeing cart. Leeming knew, however, that catching it up was easier than stopping it. Though he had a pistol in his pocket, he needed two hands to hold onto the reins. In the event, the driver lost his nerve. As Leeming galloped level with him, the man heaved hard and brought the cart to a gradual halt. It took Leeming a little longer to rein in his horse. He'd never been so pleased to jump from the saddle. Apart from anything else, it allowed him to take out the pistol.

'Don't shoot, sir!' pleaded the man.

'I'm arresting you for the theft of a painting.'

'I didn't take it – I swear it. He paid me to hand it over, that's all. I needed the money, sir. I've just been turned out of my cottage and have only the clothes I stand up in. Take pity on me,' he begged, extending both palms in supplication. 'Give me something to relieve my misery.'

'I have just the thing,' said Leeming.

And he clapped the handcuffs onto the man's wrists.

Madeleine Colbeck was overjoyed to learn that her wish had come true. When they were actually on their way to Stennard

Court the next day, she still couldn't believe it.

'This is a wonderful treat for me, Robert.'

'You deserve it, my love.'

'I never thought that Lord Stennard would agree to it.'

'You underestimate your husband's powers of persuasion,' said Colbeck with a grin. 'The truth of it is that he was so pleased to get the painting back that he could refuse me nothing – even though the case is not yet over.'

'Do you think you'll ever recover that money?'

'I'm certain of it, Madeleine. I already have two suspects in mind.'

'Will Victor Leeming be joining us at the gallery?'

'No,' replied Colbeck. 'He's too busy making enquiries about the suspects I just mentioned.'

'Shouldn't you be doing that?'

'Wait and see, my love.'

They left the train at Berkhamsted and hired a cab to take them to the house. Stennard gave Madeleine a cordial welcome and insisted on taking her by the arm to show her around the exhibition. Colbeck trailed behind them. Drooling over each painting, their host took them from one to the other in sequence. At the end of one row, they crossed the gallery to work their way along the other wall. It was when they reached Turner's painting that Stennard's happiness swelled to its peak.

'It's the painting I most covet in the whole exhibition,' he said with a grand gesture. 'I'd give anything to own it.'

'So would lots of collectors,' remarked Colbeck.

Madeleine was staring at it with open-mouthed admiration, studying once again its extraordinary use of colour. It was worth making the journey there simply to relish the work of a genius. All of a sudden, she stiffened and took a step forward to peer more closely. When she turned around, she was in evident distress.

'It pains me to say this, my lord,' she said, deferentially, 'but it's a fake.'

'How dare you even suggest it!' exclaimed Stennard.

'My wife knows the painting extremely well,' said Colbeck.

'And so do I. That's a genuine Turner – take my word for it.'

'Then where is the hare?' asked Madeleine, pointing. 'In the right-hand corner, there should be a hare. It's not very distinct in the original but it's there.'

Stennard used his monocle to scrutinise the canvas. Refusing to believe that he'd been duped, he searched for the tiny animal but to no avail. It was not there. Madeleine had exposed a fraud.

'There's one way to make certain,' said Colbeck, lifting the frame from its hood and lowering it to the floor. He turned it round to examine the back. Fresh tacks had been put into it. There were holes where the original ones had been removed. 'The evidence is fairly conclusive, I think.'

Stennard's heart missed a beat as the saw the telltale holes. Turner's work had been removed and a copy of it put in its place. His earlier delight was transformed into cold fury. He rounded on Colbeck.

'We've been tricked,' he roared. 'I paid all that money for a fake.'

'I had a feeling that it might be a clever copy,' said Colbeck, smoothly. 'They kept the original so that they could extract even more money out of you. In time, you'd have received a second demand.'

'A second demand?' Stennard goggled. 'What *is* going on?'

Colbeck moved away. 'Excuse me, my lord. I have to authorise some arrests.'

Herbert Stagg counted out the money with a gleeful chuckle. The short, stout man who'd called at his lodging was Ruthin Woodvine, an art dealer. He was paying Stagg for the valuable information he'd received. Woodvine shared his elation.

'And the best part of it is that there's more to come,' he said, smugly. 'When he realises that he paid for a fake, Stennard will stump up three times that amount to get the original back. We'll have made a small fortune.'

'Richmore would kill me if he knew what I'd done.'

'You pulled the wool over his eyes good and proper.'

'The real credit belongs to you, Mr Woodvine. You *know* about art.'

'I know about people,' corrected the other, 'and know just how much they're prepared to cough up for something they're desperate to hang on their wall. Come,' he went on, getting up from the table. 'We must go and celebrate.'

Stagg scooped up the money. 'The first drink is on me.' A loud knock on the door made him thrust the cash into his pocket. 'That's probably my landlord, asking for the rent. I'll be able to pay him now.'

He opened the door and found himself facing a determined Victor Leeming. Behind the sergeant were two uniformed policemen. Leeming doffed his hat.

'Good day to you, Mr Stagg,' he said. 'I have a warrant for your arrest.' His gaze moved to the art dealer. 'And you, I suspect, sir, may be Ruthin Woodvine. You are also wanted in connection with the theft of a painting so you'll have to come along with us. The game is up, I fear.'

Stagg was rooted to the spot but Woodvine thought only of escape. Opening his frock coat, he put a hand inside to grab his revolver but he was far too slow. Leeming was on him at once, felling him with a single, uncompromising blow to the chin. As the art dealer collapsed at his feet, Leeming relieved him of the weapon.

'Thank you, Mr Woodvine. I'll take that.'

'There must be some mistake,' gibbered Stagg.

'There was, sir, and it was your cousin, the coachman, who made it. If you tell barefaced lies to Inspector Colbeck, you're bound to come to grief in the end.'

Edward Tallis was basking in the reflected glory of his officers. A crime had been solved, the perpetrators were behind bars and he had a glowing letter of thanks from Lord Stennard on the desk in front of him. He sought clarification.

'What aroused your suspicion about the coachman?' he asked.

'It was that story about being held up on the way to the station,' said Colbeck. 'He claimed that the road was blocked. Yet when I drove a carriage along it, I couldn't see any place where he could be impeded by an overturned cart. He could simply have driven around it. You see, sir,' he continued, 'there had to be collusion with someone at Stennard Court. It was the coachman. There was no second carriage that picked up the painting at the station. Lord Stennard's coachman drove there at the agreed time with Woodvine as his passenger. Richmore wouldn't have been able to identify the coachman again because it was raining and the man was hidden beneath a cape and hat. Stagg, of course, was part of the gang. The daring theft was only made possible by the fact that the coachman was his cousin.'

'Remarkable!' said Tallis, sitting back. 'Turner's original painting is back in its frame and the malefactors will each collect a very long prison sentence. There's just one thing that puzzles me,' he added, stroking his moustache. 'Lord Stennard is an acknowledged connoisseur in the art world. Why didn't he spot that the painting he bought back was a fake?'

'Lord Stennard is blind in one eye and has such poor vision in the other that he uses a monocle. The coachman was aware of that. When the information was passed on to Woodvine, the art dealer saw his chance. I feel sorry for Lord Stennard. He can take in the sheer wonder of a painting in its entirety but his impaired eyesight means that he can't appreciate the fine detail.'

'So who *did* establish that the painting was a fake?'

Colbeck thought fondly of Madeleine. 'We were lucky to have an expert at hand, Superintendent.'

THE RAILWAY CHURCH

Old age had sapped his strength and bent his back but Simon Gillard's devotion to duty was unaffected by the passage of years. Indeed, now that he had retired, he was able to dedicate himself completely to his work as churchwarden. Gillard needed no encouragement to drag himself out of bed on the Sabbath. He was always up early, lifted by a feeling of importance and filled with pure joy. It was the one day of the week when his bones never ached. During the short walk to church that morning, he went through his usual ritual, reminding himself of what he had to do before the congregation arrived for a service of Holy Communion.

Gillard had to let himself into the church, unlock the cupboard in the vestry so that the sacristan could prepare the altar, slide the hymn numbers into the wooden display board above the pulpit, open the bible on the lectern at the appropriate page for the readings and set the offertory plate in position. There would be a number of other tasks to complete before the others turned up. Gillard knew the routine off by heart and drew immense solace from the thought that he was doing God's work and serving the community. As he turned the key in the lock, the door opened smoothly on well-oiled hinges and he stepped inside.

There were people in Wolverton who sneered at the church of St George the Martyr because it had been built fifteen years earlier by the London to Birmingham Railway Company to supply the spiritual needs of their employees and their families. Critics disliked what they saw as a church built on traditional lines with a decidedly utilitarian air about it. It blended in with the terraces of small, plain, relentlessly uniform railway houses. Some argued that the church had no history, no grandeur, no sense of being on consecrated ground and no right to be there. Gillard disagreed. To him, it was as inspiring as the greatest of medieval cathedrals. Alone in the church of St George the Martyr, he felt that he was in direct communication with the Almighty. Standing in the nave, as he did now, he looked towards heaven and offered up a silent prayer.

His gaze then alighted on the altar and he froze in horror. Stretched out in front of it was the body of a man. His head had been smashed open and was soaked in blood. He lay there like some grotesque sacrifice. It was too much for Gillard. He gasped, tottered then fell forward into oblivion.

The Sabbath was no day of rest for the detectives at Scotland Yard. If an emergency arose, they had to respond to it. Robert Colbeck and Victor Leeming had each attended services at their respective parish churches, only to return home to an urgent summons from their superintendent. Edward Tallis told them everything that could be gleaned from the telegraph he'd received from Wolverton, then he dispatched them there. An unwilling rail traveller on weekdays, Leeming was even gloomier when he was forced to catch a train on a Sunday.

'I'd hoped to spend some time with my children,' he moaned.

'I, too, had other plans,' said Colbeck.

'It's unfair on Estelle. She looks after them during the week. It's only right that I do my share whenever I can.'

'Police work often occurs at inconvenient hours, Victor. It can be irritating but we must try to see it from the point of view of the victim. He didn't get himself killed on a Sunday morning specifically to ruin our leisure time with the family.'

'Why bother us?' asked Leeming. 'This is a case for the local constabulary.'

'Because they're aware of our reputation, the LNWR asked for us by name. Doesn't that make you feel proud?'

'No, sir, it makes me feel annoyed. We're being imposed upon.'

'This murder has a unique distinction.'

'Yes, it's made me miss the best meal of the week with the family.'

'Take a less selfish view,' advised Colbeck. 'The crime took place in the first church ever built by a railway company.'

'If you ask me,' grumbled Leeming, 'the railways are a crime in themselves.'

Colbeck laughed. 'That's precisely why I *don't* ask you,

Victor. Tell me,' he went on, 'are your children still playing with the toy train I bought them?'

'That's different, sir.'

'Are they?'

'Yes,' said Leeming, reluctantly. 'They play with nothing else.'

'So the railway does have a useful purpose, after all.'

'They're too young to understand.'

'And you're far too old *not* to understand its value to us.' He became serious. 'A man has been slaughtered in a church – and on a Sunday. Doesn't that make you want to track down the killer?'

'It does, sir,' said Leeming, roused. 'What he did was unforgivable.'

When a brutal murder took place, there was, as a rule, universal sympathy for the victim. That was not the case with Claude Exton. Staff on duty at Wolverton station all knew and loathed the man. More than one of them seemed pleased at the news that he was dead. What they did do was to provide useful background details for the detectives. Leeming recorded them in his notepad. Exton was an unpopular member of the community, a shiftless man of middle years who lurched from one job to another. He'd been banned from one pub for causing an affray and was thrown out of another for trying to molest the landlord's wife. Other outrages could be laid at Exton's door.

'In other words,' said Leeming, 'he was a real reprobate.'

'That's putting it kindly,' muttered the stationmaster.

'Was he a churchgoer?' asked Colbeck.

'No, Inspector. He always boasted that the only time they'd get him across the threshold of a church was for his funeral. It seems he was right about that.'

The collective portrait of the deceased was unflattering but it gave them a starting point. Colbeck and Leeming walked swiftly to the church. Everyone had heard the news. People were standing outside their houses discussing the murder with their neighbours. A noisy debate was taking place on a street corner. There was a small crowd outside the church itself and a uniformed policeman was blocking entry to the building. When he saw them approach, the vicar guessed that they must be the detectives and he rushed across to introduce himself. In the circumstances, the Reverend John Odell was surprisingly composed. He was a short, tubby man in his fifties whose normally pleasant features were distorted by concern.

'This is an appalling crime,' he said. 'A church is supposed to be a place of sanctuary against the evils of the world. I thank God that I got here early enough to stop any of my parishioners seeing that hideous sight.'

'Were you the first to discover the body?' asked Colbeck.

'No, Inspector. That gruesome task fell to the warden, Simon Gillard. When I arrived here with the sacristan, we found the poor fellow prostrate in the aisle. He'd fainted and injured his head as he hit the floor.'

'We'll need to speak to him.'

'Then you'll have to go to his house. As soon as he'd recovered, I had him taken straight home. Then I sent for the police.'

'Is the body still inside the church?' wondered Leeming.

'Yes, it is,' replied Odell. 'I want it moved as soon as possible, obviously, but I thought you might prefer to see it exactly as it was found. Claude Exton was not a churchgoer but he nevertheless deserves to be mourned. Since we couldn't use the church, I conducted a very short, impromptu service out here and we prayed for the salvation of his soul. Then I urged the congregation to disperse to their homes but, as you see, the news has attracted people of a more ghoulish disposition.'

'Human vultures,' murmured Leeming. 'We always get those.'

'I'm assuming that the warden unlocked the church this morning,' said Colbeck. 'Who else has a key?'

'Well, I do, naturally,' said Odell, 'and so does the other warden but he's ill at the moment. Between us, we hold the only three keys.'

'So how did the killer and his victim get inside the church?'

'That's what puzzles me, Inspector. It was locked overnight.'

'Is it conceivable that any of the keys went missing?'

'Oh, no,' said Odell, firmly. 'The other warden and I are extremely careful with our keys and Simon Gillard is so dutiful that I wouldn't be surprised if he takes his to bed with him. How two people got inside the church is a mystery. Only one, alas, came out alive.'

After plying the vicar with some more questions, the detectives asked the policeman to let them into the church. He stood aside so that they could open the door. Some of those lingering nearby edged forward to take a peek but Colbeck shut the door firmly behind him. The atmosphere inside the church was eerie. It was quite warm outside but both of them shivered involuntarily. Consecrated ground had been violated by a foul murder. There was a strange sense of unease. They walked down the nave and into the chancel to view the body. Though both of them had seen many murder victims, they were shocked. Colbeck was also curious.

'What does it remind you of, Victor?' he asked.

'That man in Norwich, sir,' said Leeming. 'He'd been battered to death with a sledgehammer. His head was just like pulp.'

'Look at the way the body has been arranged in front of the altar.'

'That's just the way he fell.'

'I don't think so. There's something almost . . . artistic about it.'

Leeming frowned. 'Is there?'

'It's reminiscent of those medieval paintings that depict the slaughter of Thomas Becket. He was hacked down in front of the altar by four knights who thought they were doing the king's bidding.'

'It doesn't look like that to me, sir. And if what they say is true, he's certainly no saint like Becket. Exton was a real sinner.'

'Then we could be looking at the *punishment* for his sins.'

Colbeck knelt down to examine the corpse. Around the mouth were traces of vomit. He searched the man's pockets but they were empty. He then gently pulled back the sleeves of Exton's jacket.

Leeming was perplexed. 'What are you looking for, Inspector?'

'Something I expected to find,' said Colbeck, 'and you can

still see traces of the marks on his wrists. As we've heard, Exton abhorred churches. He'd never have come in here and stood obligingly in front of the altar so that someone could bludgeon him to death. I think that he was knocked unconscious elsewhere, tied up and gagged, then brought here to be killed.'

'Then we're looking for a strong man, sir. Exton was heavy.'

'Let's get him out of here,' said Colbeck, standing up. 'He's defiling the church. Tell the vicar to summon the undertaker and ask that constable to frighten the crowd away. We don't want an audience when we move him. However much of a rascal he was, Exton is entitled to some dignity.'

Simon Gillard was propped up in his armchair with bandaging around his head. Still shocked by the ghastly discovery in the church, he was in a complete daze. When his wife admitted Colbeck to the house and took him into the parlour, her husband was staring blankly in front of him.

'This is Inspector Colbeck from Scotland Yard,' she explained. 'He needs to talk to you, Simon.' There was no response. 'I'm sorry, Inspector,' she went on. 'He's been like this for hours.'

'That's understandable,' said Colbeck. 'Perhaps you can help me instead.'

'It was my husband who found the body.'

'Does he enjoy being a warden?'

'Oh, yes,' she said, 'he loves it. Since he retired, the church has taken over his life – both our lives, in fact. I'm one of the cleaners and I organise the flower rota.'

Winifred Gillard was a short, roly-poly woman with grey hair framing an oval face that still had traces of her youthful appeal. She talked fondly of her husband's commitment to the church since his retirement from the railway, and she spoke with great respect of the vicar.

'Does your husband ever lend the key to the church to anybody?'

'Only to me,' she replied. 'Simon guards his bunch of keys like the family jewels – not that we have any, mind you. When he first became warden, he used to sleep with them under his pillow.'

Colbeck smiled inwardly. The vicar's earlier comment had some truth in it.

'So nobody else would have access to the keys?'

'Nobody,' she insisted, 'nobody at all.'

Victor Leeming was asking the same question of the other warden, Adam Revill, an emaciated man in his sixties with a few tufts of hair on a balding head. He was patently unwell and sat in a chair with a blanket around his shoulders. Every so often, he had a fit of coughing.

'No, Sergeant,' he asserted. 'I never lend the key to the church to anybody. If I'm not using it, it stays on a hook in the kitchen. Maria will tell you the same.'

'It's true,' she said. 'Uncle Adam takes his duties seriously. It grieves him that he's been unable to carry them out for a while. The doctor told him to stay indoors and rest.'

'I'd be lost without Maria,' said Revill, giving her arm an affectionate squeeze. 'She's been a godsend. Since my wife died, I've had to fend for myself. The moment I was taken ill, Maria began popping in to look after me.'

'I only live four doors away,' she said.

Maria Vine was an attractive woman in her thirties with a soft voice and a kind smile. Fond of her uncle, she wanted no thanks for keeping an eye on him.

'I take it that you both knew Claude Exton,' said Leeming.

'Yes, we did,' replied Revill, curling a lip. 'We knew and disliked him.'

'That's not entirely true,' said his niece.

'He was a good-for-nothing, Maria.'

'I know – and he was a nuisance to everybody. But he wasn't that bad when his wife was alive.' She turned to Leeming. 'She was killed in a railway accident, Sergeant. It preyed on Mr Exton. That's when he took to drink.'

'He seems to have had a lot of enemies,' observed Leeming.

'I'm one of them,' said Revill.

'Yes, but you didn't hate him enough to kill him, sir. And even if you did, you'd hardly do it inside a church.'

'That's true, Sergeant. A church is sacred.'

'I feel sorry for Mr Gillard,' said Maria. 'He actually found the body.'

'Yes,' croaked Revill, 'I pity Simon. But don't ask me to shed any tears for Claude Exton. He's gone and I'm glad.'

'That's a terrible thing to say,' chided Maria. 'Don't speak ill of the dead.'

The rebuke set Revill off into a fit of coughing that went on for a full minute. Leeming waited patiently. Maria was embarrassed on her uncle's behalf.

'I'll make a cup of tea,' she announced. 'Would you like one, Sergeant?'

'Yes, please,' said Leeming.

As soon as she went out of the room, Revill stopped coughing. He crooked a finger to beckon Leeming closer.

'Don't listen to Maria,' he said. 'She always tries to think the best of people.'

'That's a good attitude to take, sir.'

'What she told you about Exton's wife is not true. It may have looked like an accident but we know the truth.' He lowered his voice. 'She committed suicide.'

When they met up outside the church, the detectives were pleased to see that the body had been removed, the crowd had vanished and the door was locked. As a result of their interviews, both had acquired the names of people with a particular reason to detest Claude Exton. They compared their notes.

'Let's start with the people who appear on both lists,' suggested Colbeck.

'The man that Mr Revill kept on about was George Huxtable. He and Exton came to blows once,' said Leeming. 'Exton was bothering Mrs Huxtable.'

'She wasn't the only woman who caught his eye.'

'He seems to have been a menace.'

'What would you do if someone made a nuisance of himself to Estelle?'

'Oh, I can tell you that,' said Leeming, forcefully. 'I'd have a quiet word with him and, if that didn't work, I'd punch some sense into him.'

'That might render you liable to arrest.'

'I wouldn't care, sir. Whatever it took, I'd protect my wife.'

'And I'd do the same for my wife,' said Colbeck. 'Yet neither of us would go to the lengths of killing the person inside a church. The very idea would revolt us.'

'It didn't revolt the man who murdered Exton.'

'How can you be sure it was a man, Victor?'

'No woman would be able to carry his weight, sir.'

'Two women might,' argued Colbeck. 'And one woman might move him on her own if she used a wheelbarrow. I'm not claiming that that's what happened. I just think we should keep an open mind. A woman would have been capable of luring Exton into a position where he was off guard. No man could do that.'

'Could any woman hate him enough to smash his head open?'

'Why don't you put that question to Mrs Huxtable?'

'What will you be doing, sir?'

'I'll be talking to Harry Blacker. He's the gravedigger.'

Anthony Vine more or less carried him up the narrow staircase. Revill protested but he knew that they were right. He was better off in bed where he could drift in and out of sleep. Maria was waiting in the bedroom to help her husband lift the older man into position. She plumped the pillows to make him comfortable and drew the bedclothes over him. After stifling a cough, Revill managed a smile of gratitude.

'You're both Good Samaritans – you really are.'

'We're family,' said Vine, 'and this is what families do for each other.'

'But it's so much trouble for you.'

'Don't be silly, Uncle Adam,' said Maria. 'It's no trouble at all. I haven't forgotten how good Aunt Rachel was to me when I was ill as a child. You used to come with her sometimes and tell me those wonderful ghost stories.'

'That's the first I've heard of it,' said Vine with a grin. 'I didn't know that he enjoyed scaring the daylights out of my wife.'

'I was only six at the time, Anthony,' she reminded him.

'All that I heard at that age were Bible stories.'

A few years older than his wife, Vine was a wiry individual of middle height with conventional good looks. Six days a week, he worked in the standard garb of a fireman but he now wore his suit. There was no sign of the routine dirt he picked up during his time on the footplate.

'I still think it could be George Huxtable,' whispered Revill.

'Speak up, Uncle Adam,' said Maria.

'He and Exton were always snarling at each other.'

'That doesn't mean George killed him,' reasoned Vine. 'And if he did, he'd be more likely to dump him in the river than leave him in a church. George Huxtable only ever came near the church at Easter and Christmas.'

'He and his wife are not the only ones,' said Revill, darkly. 'We have too many occasional Christians in Wolverton.'

'Don't worry about that now,' said Maria, moving to the door. 'We're off now, Uncle Adam. One of us will pop in from time to time to see if you need anything. Anthony will bring you something to read, if you like.'

'The only thing I read on the Sabbath is a Bible. And I still say it was George Huxtable,' he added. 'I've seen it coming for months.'

* * *

As soon as he laid eyes on the man, Victor Leeming could see that he'd have no trouble carrying a body over his shoulder. George Huxtable was a hulking man in his forties with a pair of angry eyes staring out of an unprepossessing face. His wife, May, by contrast, was a dainty woman with a fading prettiness. Side by side, they were an incongruous couple. When the sergeant introduced himself, Huxtable dismissed his wife with a flick of the hand and she fled to the kitchen.

'I know why you've come,' he said, arms folded. 'People have been talking. Well, you're wasting your time, Sergeant. I didn't kill that bastard. Somebody got there before me.'

'Show some respect, sir. The man is dead.'

'It's the best news I've had in years.'

'You spent the night here, presumably,' said Leeming.

'Yes, I did. I worked the late shift at the factory,' explained Huxtable. 'While everyone else was back home for the evening, I was putting rivets into a locomotive that came in for repair.'

'What time did the shift finish?'

'At ten o'clock last night. I came straight here. My wife will tell you that I got back here around twenty past ten.'

'Did your journey home take you anywhere near the church?'

'No, it didn't.'

'I can always check your departure time at the factory.'

'Please do. The foreman stands over us. I have to work until the last second.'

'We have a superintendent like that,' said Leeming, ruefully. 'He keeps our noses to the grindstone.' He looked Huxtable up and down. 'Mr Exton must have been a fool.'

'He was a fool, a liar, a drunk and a pest to women.'

'I'd have thought that the last woman he'd pester was your wife. He must have known you wouldn't take kindly to it.'

'When I heard that he'd been following May around, I wanted to tear his head off. My wife begged me not to touch him but I gave him a black eye just to let him know who he was dealing with. He didn't bother May after that.'

Leeming thought of the submissive little creature that had scurried off to the kitchen. Colbeck had suggested that he ask her if a woman could hate a man enough to kill him. The question was redundant. She was clearly incapable of violence. As for burning hatred, Huxtable had enough for the two of them.

'Do you have any idea who *did* commit the murder?' asked Leeming.

'A lot of people come to mind.'

'Would the name of Harry Blacker be among them?'

Huxtable smirked. 'He'd be top of the list,' he said. 'The surprise is that he battered Exton to death in a church. Harry would have preferred to bury him alive.'

Leeming was not convinced of his innocence. There was no point in asking the wife to confirm the time of her husband's return on the previous day. May Huxtable was so afraid of him that she'd say anything he told her to say. As he left the room, Leeming glanced through the open door of the kitchen. The woman was bent over a washboard, scrubbing away as hard as she could at what looked like Huxtable's working clothes. Two questions sprang into Leeming's mind. Why was she doing that on the day of rest and what was she so anxious to wash away?

* * *

'Where were you last night?'

'Where were *you*, Inspector?'

'I'll ask the questions, Mr Blacker.'

'Then the answer is that I can't remember.'

'Why is that?' asked Colbeck.

'I'd drunk too much.'

Harry Blacker was fishing in the river when Colbeck finally ran him to earth. He was a scrawny man in his sixties with a craggy face and an almost toothless mouth. When Colbeck asked him about the murder, the gravedigger claimed that it was the first time he'd heard of the crime. Putting his head back, he chortled merrily.

'Now there's one grave I'll really enjoy digging,' he said.

'You and Mr Exton were not exactly bosom friends, were you?'

'I despised him, Inspector.'

'Did he harass Mrs Blacker?'

'There's no Mrs Blacker to harass,' said the gravedigger with another chortle. 'Who'd marry an ugly devil like me? Besides, I like my own company. And I'd much rather catch fish all day than be chased around from breakfast to supper time by a sharp-tongued harridan. There's plenty of women like that in Wolverton.'

'I'll have to take your word for it,' said Colbeck, recoiling from the man's bad breath. 'What did you and Mr Exton fall out over?'

'What else but the churchyard?'

'Oh?'

'It's *mine*, Inspector,' said Blacker with vehemence. 'I've dug

70

every grave in that place and I'll dig a lot more before it's my turn to be buried in the ground. Exton had the nerve to sleep there when I wasn't looking. I caught him one night and poured a bucket of water over him. That kept him away for weeks but I knew he'd be back eventually. People like him never give up.'

'What did you do?'

'I got into the habit of going past there every night to make sure he wasn't using my territory as his bedroom. When he did show up,' said Blacker, bitterly, 'he did something so disgusting that I wanted to kill him on the spot. Since he had his trousers down, I smacked him across his bare arse with the flat of my spade.' He let out a cruel laugh. 'He wouldn't have been able to sit down for a week.'

Victor Leeming had a long wait outside the church and it gave him time to construct his theory about the crime. When an apologetic Colbeck turned up at last, Leeming had the solution worked out in his mind.

'We must treat George Huxtable as a prime suspect, sir.'

'Why is that, Victor?'

'He's a big, embittered man with a grudge against Exton. Huxtable worked until late at the factory last night. I believe that he could have overpowered Exton, left him bound and gagged somewhere, then slipped out in the night and taken him to the church to murder him. It was the wife who gave me the clue,' said Leeming. 'She was frantically scrubbing his working clothes. Estelle would never do anything like that on a Sunday. Mrs Huxtable is under her husband's thumb. If he ordered her to get rid of bloodstains, she'd do it without question.'

'Did you actually *see* any bloodstains?'

'No, but it's a strong possibility they were there.'

'Only if he actually committed the murder,' said Colbeck, 'and to do that, he'd need a key to the church. Where did he get it from?'

Leeming's certainty faltered. 'I'm not sure about that, sir.'

'It's the crucial factor. Is Huxtable a religious man?'

'Not as far as I could see.'

'Then the significance of that scene at the altar would mean nothing to him.'

'He just *looked* so guilty, Inspector.'

'And so did Harry Blacker when I first clapped eyes on him.'

'Is he a likely suspect?'

'No,' said Colbeck, 'but he did point me in the direction of someone who might be. Come on, Victor,' he said, moving off. 'We have a train to catch.'

Leeming fell in beside him. 'Are we going back to Euston?' he asked, hopefully.

'I'm afraid not. Do you know why the railway company chose Wolverton as a place for their depot and their factories?'

'No, I don't.'

'It's almost equidistant between London and Birmingham. When I said that we had a train to catch, there was something I forgot to mention.' Colbeck gave a teasing smile. 'It won't be the same train. You'll go in the direction of London and I'll go in the direction of Birmingham.'

When they called in on Adam Revill later that afternoon, the warden had rallied. A couple of hours' sleep had put some colour in his cheeks and given him the urge to sit up in bed and read. Anthony and Maria Vine were pleased to see the improvement in him. Maria placed a cup of tea on the bedside table.

'There you are, Uncle Adam,' she said. 'It's just as you like it.'

'You're so good to me, Maria – and so are you, Anthony.'

'We're both happy to help.'

'I feel so much better now,' said the warden. 'The person who really needs your help is Simon Gillard. After making that grisly discovery in the church, he must be in a terrible state. I just wish that I was well enough to comfort him.'

'Anthony says they've moved the body,' explained Maria. 'He walked past the church earlier on. The detectives seem to have disappeared.'

'Well, I hope they come back soon,' said Vine. 'The murder has cast a pall over the whole town. We need someone to lift it from us. As for Simon, I agree that he'll need a lot of support from us. He doesn't have the strongest constitution. It's been a real blow.'

'You must be ready to take over, Anthony.'

'I'm not a warden, my dear.'

'You will be one day and there's nobody who can compare with you when it comes to church affairs. That's the kindest thing you can do for Simon. Tell him that you'll take over his duties next Sunday. It will be a huge weight off his shoulders.'

'Maria is right,' said Revill. 'You're the man to step into the breach.'

'I'd have to speak to the vicar first,' said Vine, clearly attracted by the notion. 'I'll need his approval before I speak to Simon Gillard.'

They heard a knock at the front door. Maria went off to see who it was.

'That may be the vicar now,' said Revill. 'He promised to call this afternoon.'

'Then I'll seize my opportunity,' said Vine.

But it was not the Reverend Odell. They heard a voice talking to Maria then three sets of footsteps came up the staircase. Maria entered the bedroom with Colbeck and Leeming. Since he'd met Revill and Maria before, the sergeant took charge of the introductions. Vine shook hands with both men.

'I'm so glad that you haven't deserted us,' he said. 'We need this murder solved and solved quickly.'

'We take the same view, Mr Vine,' said Colbeck. 'That's why we went for a ride on the train. I went to Blisworth and the sergeant went to Bletchley. When he drew a blank there, he went on Leighton Buzzard.'

Maria was baffled. 'I don't understand.'

'Everything turns on that key, Mrs Vine. Only three keys to the church existed so the killer must somehow have acquired a fourth. And that,' Colbeck said, 'means that he needed a locksmith to make one. He'd be too cunning to use someone here in Wolverton so he'd go to another town – Leighton Buzzard, as it turns out.'

'The locksmith there was very helpful,' said Leeming. 'He remembered that he'd made a replica of a key to a church door only days ago and he remembered the man who asked him to do it. Of course,' he went on, turning meaningfully to Vine, 'you were careful not to give him your proper name. You called yourself Marklew.'

'That was my maiden name!' cried Maria, looking at her husband. 'Is this true, Anthony? Did you go to Leighton Buzzard?'

'No,' replied Vine, indignantly. 'The locksmith is confused.'

'We can soon clear the confusion,' said Colbeck. 'We can take you to meet the gentleman and he will confirm his identification.' He confronted Vine. 'You took advantage of Mr Revill's illness, didn't you? While he was confined to his bed, you borrowed his key, had a copy made and restored the original to its place here. Then you overpowered Mr Exton, got him into the church and committed the murder in front of the altar.'

Vine spluttered. 'I'd never dream of doing such a thing.'

'We spoke to the vicar, sir. He told us what a deeply religious man you were.'

'There's nothing religious about battering a man to death,' said Leeming.

'I also spoke to Harry Blacker,' resumed Colbeck. 'He said that you were incensed when you heard that Mr Exton had defecated on your mother's grave. There'd been bad blood between them when she was alive, apparently, but nothing excused what he did in that churchyard.'

Maria was staring at her husband in horror and Revill was scandalised.

'Did you take my key behind my back, Anthony?' he demanded.

'Yes, he did,' said Leeming.

'I can't believe I'm hearing this,' said Maria, backing away.

Abandoning denial, Vine tried to justify what he'd done.

'He deserved it, Maria,' he argued. 'Have you forgotten all the other things he did to the church? I lost count of the number of times I had to scrub off the obscenities Exton had daubed on the walls. He mocked God. He laughed at Christianity,' he cried, eyes darting wildly. 'When he . . . did what he did over my mother's grave, it was the final straw. I *had* to teach him a lesson. You must see that. I took him into church and made him beg forgiveness from God – then I killed him in front of the altar.' He raised a palm. 'Don't ask me to feel sorry for him because I don't. Divine guidance made me do it.'

Colbeck nodded to Leeming who moved forward to make an arrest. But Vine was not going to surrender. Grabbing the sergeant by the shoulders, he flung him away then lifted the sash window in order to jump out. A yell of pain told them that he'd fallen badly and injured himself.

'I'll arrest him outside,' said Leeming, leaving the bedroom.

'Yes,' said Colbeck, peering through the window. 'From the look of it, you won't get much resistance this time.'

'Anthony can't plead divine guidance,' said Revill in bewilderment. '*Thou shalt not kill.* That's what we're taught. What Anthony did was . . . dreadful.'

Maria was still transfixed by what she'd learnt about her husband. As she tried to take in the full horror of it all, her face crumpled and the tears gushed out. After a few moments, she collapsed into Colbeck's arms.

When the train pulled into Euston station, the detectives got out and walked along the platform. Both were pleased to have solved the crime so quickly and to have restored a degree of calm to Wolverton.

'There you are, Victor,' said Colbeck. 'You'll still be able to see your children before they go to bed.'

'I'm sorry that I was so churlish on the way there, sir.'

'Our interrupted Sunday was redeemed by an important arrest.'

'I'm glad we don't have people like Anthony Vine in our congregation,' said Leeming. 'He's got a very twisted view of Christianity.'

'He's a devout man with a fatal weakness. He forgot one of the main precepts of the Bible – *Vengeance is mine; I will repay, saith the Lord*. Mr Vine took too much upon himself,' said Colbeck. 'In trying to play God, he created a disaster for the very church he loved and served. It will be something to reflect upon as he's waiting to mount the gallows.'

A FAMILY AFFAIR

In a sense, Caleb Andrews had never actually retired from the railway. He continued to turn up at Euston on an unpaid, unofficial basis in order to hear the latest gossip and to offer unsought advice to his former colleagues over a pint of beer at the pub they patronised. Andrews was a short, stringy man with a fringe beard decorating a leathery face. Known for his pugnacity, he also had a softer side and it was in evidence that evening as he listened to the harpist. A small crowd had gathered around the old man as he worked his way through his repertoire. Andrews was not the only onlooker who had to hold back a tear when he heard the strains of 'Home, Sweet Home'. He marvelled at the way that the decrepit figure could pluck such sweet melodies from his strings. Well into his seventies, the harpist wore an ancient, ragged suit and a top hat battered into concertina shape. Beside him on the ground was a cap to collect any money from his transient audiences. Curled up asleep near the cap was a mangy dog of uncertain parentage.

The harpist's musical taste was catholic, embracing everything from operatic arias to bawdy music hall songs and stretching to stirring marches more suited to a regimental brass band. Passers-by hovered long enough to hear a favourite tune and, in some cases, tossed a coin into the cap. Andrews did the same, then his sharp eye spotted a threat to the money. Lurking on the edge of the crowd was a ragamuffin who could be no more than nine or ten. He sidled towards the cap and was about to snatch it up when Andrews shouted a warning.

'Watch out!'

His yell was unnecessary because the dog had already come to life to protect its master's income and bitten the boy's wrist. Howling in pain, the ragamuffin darted off. As he turned to look after the thief, Andrews bumped into a well-dressed man who muttered an apology then walked swiftly past him. Thinking no more of the incident, Andrews listened to the harpist for another few minutes then headed for the pub where he'd spent so many happy times with his friends over the years. They gave him a warm welcome and someone bought him a drink. He revelled in the banter. Dirk Sowerby, his erstwhile fireman, then came in. Andrews insisted on treating him and moved to the bar counter. When he reached inside his coat for his wallet, however, it was not there. He came to an immediate conclusion.

'I've been robbed!' he protested.

'It was embarrassing, Maddy.'

'I can see that.'

'Instead of buying Dirk Sowerby a drink, I had to borrow

money off him to pay my way. I felt such a fool.'

'Are you absolutely sure that you had the wallet in your coat?'

'Yes,' replied Andrews, irritably. 'Of course, I'm sure.'

'I've known you forget things before,' Madeleine reminded him.

'I've never forgotten my wallet and my watch, Maddy. I wouldn't leave the house without them. You know that.'

Madeleine nodded. During all the years she'd lived with her father, she couldn't remember him forgetting anything of real importance. Andrews had a routine from which he never wavered. The truth had to be faced. Her father was the victim of a pickpocket. She was angry on his behalf but schooled herself to think calmly.

'Do you have any idea when it might have happened, Father?'

'I think so. It was when I listened to that harpist.'

'Go on.'

He recounted the events at Euston station and declared that the man who'd bumped into him was the culprit. Distracted by the music, Andrews felt, he'd been targeted. He was determined to get his money back.

'I didn't come here to seek Robert's help,' he said. 'A detective inspector has more important things to worry about than a pickpocket. I just wanted to talk it through with you so that it became clear in my mind. It's *my* turn to be a detective now,' he went on, rubbing his hands. 'I'll show my son-in-law that he isn't the only clever policeman in the family.'

They were in the drawing room of the house that Madeleine shared with her husband, Robert Colbeck. She was an alert, attractive

woman who had moved from a modest dwelling in Camden Town
to a more luxurious home in John Islip Street in Westminster, slowly
settling into the latter. Always pleased to see her father, she was sorry
that he'd brought such bad news on this occasion.

'Would you recognise the man again?' she asked.

'I think so. He wore a frock coat and top hat.'

'Hundreds of men answer to that description, Father.'

'I may only have seen him for a second but I'm sure I can
pick him out.'

She was dubious. 'Be very careful,' she said.

'They're obviously in this together, Maddy.'

'Who are?'

'The harpist and the pickpocket,' he told her. 'The one holds
your attention while the other moves among the crowd, looking
for prey.'

'I think that's unlikely,' she said. 'An old man with a mangy
dog doesn't sound as if he'd have anything to do with a well-
dressed gentleman.'

'He was no gentleman – he was a thief!'

'What do you propose to do?'

'I'll go back to the station tomorrow to see if the harpist is
there. If he is, I'll watch from a distance to see if the dipper is
there with him.'

Madeleine was alarmed. 'Don't do anything rash,' she said.
'It might be better if I came with you tomorrow.'

'I can manage on my own,' he insisted. 'I don't need you
and I don't need the famous Railway Detective. This is my case,
Maddy, and I mean to solve it.'

* * *

Early next morning, Andrews was part of the hustle and bustle of a major railway station once again. People queued for tickets then went in search of the appropriate platforms. There was constant noise and movement. From a vantage point near the main entrance, Andrews kept his eyes peeled. Hours oozed past but there was no sign of the harpist. What he did see were several men who looked vaguely like the one who'd bumped into him the previous evening. Madeleine had been right. His loose description of the supposed pickpocket fitted any number of male passengers. During their brief encounter, Andrews had had no time to register the man's height, age or colouring. He couldn't even decide if he'd heard an educated voice or a Cockney twang. Detective work was not as straightforward as he'd imagined.

The musician finally arrived around noon. Covered by a piece of cloth, his Irish harp was small enough to be carried under his arm. The mangy dog trailed after him. He took up a different position this time, squatting down on the ground near a cloakroom where luggage could be deposited. Music soon filled the air. Andrews drifted across so that he could keep the old man under surveillance. Busy people rushed past but there were small groups that loitered for short periods to listen. The first few coins clinked into the cap. The dog fell asleep.

After an hour or so, the harpist stopped for refreshment. From inside his coat, he pulled out a hunk of bread and a piece of cheese. His audience vanished instantly. Once he resumed, however, more and more people moved across to hear him. When the crowd thickened, an impeccably tailored man walked slowly towards the cluster. Andrews watched him like a hawk.

As he eased his way to the front of the queue, the man rubbed against several other people with gestures of apology. Andrews recalled the polite gentleman who'd bumped into him. Was he looking at the same man? It was a strong possibility. Indeed, the more he studied the newcomer, the more certain he became that he'd identified a pickpocket.

When the man broke away from the crowd, he bumped accidentally into a woman and immediately raised his hat to her before striding off. It was exactly what had happened to Andrews. What looked like a chance collision was, in fact, an opportunity for the pickpocket to claim another victim. The evidence, Andrews decided, was now overwhelming. It was him.

Disregarding the fact that he had no power of arrest, Andrews ran after the man and clutched at his arm. The stranger turned to face him.

'May I help you, sir?' he asked.

'Yes,' said Andrews, 'you can return my wallet for a start. You stole it from me yesterday evening when I was listening to your accomplice playing his harp.'

'What the devil are you talking about?'

'You're a pickpocket. I've been watching you at work.'

'I work in a bank,' said the man, testily, 'and I'll be late if I miss my train.'

'You're going nowhere,' said Andrews, tightening his grip.

'Leave go of me,' ordered the man, 'or I'll call a policeman.'

'That's exactly what *I* wish to do.'

Train passengers were treated to the extraordinary sight of a wiry old character, clinging like a limpet to the arm of an elegant gentleman who was doing everything he could to shake him off.

Both were yelling simultaneously for a policeman. It was only a minute before one came over to see what the commotion was. He was a hefty individual in his thirties with rubicund cheeks.

'What's going on here, then?' he asked.

'Get this imbecile off me!' pleaded the man.

Andrews released him. 'Arrest him, constable,' he said. 'He's the pickpocket who stole my wallet yesterday. That harpist is his accomplice.'

'I've never set eyes on the fellow before.'

'The two of you work hand in glove.'

'Now calm down, the pair of you!' said the policeman. 'We'll get nowhere if you both jabber away.' He turned to the man. 'You tell me your story first, sir.'

Angered by the deference in his tone, Andrews tried to complain but he was silenced by the policeman with the threat of arrest. The man gave his account of what had happened then opened his frock coat wide.

'If you think I stole anything,' he challenged, 'search me.'

Andrews had the unsettling feeling that he may have been mistaken, after all.

'Go on,' urged the man. 'You called me a pickpocket. Prove it.'

'I'm sorry,' murmured Andrews. 'I took you for someone else.'

'You assaulted me, you ruffian. Dozens of witnesses will testify to that.' He appealed to people standing by. 'You all saw him, didn't you?'

Several of them nodded their heads. An unprovoked assault had occurred.

The policeman put a hand on Andrews' shoulder. 'You'd better come with me,' he said, trying to lead him away.

'You can't arrest me!' howled Andrews, brushing him off. 'My son-in-law is a detective inspector at Scotland Yard.'

'I don't care if he's the Archbishop of Canterbury,' said the policeman, taking a firmer grip. 'I'm taking you into custody to face charges of assault and resisting an arrest.'

To a round of applause from onlookers, Andrews was marched away.

It was late afternoon before Colbeck was able to get across to the police station near Euston. By that time, his father-in-law had been cooling his heels in a dank and cheerless cell for hours. When he was released by the duty sergeant, Andrews made wild threats about suing the police for wrongful arrest. Colbeck hustled him out of the building.

'You don't need to tell me the story,' he said. 'I read the report. Because I was ready to vouch for you, all charges have been dropped. Please don't antagonise the police, Mr Andrews, or you may get yourself into a situation from which I'm unable to rescue you.'

Andrews took a deep breath and tried to master his sense of humiliation.

'Thank you, Robert,' he said at length. 'They laughed at me when I said that the Railway Detective was my son-in-law. Now they know better.'

'Forget what happened at Euston station today. Go back to the events of yesterday. Madeleine told me that a pickpocket had stolen your wallet. How exactly did it happen?'

Andrews gave a vivid account, describing both the pickpocket and his alleged accomplice. Colbeck was not persuaded that either of the men was guilty of the crime or that they were in any way connected.

'What did the man do after he'd apologised?' he asked.

'He rushed straight off towards the platforms.'

'Then the logical supposition is that he was about to catch a train.'

'Yes,' said Andrews, peevishly, 'and he'd have had my wallet in his pocket.'

'I beg leave to doubt that, Mr Andrews. Dippers are after rich pickings. With respect, you don't look like the sort of person who might be carrying a large amount of money.'

'That doesn't matter. It still hurt when he took the little I had on me.'

'In my view,' said Colbeck, 'the fact that this man went off to catch a train absolves him of the crime. If Euston was his patch, he'd have stayed there in search of more victims. There's another point. Pickpockets often have an accomplice to whom they can slip what they've stolen. If they're confronted by a policeman, they're happy to be searched because they have nothing on them that they don't legitimately own.'

'This man *did* have an accomplice,' said Andrews. 'It was the harpist.'

'Did you actually see him pass any wallets or purses to the old man?'

'Well, no . . .'

'What gave you the impression that they worked together?'

'I was distracted by the music, Robert.'

'All that the harpist was doing was to earn a few pennies,' reasoned Colbeck. 'Pickpockets expect more than that. The one who stole your wallet simply seized a moment when your mind was elsewhere. But let me ask you another question,' he added. 'Why did you try to solve the crime yourself instead of reporting it to the police the moment you became aware that you'd been robbed?'

Andrews was shamefaced. 'I thought I could do your job for you,' he said before thrusting out his chest. 'And I still might.'

Colbeck asserted his authority and told his father-in-law that his days as an amateur detective were over. A professional criminal would only be caught by those with the requisite experience. He had a surprise for Andrews.

'I appreciate how you must feel,' he said, sympathetically. 'Being the victim of theft is always unpleasant but you were not the only one. There were six other reports yesterday of money being stolen by a pickpocket at Euston. However, no less than fifteen victims came forward at Paddington with the same complaint and the harpist was not playing there. Where crowds gather, there'll always be dippers on the prowl. Railway stations are their natural habitat.'

Andrews was dejected. 'Have I lost that money forever, then?'

'Not necessarily,' replied Colbeck. 'I'll ask Sergeant Leeming to look into the case. When he was in uniform, he had a reputation for being able to spot pickpockets at work. Let's see if he can still do it.'

When she heard what had occurred, Madeleine was torn between sympathy and amusement, sorry that her father had suffered the indignity of arrest yet able to see the irony of a self-appointed detective ending up behind bars. Over dinner with her husband, she thanked him for his intervention.

'It was very kind of you to step in, Robert.'

'I couldn't let my father-in-law get an undeserved criminal record. He was his own worst enemy, Madeleine. He should have come to us right away,' said Colbeck. 'How would *he* feel if I tried to drive a train without any qualifications for doing so?'

'That's an unfair comparison.'

'I fancy that I'd make a better job of it than he did of being a detective.'

'But you'd have the sense not even to try. Father, on the other hand, couldn't be held back. He was determined that it would be his case. He's always been rather impulsive. This is only the latest example.'

'In principle, I admire what he did but I deplore the way he went about it.'

'He'll be terribly upset. I'd better go and see him tomorrow.'

'That's an excellent idea, Madeleine,' said Colbeck. 'Apart from anything else, it will keep him away from Euston. I don't want him going there and stepping on Victor Leeming's toes.'

'What will the sergeant be doing there?'

'He'll be on the lookout for an old harpist and a cunning pickpocket.'

Victor Leeming was very unhappy about being sent to Euston on what he perceived as a rather demeaning errand. As a detective, he dealt with dangerous criminals and helped to solve major crimes. In his eyes, looking for a pickpocket was in the nature of a demotion. The harpist arrived and selected a spot near the ticket office. Dog and cap lay beside him. As the old man began his recital, Leeming rolled his eyes and turned to the uniformed policeman next to him.

'I hate street musicians,' he said, bitterly. 'When I set off for work this morning, there was a hurdy-gurdy man outside my front door. I turned the corner and almost walked into a barrel organ. Farther down the street, someone was playing a violin – it sounded as if he was trying to strangle a cat. But the worst of all was these two lads in kilts,' he went on with a groan. 'They were playing bagpipes and going from house to house in search of Scotsmen. The noise was deafening. People gave them money just to get rid of them.'

'I quite like the harpist,' said the policeman, defensively.

'Then you shouldn't be listening. You're on duty.'

'I could say the same of you, sir.'

'Point towards the waiting room,' suggested Leeming. 'If anyone is watching me, I don't want them to think I'm a policeman. Let them believe I just asked you for directions.'

The policeman obeyed. Leeming pretended to thank him before walking over to the waiting room. Once inside, he stood by the window so that he could see the ever-changing crowd around the harpist. Nothing remotely suspicious occurred. After a barren half an hour, he stamped his foot in irritation and went outside again, making for the bookstall where he bought a newspaper. While opening it up as if reading it, he kept one eye firmly fixed on the people enjoying the music.

By early afternoon, Leeming was becoming increasingly annoyed. He was even tempted to abandon his vigil and return to more important duties at Scotland Yard. Then something of interest finally took place. A man came out of the ticket office in obvious distress. He scuttled across to the policeman to whom Leeming had spoken earlier. From the way that he patted one side of his chest and pointed towards the harpist, the sergeant deduced that the man's wallet had been stolen and that the crime had only come to light when he went to buy a ticket. The policeman nodded soulfully as he heard the tale of woe but he didn't walk towards the harpist to investigate. Having been warned why Leeming was there, he kept well away from the harpist for fear of frightening the pickpocket and accomplice – if such a person existed – away from the station altogether. But at least it was clear that a deft hand was at work. Leeming cheered up. His presence might be justified, after all.

Drifting towards the harpist, he stood a few yards away from the crowd around him, blocking out the music so that he could concentrate solely on watching them. The long wait eventually yielded a reward but it was an unexpected one. Having been certain that he was looking for a man, he was astonished when his chief suspect was a buxom woman of middle years with an expensive dressmaker. She looked altogether too grand to bother with an itinerant musician yet she produced a purse and took out a handful of coins to drop into his cap. The dog yawned in gratitude. What she did next alerted Leeming at once. She bumped into someone, apologised profusely to him then pushed her way gently through the crowd and headed for the exit. Leeming was after her immediately. Though she had a good start on him, he soon overhauled her.

'Good day to you, madam,' he said. 'I wonder if I may have a word.'

'I'm in rather a hurry,' she said, sizing him up at a glance and deciding that he was not fit company. 'You'll have to excuse me.'

Leeming stood in her path. 'I'm afraid that I can't do that.'

'If you don't get out of my way, I'll summon a policeman.'

'I *am* a policeman,' he told her, 'and I'm here to arrest pickpockets. I've every reason to believe that you stole a man's wallet earlier on and have just deprived another victim of his money. You'll have to accompany me to the police station.'

'I'll be delighted to do so,' she said, angrily, 'because I wish to complain about the sheer impertinence of one of their officers. When he was alive – you may be interested to know – my late husband was an archdeacon. We led lives of absolute piety. Arthur would have been outraged to hear of the monstrous accusation that I was a criminal.'

She glared angrily at Leeming but he stood his ground resolutely.

'I saw what I saw, madam,' he said.

'Then take me to the police station and search me,' she said, defiantly. 'You'll find nothing incriminating.'

'I don't expect to – someone as intelligent as you would never risk being caught with any of the stolen items on you. An accomplice was at hand so that you could slip him wallets and purses as and when you lifted them from their owners. As soon as he sees me hauling you off,' explained Leeming, 'he'll follow in order to rescue you. When he spots someone breaking away from the crowd, the policeman I alerted earlier will intercept him.'

The woman drew herself up to her full height. 'This is absolute lunacy.'

'Come this way, madam,' he said, taking her arm.

She shook him off. 'Unhand me, sir! Don't you dare touch me!'

'If you don't do as I say, I'll be forced to handcuff you.'

'I'm a respectable woman and – on my word of honour – I've done nothing wrong. Surely, that's all you need to hear, man.'

'That excuse may have worked on the archdeacon – if that's what your late husband really was – but it will not do for me. Every person I've ever arrested has pleaded innocence.'

'If you don't believe *me*, ask my sister.'

'Yes,' said a voice behind him, 'I'll vouch for Maud.'

Leeming turned to see a much smaller woman of similar age. Her benign appearance belied her character because she suddenly pushed him hard in the chest with both hands. As he staggered backwards, the other woman stuck out a leg and tripped him up. Both of them then lifted up their skirts and showed a surprising turn of speed. Before Leeming could drag himself up, they'd got to the exit and headed for the cab rank. He sprinted after them and gained ground at once. But he was too late to stop them reaching a cab and climbing into it. Before it could be driven away, however, a sprightly old man jumped into the road and grabbed the horse's bridle to prevent it moving.

As Leeming came running up, Caleb Andrews cackled in triumph.

'I was watching you all the time, Sergeant,' he explained, 'in case you needed help. Maddy tried to stop me coming here but I was determined to get that wallet of mine back.'

Maud and Lilian Grieves were indeed sisters and they lived in a fine house in a street just off Park Lane. Now that they'd been caught, they showed neither fear nor remorse. They insisted on taking the two men to their home and handing back the stolen property they'd accumulated. When they entered the premises, Leeming and Andrews were taken to a room that was filled with the spoils of the two pickpockets. Laid out on tables like museum exhibits were dozens and dozens of wallets, purses, handbags and other assorted items. Andrews spotted his wallet and dived forward to reclaim it.

'The money is still inside,' said Maud, piously. 'We're not thieves. We just like the thrill of relieving people of whatever they have in their pockets and handbags.'

'It's a sort of hobby,' said Lilian, stroking a stolen cigar case. 'Maud and I are well provided for, as you can see, but our lives lack excitement. Since our husbands died, life became very dull until we discovered how light-fingered we were. We take it in turns to pick pockets then pass it on for safekeeping to whoever is acting as a lookout. You've no idea how careless people are in a crowd.'

'Yes, I do,' said Leeming. 'I've seen too many examples of it.'

'I was careless,' admitted Andrews. 'I never felt a thing.'

Maud beamed. 'That's because I lifted your wallet when you were listening to that old man on the harp. Unbeknownst to him, he's been very helpful to us.'

'All this will be advertised,' said Leeming, indicating the

display. 'A lot of people are going to be very glad that we've recovered what was stolen from them.'

'I'm one of them,' said Andrews, holding up his wallet. 'It never crossed my mind that I'd been robbed by a woman.'

'Nor me,' confessed the sergeant. 'You fooled me completely. I was looking for two hardened criminals, not a pair of respectable ladies who happened to be sisters.'

'That was our disguise,' boasted Lilian. 'Nobody suspected us.'

'It was wonderful while it lasted,' added Maud. 'It was a family business, so to speak. I'm sorry that it's over but we always knew it would have to end one day.'

'It's finished for good,' said Leeming, bluntly. 'You'll have to come with me to the police station. Oh,' he went on, turning to Maud. 'There's one thing I'm curious to know. Was your husband *really* an archdeacon?'

'That's exactly what Arthur was,' replied Maud with a nostalgic smile, 'and Lilian will confirm it. He was the light of my life in every way. I would never lie to you about his eminent position in the church. There was, however, some deception involved,' she conceded. 'Unfortunately, Arthur was not my husband. We simply pretended that he was.' Her eyes twinkled. 'He and I had an understanding, you see.'

THE HAT TRICK

As they walked hand in hand beside the rippling stream, they felt the early morning sun on their backs. Alaric and Liza Bignall had been married for over nine months now but they still had the glow of newly-weds. The route was among their favourites and held a special significance because it was beside that same stream that Bignall had proposed to her. Since they'd both been overwhelmed by excitement at the time, they could not remember the exact spot where the event had taken place. All that Bignall could recall was that it was near a point where they'd been able to cross the stream by using a series of small boulders as stepping stones. The problem was that boulders were strewn everywhere in the water, creating eddies and miniature cascades at irregular intervals.

'I think that it was here,' he said, coming to a halt.

'No, it wasn't, Alaric. It was much farther on than this.'

'It feels like the right place, Liza.'

'Not to me, it doesn't,' she said.

'Look at the way the stepping stones are set.'

'That's what I am doing and they're wrong. There was a very large boulder in the middle of the stream, much bigger than the one here.'

'Your memory's playing tricks on you.'

'When we find the right place,' she said, firmly, 'I'll know it at once.'

Their discussion was interrupted by the sound of an approaching train. It was travelling at full speed. They turned to look up the embankment and watched the train thunder past. From an open window, a top hat suddenly shot out and rolled crazily down the embankment. The door of a compartment was then flung open and a man dived out, hitting solid earth and tumbling helplessly towards them. Gathering pace, he fell on and on until he reached the stream itself, plunging into the water and striking his head against a jagged rock.

By the time they got to him, the blood gushing from the wound was being carried away by the stream. Liza was aghast.

'He's dead!' she cried.

When they eventually got to Sheffield station, they alighted from the train and hired a cab to take them to the outskirts of the town. Victor Leeming was not at all convinced that their journey was necessary.

'All this fuss over a top hat,' he moaned. 'When carriages had no roofs on them, hats were being blown off all the time and there were dozens of cases of people chasing after them. That's obviously what happened here, sir.'

'Unlike you,' said Colbeck, wryly, 'I'm not gifted with second sight so I can't make such an authoritative judgement. Neither, it seems, can the railway company that asked us to investigate. They want an answer to a simple question – did he jump out of the train or was he pushed?'

'He jumped out after his hat, sir.'

'When the train was going full pelt?'

'Some people are very vain about their appearance,' said Leeming, pointedly. 'They'd die rather than be seen in public without a hat.'

'I'm one of them,' said the other with a laugh, 'and I freely admit it. But even my vanity doesn't extend to risking my life in order to retrieve a top hat. Headgear can be easily replaced, albeit at a cost. I'm conceited enough to believe that Detective Inspector Robert Colbeck would not be so easily substituted.'

They lapsed into silence and watched houses, civic buildings and factories slide past. Earlier in the century, Sheffield had been a pretty South Yorkshire town with the most famous cutlery industry in England. The advent of railways had increased its population markedly, pushed out its boundaries and given its burgeoning enterprises an international market. Cutlery remained its main product but steel, carpets and furniture were also produced. The invention of the silver-plating process enabled the town to manufacture Sheffield Plate, another claim to fame. Growth came at a price. Billowing smoke and industrial clamour seemed to be everywhere.

'Do you know what a hat trick is?' asked Colbeck, resuming the conversation.

'Yes, sir,' replied Leeming with a grin. 'It's keeping the thing on your head instead of letting it blow off.'

'I can see that you don't follow events in the world of cricket.'

'Tug-of-war is the only sport that I was any good at. When I was a young constable, I was part of a winning team.'

'To some degree,' said Colbeck, 'you still are. We're engaged in a non-stop tug-of-war against the criminal fraternity. We have to fight hard to retain our footing. However,' he continued, 'I ask about a cricketing term because it recently came into being in this very town. Sheffield has a long association with the sport. Does the name H. H. Stephenson mean anything to you?'

Leeming shook his head. 'I've never heard of the man, Inspector.'

'His remarkable feat has introduced a new phrase into the English language. A mere fortnight ago, Stephenson was playing for the All-England Eleven here in Sheffield. With three consecutive balls, he bowled out three of the opposing batsmen.'

'Is that unusual?'

'It's extremely unusual, Victor. I daresay that it's happened before but it's never been accorded its full merit. In this instance, a hat was taken round the spectators and they tossed coins into it in appreciation of what they'd seen.'

'Nobody did that when we won a tug-of-war. The most we got was a free pint of beer and – if we were lucky – a stale pork pie.'

'Anyway,' concluded Colbeck, 'that's how the notion of a hat trick emerged into the light of day. I fancy that the expression will stick. The fact that it was coined in the very place we're visiting is a pleasing coincidence.'

'It doesn't please me,' murmured Leeming.

Alaric and Liza Bignall were practical. When they'd got over the initial shock, they established that the man was still alive though knocked unconscious. From the unnatural angle at which he lay, they realised that one of his legs had been broken. They pulled him carefully out of the water. Since the head wound was the major concern, Liza tore a strip off her petticoat to use as a bandage. Leaving his wife to look after the man, Bignall had run off to summon help. He later returned in a horse and cart driven by a farmer. While the two men lifted the patient gently onto the cart, Liza retrieved his top hat and set it down beside him. The farmer had driven them to the home of a doctor who lived on the very edge of Sheffield and it was there that the detectives made the acquaintance of James Scanlan, a portly man in his late fifties with heavy jowls and watery eyes.

'He's still in a coma,' Scanlan explained, 'and is very unlikely ever to come out of it. To be quite frank, he already has one foot in the grave. I've put splints on a broken leg but it's the internal injuries that are the real threat.'

'Shouldn't he be moved to an infirmary?' said Leeming.

'There's no point. He'd probably die on the way there. The journey here all but killed him. I can make his last few hours alive as dignified as possible.'

'What do we know about him?' asked Colbeck.

'This may help you, Inspector.'

Scanlan handed over the injured man's wallet and Colbeck

examined the contents. There were several five-pound notes inside and a first-class return ticket to Sheffield but the most useful item was a business card, identifying him as Rufus Moyle, a solicitor from York.

'He was brought here by a farmer who's one of my patients,' said Scanlan, 'but he was actually found by a young man and his wife. Their prompt action probably saved his life – for a time at least.'

'Do you have their names and address?'

'I do, Inspector. I imagined that you'd wish to speak to them.'

'Thank you,' said Colbeck, taking the sheet of paper that was offered to him. After a glance at the address, he handed the paper to Leeming. 'There you are, Sergeant. Take the cab and see what Mr and Mrs Bignall have to say.'

'Yes, sir – where shall we meet?'

'I'll see you at the police station.'

When Leeming had gone, Colbeck was conducted into a room at the rear of the house. Stripped of most of his clothing, Rufus Moyle lay on a bed with a sheet over his body. Heavy bandaging encircled his head and his face was bruised. He was a tall, slim man in his fifties. His elegant frock coat had been ripped apart, his trousers were covered in dirt and his shoes were badly scuffed. At a glance, Colbeck could see that the top hat, though soiled, was of the finest quality. Clearly, Rufus Moyle was something of a dandy.

Eyes closed tight, the patient hardly seemed to be breathing.

'He was obviously a successful man,' decided Colbeck. 'He can afford an excellent tailor. In the course of my work,

I've dealt with many solicitors. They are usually sharp-witted gentlemen. They're highly unlikely to plunge out of a moving train in pursuit of a hat.'

'Could it have been a suicide attempt, Inspector?'

'I doubt that very much. Had that been his intention, Mr Moyle would have left nothing to chance and – as you can see – he survived. There are much quicker and more foolproof ways of killing oneself. Also, of course, he'd bought a return ticket. Nobody would spend money on a journey they never intended to make.'

He searched the pockets of the coat, waistcoat and trousers but found nothing apart from a handkerchief and an enamelled snuffbox.

'His family needs to be informed as soon as possible,' he said, considerately. 'Sergeant Leeming has taken our cab. Could I prevail upon you to get me to the police station somehow?'

'One of my servants will drive you there in the trap.'

'Thank you.' Colbeck glanced down at the patient. 'I hope to find him still alive when we get back here.'

Doctor Scanlan shrugged. 'That's in God's hands, Inspector.'

Alaric and Liza Bignall were both at home when Leeming arrived. The cobbler's shop where Bignall worked was closed for renovation so he'd brought some of the boots and shoes in need of repair back to the house. He was hammering away in the garden shed when the visitor called. Liza called him into the house and introduced him to the sergeant. Bignall was impressed.

'You've come all the way from Scotland Yard because

someone jumped out of a train?' he said in amazement.

'There may be more to it than that, sir,' said Leeming. 'What I need you and your wife to do is to tell me what exactly happened and where you were at the time. I've brought this so that you can give me a precise location.'

Producing an Ordnance Survey map from his pocket, he opened it out and set it on the table. Husband and wife pored over it. After a while, Bignall jabbed his finger at a spot on the map but Liza felt that it was slightly further to the left. When they'd reached a compromise, Leeming marked the place with a pencil that he then used to make notes. Bignall recalled the events of the morning and his wife either confirmed or amended the details.

'You are to be congratulated,' said Leeming when the joint recitation ended. 'You did the right thing in a difficult situation. Let me come back to something you said, sir,' he went on, referring to his notebook. 'According to you, the man *dived* from the train? Is that correct?'

'Yes, it is,' replied Bignall.

'Are you certain that he didn't jump?'

'I am, Sergeant. My wife will confirm it.'

'The man dived out headfirst,' she said. 'We both saw him.'

Leeming's interest in the case quickened. Ready to dismiss what occurred as an act of folly on the part of Rufus Moyle, he was now forced to confront the possibility that a crime had taken place. Someone in pursuit of a hat would surely jump from a train and land on his feet before tumbling down the embankment. A man who dived might well have been pushed from behind.

'I hope that we've been helpful,' said Bignall.

'You've been very helpful indeed, sir,' said Leeming. 'This case is not as trivial as I first thought. I'm grateful to both of you.'

As soon as he saw the return ticket in the injured man's wallet, Colbeck felt certain that Moyle had somehow been ejected from the train. Other passengers might have seen him careering down the embankment but they couldn't be sure from which compartment he'd been shoved out and the person responsible would hardly admit what he had done. The accident had been reported at Sheffield station and a telegraph was sent to the headquarters of the railway company. They, in turn, fearing foul play, had contacted Scotland Yard. Colbeck knew that the anonymous attacker could be hundreds of miles away. The case might never be solved.

Dropped off at the police station, he thanked the driver of the trap and went into the building. His assumptions were immediately challenged.

'We *know* who was in the same compartment with him, Inspector,' said the duty sergeant, Will Fox, 'because he was kind enough to come here and report the accident.'

Colbeck was surprised. 'Did he claim it was an *accident*?'

'Oh, yes. There were only two of them in the compartment, apparently, and they were strangers to each other. A few miles outside Sheffield, one of them peeped out of the open window and his hat blew off. On impulse,' said Fox, 'he opened the door and went after it. He was well dressed, I'm told, and he obviously cherished the top hat.'

'Then why didn't he take more care of it? I always remove my hat before I look out of a window on a train. It saves me a lot of money and inconvenience. Mr Moyle must have known there was a risk of losing the hat.'

'We all do odd things in some situations, sir.'

'What was the name of the gentleman who came forward?'

'He left his business card,' replied Fox, picking it up from the desk and handing it to Colbeck. 'He's a Mr Humphrey Welling, a company director.'

'He's rather more than that,' observed Colbeck when he saw the card. 'He's a director of the Midland Railway. Did he have business in the town?'

'So I would imagine.'

'Where is he now?'

'He was planning to return home to York this afternoon.'

'Then that's where we'll seek him out,' said Colbeck. 'We have to go to there to break the sad news to Mr Moyle's family. We can call on Mr Welling afterwards.' He glanced at the card. 'What manner of man was he?'

'Oh, he was as proper a gentleman as you could wish to meet,' answered Fox. 'His hair was white and he was on the stout side. I had the feeling that Mr Welling looked older than he really was. He was well educated and well spoken. He used a walking stick and seemed to be in some pain when he moved. I just wish that all our witnesses could give such clear statements.'

'May I see exactly what he said, please?'

Fox opened the desk and took out some sheets of paper before passing them over. Colbeck read the statement with interest. Before the inspector had finished it, Leeming came into the police station. After introducing himself to the duty sergeant, he waited until Colbeck had finished.

'Have you learnt anything new, sir?' he asked.

'I have indeed – what about you?'

'Mr and Mrs Bignall were well worth the visit.'

'I suspect that what they told you may be contradicted by what I've just read,' said Colbeck, returning the statement to Fox. 'It seems as if all roads lead to York. Let's be on our way, shall we?'

On the train journey north, the first thing that the detectives did was to look for the spot where Moyle had lost his hat. Using the Ordnance Survey map to locate the area, they gazed through the window and noticed how steep the embankment was. The stream below was still gurgling merrily on. As he recounted what the Bignalls had told him, Leeming referred to his notebook. He described them as reliable witnesses and accepted their word without question. When he heard what the police statement had contained, however, the sergeant hoped that it was an accurate one.

'If what Mr Welling says is true,' he pointed out, 'we can declare that it was a tragic accident and go back home to London.'

'Not so fast, Victor – we need to dig under the surface first.'

'What do you expect to find?'

'I have no idea. That's what makes this case so intriguing.'

'Mr Moyle's family is going to have the most dreadful shock.'

'We can't even be sure if we're telling them the truth,' said

Colbeck, sadly. 'When they hear that he's been badly injured, he may, in fact, already be dead.'

'And all because of a top hat,' sighed Leeming.

'Never underestimate the importance people attach to certain possessions. Since you never go to the theatre, you'll be unfamiliar with Shakespeare's *Othello*.'

'Is that the play with the three witches, sir?'

'No, Victor, it features a man who's driven to murder his wife because she appears to have given away the handkerchief he pressed upon her as a gift. What if the top hat was a gift from Mrs Moyle?' continued Colbeck, thoughtfully. 'That would lend substance to the theory that he felt impelled to go after it.' He smiled at Leeming. 'What's your opinion of Sheffield?'

'It's the most awkward place to get to, Inspector.'

'Yet it's served by two rival companies – the Midland Railway and the Manchester Sheffield and Lincoln. When they were built, neither of them saw fit to give Sheffield the prominence it patently deserves. It was neglected by the North Midland Railway, as it then was, and had to endure the humiliation of being bypassed. The only way to get there was by a branch line.'

'What do you think, Inspector?'

'Oh, I'm certain that Sheffield is going to be a major city one day.'

'I was asking about this case. Was it an accident or a crime?'

Colbeck pondered. 'It could be either.'

Rufus Moyle owned a large house in the most desirable part of the city. When the detectives arrived from the station in a cab, they realised that it was possible to see York Minster from the steps leading up to the front door. Leeming rang the bell and the door was opened by a servant. A woman came rushing into the hallway. Her face was a study in anxiety. As soon as Colbeck explained who they were, she gave a visible shudder.

'Is it about my husband?' she asked. 'I expected Rufus home hours ago.'

'May we come in, please, Mrs Moyle?'

'Yes, yes, of course.'

Beatrice Moyle beckoned them in and took them to the drawing room. She was a tall, slender woman ten years or so younger than her husband. Had she not been so distraught, she would have been strikingly beautiful. Colbeck invited her to sit down before he broke the news to her. He and Leeming also took a seat.

'I'm afraid that your husband was involved in an accident,' said Colbeck.

'I knew it,' she said, biting her lip. 'I had a premonition.'

'What sort of premonition, Mrs Moyle?'

'I just felt that something terrible was going to happen today. I begged Rufus not to go to work but he brushed aside my fears. What happened, Inspector?'

'Suffice it to say that he was badly injured in a fall. He's being cared for by a doctor in Sheffield. The accident has left him in a coma.'

'Dear God!' she exclaimed, leaping to her feet. 'I must go to him.'

'Sergeant Leeming will accompany you.'

'I'll pack some things in case I have to stay there.'

'Do the rest of the family need to be informed?'

'We have no children, Inspector, and our parents are all dead.'

'You might find it comforting to have a close friend with you, Mrs Moyle.'

'I'll be all right,' she said, bravely. 'Please excuse me.'

When she'd left, they had a chance to appraise their surroundings. They were in a large, well-proportioned room with a high ceiling. It was filled with costly and tasteful furniture from a century earlier. Over the mantelpiece was a full-length portrait of Rufus Moyle, a handsome man with long, wavy dark hair. Colbeck felt a pang of envy when he saw the exquisite apparel he was wearing. Leeming was quick to see a faint resemblance.

'He looks a bit like you, Inspector,' he remarked.

'I always think there's an element of narcissism in having one's portrait painted,' said Colbeck, 'and, happily, that's something I lack. I'd be much more likely to commission a portrait of Madeleine. She would adorn our home whereas I would feel embarrassed to see myself glaring down from a portrait.'

'Like you, Mr Moyle has a lovely wife. I wonder why *she* isn't hanging over the mantelpiece – or a portrait of both of them, maybe.'

'We may never know, Victor.'

'I noticed that you didn't tell her what had actually happened to him.'

'Mrs Moyle was clearly worried before we even got here,' said Colbeck. 'I didn't want to distress her even more by telling her that her husband had jumped out of a train. If she presses you for information, don't give too much away.'

'Where will you be, sir?'

'I intend to call on Mr Welling. When I've spoken to him, I'll catch the next train to Sheffield and join you at Doctor Scanlan's house. One last thing,' he added. 'If you can get her to volunteer the information, see what you can learn about Mrs Moyle and her husband. This room is telling me an interesting story. I'd like to know if my instincts about it are sound.'

Humphrey Welling was an affable man in his early fifties with prematurely white hair and a paunch. When he called at the house, Colbeck was given a cordial welcome and ushered into the library. Welling was surprised that a senior detective from Scotland Yard had been summoned to investigate what was simply an unfortunate accident.

'They happen all the time on the railways,' he said. 'I would have thought that it was too starved a subject for your sword, Inspector.'

'It may well be,' said Colbeck, noting the quotation from Shakespeare.

'Have you been in touch with the man's family?'

'We called on his wife earlier, sir. Mrs Moyle is now on her way to Sheffield.'

'Moyle, is it? The fellow didn't give me his name. To be honest, he was not the most communicative travelling companion. He spent most of the journey with his head buried in a newspaper.'

Welling described what had happened, telling a story that tallied to the last detail with the statement he'd given at the police station. He expressed sympathy at what he assumed was the death of Rufus Moyle.

'The gentleman is still alive,' said Colbeck, 'though he's in a coma and his life is hanging by a thread. I didn't want to alarm his wife by telling her that. Mrs Moyle will learn the full truth when she gets to Sheffield.' He looked at the well-stocked shelves. 'You're a reading man, I see.'

'I've only become one since my wife died,' explained Welling. 'That's when I had this room converted into a library. It helps to stave off loneliness.' He picked up the book on the table beside him. 'This is what's engrossing me at the moment. It's a history of cricket. Do you take an interest in the game, Inspector?'

'I try to, sir. In fact, I was telling my colleague about the report I read in *The Times* about Stephenson's hat trick. It was achieved at Hyde Park in Sheffield.'

'Yes and I kicked myself that I wasn't there to witness the feat. I've seen Stephenson bat and bowl many times. He's a born cricketer.'

Having got him on a subject in which they were both interested, Colbeck let him roll on, feeling that he'd discover far more about the man if he learnt about his passions. When there was a lull in the conversation, he shifted its direction.

'I gather that you're a director of the Midland Railway.'

'That's right, Inspector.'

'When it first came into existence, why didn't the NMR, as it was called then, build a direct line to Sheffield?'

'Ah,' said Welling, settling back into his chair, 'that's a long story.'

* * *

112

Having taken Beatrice Moyle to the house in a cab, Leeming bided his time. Doctor Scanlan gave his prognosis as gently as he could but it nevertheless had a stunning effect on Beatrice. She staggered backwards and would have fallen to the floor if Leeming had not caught her. He lowered her into a chair. It was several minutes before she recovered. When she did so, she insisted on seeing her husband. The doctor took her off into the room where the patient lay and Leeming heard her cry of horror. He waited for a long time before she emerged. The doctor was more or less supporting her. He helped her into a chair where she sobbed into a handkerchief. Scanlan took Leeming aside.

'The situation is this,' he whispered. 'Mr Moyle is very near his end. His wife wanted to stay with him but feels she'd be unequal to the ordeal. She's already overwrought. There's a hotel where she's stayed before. I suggest that you take her there, Sergeant. If there's any change in his condition, I've promised that word will be sent at once – whatever time it might be.'

'That's very good of you.'

'I'm surprised that he's held out this long.'

'I'll take Mrs Moyle away for a while.'

Overcome with grief, Beatrice took a last look at her husband before leaving. Their cab had been waiting outside so they were able to go straight to a hotel at the heart of the town. When Leeming tried to reserve a room for her, Beatrice insisted that she could manage that. After thanking him for his help, she went slowly upstairs. Leeming walked across to the reception desk and spoke to the duty manager.

'Take good care of the lady,' he said. 'She's had to bear some terrible news.'

'I understand, sir.'

'This is not her first visit here, I believe.'

'No, sir,' said the man. 'They've stayed here a few times in the last year.'

'When did you last have Mr and Mrs Moyle as your guests?'

The duty manager raised a quizzical eyebrow. 'I beg your pardon, sir?'

When Colbeck left the train at Sheffield, he went quickly into the waiting room and stayed there until all the passengers had got off. Only when everyone had gone past did he take a cab to Scanlan's house. Leeming had returned but there was no sign of the doctor. He came into the room with a gesture of helplessness.

'Mr Moyle has passed away,' he declared. 'There was nothing I could do.'

'You did all that was humanly possible,' said Colbeck.

'The astonishing thing is that he survived that fall from the train.'

'I don't believe that he was meant to, Doctor.'

'Well,' said Leeming, 'I suppose I'd better go to the hotel where Mrs Moyle is staying and . . . pass on the sad news.'

'Please do that.'

'I discovered a strange thing, sir. She and her husband have stayed there before but she reserved the room under a very different name.'

'That's only natural,' said Colbeck, 'because the man with

whom she stayed there was not her husband. I don't know what alias he used but I'd wager anything that his real name is Humphrey Welling.'

Leeming was astounded. 'How did you find that out?'

'I listened and then I looked. Mr Welling is altogether too plausible. He gave me an account of Mr Moyle's leap from the train as if he'd been rehearsing it from a prepared text. He pretended to be hearing Moyle's name for the first time when I mentioned it,' recalled Colbeck, 'but I saw a light in his eye when I told him that Mrs Moyle was on her way to Sheffield. As a result, he came here as well. My guess is that he will already have joined Mrs Moyle.'

'Are you *sure* he's here, Inspector?'

'He caught the same train that I did, making certain that I didn't see him board it. When we got to the station here, however, I lingered in the waiting room so that I could watch them both go by.'

'Them?' echoed Scanlan.

'It was Mr Welling and a servant of his, a broad-shouldered fellow who admitted me to the house. Welling wouldn't have the strength to overpower another man. Besides, he has a game leg. His servant, however, has the look of someone who'd do anything for which he was paid. In short,' said Colbeck, 'there were *three* of them in that compartment.'

'Do you have any proof of that, sir?' asked Leeming. 'If you confront them, they'll simply deny it and Mr Moyle is no longer alive to challenge them.'

'Yes, he is, Victor.'

'But I've just pronounced him dead,' said Scanlan, confused.

'*We* know that,' said Colbeck, 'but they don't. I think we should bring him back to life like a latter-day Lazarus. The message that the sergeant will take to the hotel is that Mr Moyle has rallied a little and should recover consciousness.' His smile broadened into a grin. 'That should produce a result, I fancy.'

It was in the early hours of the morning when a figure crept stealthily around to the rear of the house. There was enough moonlight to help him find his way to a particular window. Since the curtains had been left slightly open, he was able to make out the shape of a body in the bed. Making as little noise as possible, he inserted a knife and flicked the catch on the sash window. He then lifted the window up and stepped cautiously through it, intending to grab the pillow to smother the patient to death. When he approached the bed, however, he found that he'd have a lot more resistance than he'd expected. A man leapt suddenly out of bed, grappled with him then flung him hard against the wall before felling him with a vicious right hook. As he collapsed to the floor, the visitor heard the door open and someone came in with an oil lamp to illumine the scene.

'Well done, Victor!' said Colbeck. 'Put the handcuffs on him.'

Having driven to the police station in the trap borrowed from the doctor, they left their prisoner in custody and went on to the hotel. After explaining the purpose of their visit to the duty manager, they went upstairs and roused the occupants of one room by pounding on the door. It was Beatrice Moyle who

116

opened it a few inches, blinking in bewilderment when she saw the detectives. Colbeck gave Leeming the privilege of arresting both her and Humphrey Welling on a charge of conspiracy to murder. The prisoners were given time to dress then taken off to the police station to join their accomplice. As they left the building, Leeming wanted clarification.

'However did you link Mr Welling with Mrs Moyle?' he asked. 'They just didn't look like a married couple. Welling was so much older.'

'So was her real husband, Victor. The lady is obviously drawn to more mature men. Unfortunately, marriage to Rufus Moyle did not live up to her expectations. She was a neglected wife in a house that reflected his personality and not hers.'

'There was that portrait of him.'

'It was only one of the indications that told me he was a strutting peacock.'

'Then there was the fact that they had no children.'

'I did say that she was a neglected wife and I meant it in the fullest sense. Mr Welling may not have seemed the ideal replacement but he was rich, indulgent and knew how to talk to a woman. How they first met,' said Colbeck, 'I don't know but I believe there was genuine love on both sides. There had to be because that's what drove them to the extreme of murder.'

'Welling could have found out from Mrs Moyle when exactly her husband would be travelling to Sheffield,' said Leeming. 'He made sure that he shared the same compartment and his servant did the rest.'

'Oddly enough, I rather liked Welling. He was an engaging

companion and his love of cricket almost won me over. But he was also a ladies' man whereas Moyle – remember the portrait and the attention to his appearance – sought company among his own sex.'

'I can never understand people like that, sir.'

'You don't have to, Victor. You can simply bask in your glory.'

'What glory?'

'Don't be modest,' said Colbeck, patting him on the back. 'You made three arrests in succession – Welling, his servant and Mrs Moyle. That's what I'd call a hat trick.'

HELPING HAND

Having spent so many years in the army, Edward Tallis knew the importance of a disciplined way of life. As far as possible, he kept everything to an unvarying routine, leaving for work at precisely the same time every morning and organising each day in a similar manner. No matter how busy he was, he always found time for a brisk walk around noon to maintain fitness and to disperse the stink of cigar smoke that always clung to him. After leaving Scotland Yard that morning, he walked along Victoria Street. He was a big, straight-backed man with a moustache that he liked to stroke as if it were a favourite cat. His stride was long and his speed impressive. Few people could keep pace with him.

Tallis was about to cross a side street when he became aware of commotion to his left. Farther down the street, people were yelling and jeering at someone. Unable to see the object of their scorn, Tallis walked towards the crowd. They were gathered around the window of a butcher's shop, howling abuse at a man who'd just emerged from the alley that ran alongside the building. Leading the verbal assault was the butcher himself, a solid man in a long apron that almost touched the floor.

'Bugger off!' he shouted, waving a fist. 'Take that lousy cur of yours away or I'll be after the pair of you with my cleaver!'

Other people felt obliged to add their own threats and some of the worst insults came from women. Tallis's voice rose above the hubbub.

'What's going on?' he asked, the authority in his tone imposing an instant silence. 'What is this fellow supposed to have done?'

'Just look at him, sir,' replied the butcher. 'You can see that he's a miserable good-for-nothing. I caught him sleeping in the yard at the rear of my shop. These people are my neighbours. We don't want him here but he just won't leave.'

'You're not giving him any chance to leave,' argued Tallis. 'How can he move when you've got him trapped here? If you all disappear, I'm sure that he'll take the opportunity to be on his way.' When they hesitated, his voice became peremptory. 'Go home,' he ordered. 'I'm a detective superintendent in the Metropolitan Police. I'll deal with this situation.'

Deprived of the pleasure of baiting the man, some complained and others rid themselves of a few expletives but they all drifted away under Tallis's stern gaze. With a dark scowl, the angry butcher withdrew into his shop and slammed the door behind him. Tallis was at last able to take a proper look at the person who had been at the centre of the rumpus. Tall, skinny and dishevelled, he was of indeterminate age. The lank hair that hung down from under his battered hat merged with his ragged beard. His clothing was tattered, his boots falling apart. What had enraged the crowd was his sinister appearance. One eye was closed shut and there was a livid scar down his cheek. Cowering behind him was a small, bedraggled dog with its tongue hanging out. The animal had been frightened by the crowd but the man had shown no fear, taking their invective on the chin as if used to such contempt.

'What's your name?' asked Tallis.

'Joel Anstey, sir.'

'I fancy that you've been in the army.'

'Yes, sir,' said Anstey, saluting. 'I was proud to serve Queen and Country.'

'I feel the same.' He stepped forward to examine the man's face. 'Where did you get those injuries?'

'It was in the Crimea. A few weeks after we arrived there, I had my cheek sliced open by a Russian sabre. A year later, I lost my eye. But I don't regret my days in the army, sir,' he went on. 'I spent the happiest years of my life in uniform.' He gave a dry laugh. 'Would it surprise you to know that I was considered handsome at one time? What woman would look twice at me now?'

'And *did* you sleep in the butcher's yard?'

'No, sir – I merely climbed in there to see if he'd thrown out any old bones.' He indicated the dog. 'Sam is hungry.'

'You look as if you both are.'

'When the butcher found us, he threw a bucket of water over Sam.'

'Well, you were trespassing.'

'We did no harm, sir.'

Tallis sized him up. The man was articulate and respectful. There was no trace of self-pity. Evidently, he cared more for the dog than for his own welfare.

'You sound as if you were born here in London,' observed Tallis.

'I was, sir – in the parish of St Martin-in-the-Fields.'

'There's a workhouse just behind the National Gallery.'

'I'm not so desperate as to go there,' said Anstey with a flash of indignation. 'Besides, they'd turn me away. I'm able-bodied and far too young. I'm still well short of forty.'

Tallis was taken aback because the man looked considerably older.

'What was your trade, Anstey?'

'Before I went in the army,' replied the other, 'I was a saddler but you need two good eyes to handle leather and, in any case, I've lost the trick of it. I'm not asking for money, sir,' he insisted. 'I just want work so that I can earn my keep and feed Sam properly. We need a helping hand, that's all.'

Tallis was moved by his plea. Poverty and homelessness were ever-present in the nation's capital. Untold thousands lived on the streets and scratched out a bare existence as best they could. Joel Anstey's story was a familiar one but it somehow touched the superintendent at a deep level.

'I'll see what I can do,' he said.

'I'm surprised at the superintendent,' said Madeleine. 'I don't wish to be unkind but he never struck me as a compassionate man.'

'Tallis has the occasional impulse to help someone,' said Colbeck with a smile, 'and he's a good Christian. Something about this person obviously spoke to him. When he asked me if we could find him a few days' work, I said that we could.'

'Why can't this man tend the superintendent's garden?'

'He doesn't have one, Madeleine. He lives alone in a set of rooms. And as you know, Victor's little house has no garden at all. That's why Tallis turned to me.' He put affectionate hands on her shoulders. 'I didn't think that you'd mind.'

'I don't, Robert,' she said, 'but I suspect that Draycott will.'

Colbeck groaned. 'Ah, I was forgetting him.'

'He likes to rule the roost in the garden.'

'I'll warn Anstey not to tread on his toes.'

'Draycott can be very touchy.'

'We're not having him throwing his weight around, Madeleine. When all's said and done, we pay Draycott's wages. If we choose to let someone else work in the garden,' said Colbeck, reasonably, 'then nobody is in a position to stop us.'

'I still foresee trouble.'

'Keep the two of them apart – that's the secret.'

When Anstey reported for work on the following day, he snatched off his hat and stood in front of Madeleine with his head bowed. Forewarned about his rather menacing appearance, she pretended not to notice his face and took him around to the garden with his dog. Long and fairly narrow, it featured a series of small, rectangular lawns edged with flower beds.

'My husband likes a formal garden,' she explained.

'I can see that, Mrs Colbeck. It's well looked after.'

'The gardener pops in two or three times a week. His name is Draycott. There's no telling if he'll turn up today. What I'd suggest you do is to weed the patch at the far end. It's hidden behind the trellis and is badly overgrown.'

'What about a rake and such like?'

'I'll unlock the shed for you,' she said, holding up the key. 'Then I'll see if I can't find a bone for the dog as well as a bowl of water.'

'His name is Sam,' said Anstey, 'and he's as thankful as I am.'

'That's good to hear.'

'I'm not afraid of hard work, Mrs Colbeck. I'll soon prove that.'

Madeleine warmed to him. Though his facial injuries were unsightly, his voice and manner suggested a decent, honest man who'd fallen on hard times. Like Tallis, she was ready to offer a helping hand.

'It's never happened before,' he said.

'What hasn't?'

'Having a favour done by the police. Between you and me, I usually steer clear of them. Police don't like the look of me. They're always moving me on.'

Madeleine unlocked the shed and showed him the range of garden implements inside. After selecting a hoe and a rake, he walked to the end of the garden with the dog trotting after him. Coat off and sleeves rolled up, Anstey was soon at work. It was time for Madeleine to go up to her studio and she was soon absorbed in putting the finishing touches to her latest painting. With a brush in her hand, she lost all track of time and her concentration was only broken when she heard the sound of a raised voice in the garden. Rushing to the window, she looked down to see Nathaniel Draycott, brandishing a sickle and berating his new assistant. Madeleine rushed off to separate them before the argument got out of hand.

Robert Colbeck spent the morning in court, giving evidence against a man he'd caught stealing a substantial amount of money from the railway company employing him. When he got back to Scotland Yard, he went straight to the superintendent to give his report. Embezzlement had been going on for almost a year and had only been halted by Colbeck's intervention. Tallis was pleased to hear that a guilty verdict was almost guaranteed and that the man in question would face a long prison sentence.

'Did you enjoy your time in court?' he asked.

'I always do, sir. I loved working as a barrister until I reached a point where I decided it was more important to catch criminals than simply prosecute them. I'd never trade my life at Scotland Yard for a return to the bar.'

'I'm relieved to hear it, Colbeck.'

'Will that be all, sir? The sergeant and I have suspects to interview.'

'Then off you go,' said Tallis, waving a hand. 'No, wait,' he added. 'I meant to thank you for taking Anstey on.'

'It's only for a few days,' Colbeck pointed out.

'It makes no difference. It's paid employment and it will boost his spirits. Do you know what his last job was?'

'No, Superintendent, I don't.'

'He was earning nine pence a day breaking up stones with a sledgehammer. Anstey had to work alongside convicts. It was demeaning. That's why he left.'

'I hope that he won't find gardening beneath him.'

'He'll be very appreciative of the kindness you and Mrs Colbeck have shown him. He won't have to rub shoulders with desperate criminals and he'll be able to work in pleasant surroundings. After sleeping rough and being hustled from pillar to post, Anstey will find your house a haven of peace.'

Madeleine had difficulty calming down the two men. Anstey was plainly upset at being called an interloper while Draycott was throbbing with fury at the thought that he'd be supplanted. He was also livid that Sam had relieved himself in one of the flower beds. Madeleine explained that Anstey was there to do the kind of menial jobs that would actually help the gardener but Draycott was in no mood for appeasement. He was a short, squat man in his late fifties with a wrinkled face and an expression of permanent disapproval. Because he was so dependable, Colbeck and his wife tolerated his many idiosyncrasies and learnt not to interfere. As long as he was in charge, Draycott lapsed into a kind of contented cantankerousness. There was no whiff of contentment now.

'If I *must* put up with this . . .' he said, pointedly.

Madeleine was firm. 'You must, Mr Draycott.'

'Then I insist on telling him what to do.'

'That seems fair enough to me. Don't you think so, Mr Anstey?'

'Yes, I do,' said Anstey, guardedly.

'You're not to touch anything in the shed unless I say so,' cautioned the gardener, 'and that dog of yours is to be kept off the lawns and the flower beds.'

'Yes, Mr Draycott.'

Anstey spoke through gritted teeth but he nodded politely when he was given a list of tasks. Since it was clear that the two men had hated each other on sight, Madeleine was having second thoughts about taking Anstey on but she did not wish to upset her husband or, indirectly, Edward Tallis. She stayed with them until a form of truce had been established. Draycott then announced that he had other gardens to visit and stalked off. Though Madeleine was glad to see him go, Anstey stared after him with muted hostility. During the fierce argument, his pride had been wounded. She sought to soothe his hurt feelings.

'Don't be put off by Draycott's manner,' she said, airily. 'He's always rather prickly, even with us at times. It's just his way.'

'I see, Mrs Colbeck.'

Anstey attempted a smile but there was no warmth in it. He was still simmering. In the irascible gardener, he'd clearly made an enemy.

For the rest of the day, Madeleine heard no more from him. Whenever she glanced through the window, she saw him working away at the various chores he'd been given by Draycott. She sent out refreshments on a tray and didn't forget the promise of a bone and some water for Sam. Colbeck had suggested that he was paid at the end of each day so that he had money in his pocket. Madeleine could see the pleasure Anstey felt as the coins were pressed into his hand. He and the dog went off happily.

When he got back that evening, Colbeck asked his wife what had happened. On hearing about the clash between Anstey and Draycott, he was disturbed.

'It's just as well that you were here to hold them apart,' he said worriedly. 'I know that Draycott has given us good service but I'm not having him threatening anyone with a sickle. When I next see him, I'll have a word with him.'

'I fancy that he won't be around for a while, Robert. He loathed Anstey and may well wait until he's gone.'

'The superintendent is bound to ask after Anstey. What will I tell him?'

'Say that he's been an asset to us. He worked really hard.'

'What about his brush with Draycott?' asked Colbeck.

'Oh, I shouldn't mention that to him. It's all in the past now. We won't get any more unpleasantness like that.'

Joel Anstey arrived early the following morning so Colbeck had the opportunity of making his own estimation of the man. Though he wore the same clothes, Anstey had paid to have his hair cut and beard trimmed. He'd also bought a pair of second-hand boots. He removed his hat when he met Colbeck and thanked him time and again for taking him on. He promised that the dog would keep well away from the lawns and the flower beds. For his part, Colbeck was impressed by the man's manner and by his willingness to work at a tedious job. Unlike many who lived on the streets, Anstey could read, write and had served an apprenticeship in a reputable trade. Army life had equipped him with other skills.

'You deserve better than we can offer, I fear,' said Colbeck.

'I'll take what I can get, sir.'

'Then I'll leave you to get on with it.'

* * *

It was a glorious day with the sun beating down on the garden. Sweating profusely, Anstey worked steadily on. Madeleine made sure that he had plenty of water to drink and gave orders for food to be sent out to him. She was able to immerse herself in her own work and forget all about her assistant gardener. Draycott's absence allowed peace to reign in the garden. It was late afternoon when a servant came up to her studio. The gardener was asking to speak to her. Madeleine went downstairs at once. Expecting to meet Anstey, she was put out when she was confronted by the bristling Nathaniel Draycott.

'Call the police, Mrs Colbeck,' he advised.

'Why ever should I do that?'

'You've got a thief on the premises.'

'I don't believe that, Mr Draycott.'

'You heard me,' he said, impatiently. 'I warned Anstey not to poke about in my shed. I let him borrow some of my tools but he was not to touch anything else. He disobeyed my orders.'

'I can't believe that,' she said.

'It's true, Mrs Colbeck. He's the only other person who's been in that shed.'

'I know. I watched him put all the tools carefully back in there before I locked it. I opened the shed again this morning and he took out the same things. Whenever I've glanced into the garden, he's been nowhere near the shed.'

'He's a sly devil,' said Draycott. 'He sneaked in there when you weren't looking, I daresay. I wouldn't trust him an inch.'

'Did you challenge him about the missing items?'

'No, I didn't because I'd only have lost my temper. I need

you present, Mrs Colbeck.' His lip curled. 'I hate thieves. They're the lowest of the low.'

If there was going to be another explosive meeting between the two men, Madeleine wanted to be there. While she retained her trust in Anstey, she didn't think that Draycott would make empty accusations. She went with him into the garden and summoned the other man. As he walked towards them, Anstey looked defensive.

'What have you done with my pipe and tobacco?' demanded Draycott.

'Let me handle this,' said Madeleine, exerting control. She turned to Anstey. 'It seems that certain things are missing from the shed. Do you know anything about them?'

'He stole them – it's as clear as day!'

'If you keep shouting like that, Mr Draycott, I'll have to ask you to leave.' He took a step back and glared sullenly. 'Let me repeat the question, Mr Anstey.'

'There's no need,' said Anstey. 'I haven't touched his pipe and tobacco.'

'What about my trowel, my sickle and the knife I use to sharpen sticks? Yes,' Draycott went on, 'and other small things have gone missing as well.'

'Well, I never took them.'

'You're a thief and a liar!'

'I told you to keep your voice down, Mr Draycott,' said Madeleine, sharply. 'Since you can't do that, I suggest that you go home until you can speak in a more civilised manner. Go on – off you go.'

Draycott issued a flood of apologies but Madeleine was immune to his pleas.

'*He's* the thief,' he protested, 'and I'm the one who has to go.'

Shooting a look of disgust at Anstey, he slunk off. Madeleine waited until he'd left before she repeated her question once more. Anstey spread his arms.

'What possible use do I have for a trowel, a sickle and a knife?' he asked. 'I've got all I need for my work. If you still think I'm a thief, search my coat. It's hanging on the trellis.' He pulled out the pockets of his trousers. 'As you can see, I have nothing about me. You and your husband have been *good* to me, Mrs Colbeck. I'd never let you down, I swear it.'

Madeleine was in a quandary. She wasn't sure whether to pay Anstey off so that she could get rid of him altogether or to give him a day's wage and invite him back for the morrow. The latter course of action would infuriate Draycott and suggest that she rated the word of a casual labourer above that of a loyal employee. Whatever decision she made would upset one of the men. She even toyed with the idea of paying Anstey for another day's work but telling him not to return. To know that the man had been effectively dismissed might assuage Draycott's anger a little but nothing short of arrest would really satisfy him.

She wrestled with the problem for a long time before asking herself a simple question. What was the point of being married to a famous detective if she didn't make use of him when a crime had allegedly taken place?

'Come back early in the morning,' she said to Anstey, 'before my husband leaves for work. I'll pay you for today, of course, then there's another day's work if you wish to take it.'

'I'll take it,' said Anstey, gratefully. He studied her for a few moments. 'Before I go, I need to ask you something, Mrs Colbeck.'

'Go on.'

'Did you believe what Mr Draycott said about me?'

Feeling great discomfort, Madeleine searched hard for a noncommittal answer.

'Let's discuss it tomorrow,' she said.

Because he got back home very late, she didn't burden Colbeck with the problem she'd encountered. Madeleine waited until they were having breakfast next morning. She freely confessed that she didn't know if she'd done the right thing.

'I don't think that Anstey will come back,' she said.

'Oh, he'll be back, I assure you.'

'What if he *did* steal those things?'

'Then he's hidden them somewhere in the garden so that he can take them with him today and sell them for a small profit. Draycott could be mistaken, of course,' said Colbeck, reaching for his cup of tea. 'We've noticed before that he has lapses of memory. He might just have mislaid the items he thinks were stolen.'

'No, Robert, he wouldn't do that. He's very possessive about his tools.'

'Who else does he work for?'

'He has three or four gardens to look after, including the one next door, of course. I've spoken about him to Mr and Mrs Grayston.'

'What's their opinion of him?'

'Much the same as ours,' she replied. 'They say that Draycott is inclined to be grumpy but he's as honest as the day is long. He's been their gardener for years.'

'So who do we believe – a man like Draycott with a good record of service or some fellow plucked off the street by the superintendent?'

'Anstey did it,' she decided. 'That's why we'll never see him again.'

The doorbell rang. 'I fancy that may be wrong,' said Colbeck with a grin. After draining his cup, he stood up. 'I'll get to the bottom of this.'

Taking him into the garden, Colbeck asked Anstey to show him exactly what he'd done on the previous day. The man responded quickly. While Sam went scampering off towards the far end of the garden, Colbeck was given a brief tour by Anstey who pointed out a whole range of things he'd done. Colbeck glanced down at the green patches on the man's knees.

'You forgot to mention the weeding,' he said. 'I think you spent a lot of time kneeling on the grass in that neglected area behind the trellis.'

'My back was breaking by the time I'd finished.'

'I can imagine.'

Anstey licked his lips. 'It wasn't me, sir,' he said. 'I'm no thief.'

'I haven't accused you of anything.'

'Mr Draycott did. He'll say anything to get rid of me.'

'Let's have no criticism of Draycott,' warned Colbeck. 'He's an experienced gardener. The truth is that I simply don't have time to take a proper interest in what happens out here. If it were not for Draycott, all this would be a jungle.'

'He's done a good job,' conceded Anstey, 'though he's let those bushes at the far end grow far too much. They'll need pruning in the autumn.'

'I'll take your word for it.'

Colbeck asked him a series of apparently innocuous questions about his past, probing away in the hope that he'd find the true measure of the man. Anstey's replies became more and more hesitant. For the first time, he began to look shifty. They were still deep in conversation when Madeleine brought Draycott into view. The gardener surged towards the two figures.

'Lay hold on him, Inspector!' he cried. 'He stole my tools.'

'What evidence do you have of that?' asked Colbeck.

'I have the evidence of my own eyes, sir. Only one person has been working near my shed over the last couple of days and that's the rogue standing next to you. Nobody else could have taken my things,' he stressed, 'unless, of course, you think that Mrs Colbeck is guilty.'

'Heaven forbid!' exclaimed Madeleine.

'I think we can rule out my wife,' said Colbeck, good-humouredly, 'but suspicion is bound to fall on you, Anstey. Did you go into that shed?'

'Yes, I did,' admitted the other, 'but it was only to put some things away.'

'And to take others out,' sneered Draycott. 'Admit it – you were tempted.'

All eyes were turned on Anstey. He looked away and moved his feet uneasily.

'Is that right?' pressed Colbeck. '*Did* you yield to temptation?'

'No,' said Anstey, meeting his gaze. 'I didn't. When I found those flagons of beer hidden away in there, I wanted to slake my thirst because it had been hot work. But I held back. Because that beer was not mine, I never even touched it.'

It was Draycott's turn to look hunted. Madeleine was shocked.

'What's this about beer?' asked Colbeck, fixing him with a stare. 'You were told when you first came here that no alcohol was allowed. How long have you been drinking in secret in the shed?'

'Oh, I don't drink it, sir,' gabbled Draycott, 'I'm looking after it for a friend.'

'Don't insult my intelligence, man!'

'I'm not the criminal here, Mr Colbeck – *he* is.'

He pointed at Anstey but nobody else was looking. Colbeck and Madeleine were diverted by some excited yapping. The dog had obviously found something. Anstey ran to the bottom of the garden to see what was happening and the others followed. Sam had been thorough. Having sniffed around the base of some bushes, he'd found that he could easily get through to the neighbouring garden by moving a loose branch. At his feet was a trowel that he'd retrieved from next door.

'I'll wager that it belongs to you, Draycott,' said Colbeck, guessing what must have happened. 'You're employed by Mr and Mrs Grayston, aren't you? I wonder if they know that you can get from their garden into ours and back again with relative ease. I believe that, on the first day we had Anstey, you came back when nobody was looking and moved some tools from the shed to the other side of those bushes. Then you had the gall to accuse him of a crime.'

'I told you it wasn't me,' said Anstey.

Draycott gave a nervous laugh. 'It was only in fun,' he said. 'I was playing a little joke, that's all. I never really meant to get him into trouble.'

'Well, I mean to get *you* into trouble,' said Colbeck, clapping a hand on his shoulder. 'You've been hiding beer in the shed, gaining illegal access between this garden and the one next door, subjecting Mr Anstey to threatening language and behaviour, contriving to incriminate him and lying your head off when you're caught out. I'm sure that I can think of a few other charges to add to the list. But don't worry,' he continued, 'it's only in fun. It's *my* little joke.' Draycott hung his head in shame. Colbeck's gaze shifted to Anstey. 'It seems that we've just lost a gardener. I don't suppose that you'd care to help us out a little longer, would you?'

'Yes, please!' cried Anstey in delight.

'The first thing you can do is to repair that gap between the two houses. Like us, our neighbours are entitled to privacy. Neither we nor they want anyone coming in from next door whenever they choose.'

'Oh,' said Madeleine, fondling the dog, 'I think there's something we must do before that. We must find Sam another bone. He deserves it. I yield to none in my admiration of my husband's abilities as a policeman but – just for today – Sam is the *real* detective.'

SONGS FOR A SWEDISH
NIGHTINGALE

'Jenny Lind?'

'Even *you* must have heard of her,' said Colbeck.

'No, sir, I haven't.'

'She's one of the most famous sopranos in the world, Victor. Have you never heard mention of the Swedish Nightingale?'

'I'm not very interested in birds,' said Leeming.

'It's the nickname of Jenny Lind because she sings with the purity of a nightingale. People used to fight to get tickets to see her. Her operatic career made her a fortune. When she was in America, she's reputed to have earned enormous amounts of money.'

Leeming was astounded. 'She got all that just for imitating a bird?'

'Even the most gifted nightingale couldn't sing the great arias that she made her own. As for the money,' said Colbeck, 'she gave a large amount of it away to found and endow scholarships in Sweden. I once had the privilege of hearing her in *La Sonnambula* . . .'

He broke off as he saw the look of bewilderment on the sergeant's face. It was not Leeming's fault that he was ignorant of opera. Detectives at Scotland Yard were not well paid and someone like Leeming would need every penny of his wage to house, clothe and feed his young family. There'd no money left to indulge an interest in classical music and opera. Colbeck chided himself for boasting about the fact that he'd actually heard the Swedish soprano. It was unfair on a man to whom names of such operatic luminaries as Jenny Lind, Alboni, Mario and Grisi meant nothing whatsoever.

'What has this lady got to do with us, Inspector?'

'We are going to accompany her to Birmingham,' replied Colbeck.

'Why?'

'Her husband, Mr Goldschmidt, has requested police protection for her.'

Leeming was dismayed. 'That's no job for us,' he protested. 'A pair of country constables could look after her, leaving us to solve serious crimes.'

'In this case,' explained Colbeck, 'we're there to prevent a crime rather than solve one. It seems that there have been threatening letters, some of them no doubt sent by jealous rivals and therefore written out of spite. Whether or not there's any real danger, I don't know, but we have been assigned to look after her.'

'The superintendent will be very annoyed to lose us on such trivial grounds.'

'It was his idea that you and I should be chosen.'

Leeming was flabbergasted. '*His* idea?'

'Yes, Victor, and it was a surprise to me as well. Tallis is so hostile to the female sex in general that I couldn't believe he actually admired a member of it. But he does, apparently, and her name is Jenny Lind.'

'Then I'll be very pleased to meet her. If she can arouse the superintendent's interest, she must be a very special lady.'

'She is,' said Colbeck. 'That's why we must take great care of her.'

When she boarded the train at Euston station, Jenny Lind wore a hat with a veil in order to avoid recognition by any admirers. She was travelling with her husband, Otto Goldschmidt, a composer and conductor of international standing. The Swedish Nightingale was going to Birmingham to perform in a concert at the Town Hall. She was a short woman in her late thirties but motherhood had robbed her of her earlier daintiness. Her face was quite plain in repose but, when she smiled, it became radiant. With her veil lifted up and with her delightful broken English, she entranced Victor Leeming. He and Colbeck shared a first-class compartment with the pair. Goldschmidt was younger, taller and wore muttonchop whiskers but the detectives paid him scant attention. Their eyes were fixed on his wife.

'It's a pity that we're not going to Brighton,' suggested Colbeck.

'Oh?' said Jenny. 'Why is that, Inspector?'

'Because we might be taken there by a locomotive that bears

your name. As you know, the original *Jenny Lind* was built just over a decade ago for the London Brighton and South Coast Railway. It was such a success that its design was adopted for use on other railways. In other words,' he said, gallantly, 'both on the track and on the stage, you have set the standard.'

'There is only one Jenny Lind,' said Goldschmidt, proudly.

'I couldn't agree more, sir. I had the good fortune to see your wife giving a recital in London. It was a memorable experience.'

'Thank you.'

Conscious that Leeming was being excluded from the conversation, Colbeck sought to bring him into it by recalling an investigation they'd once made into a major crash on the Brighton line. What Leeming remembered most about the case was that it resulted in a rare treat for his family.

'The railway company was so grateful when we'd arrested the man who'd caused the crash that it gave us first-class return tickets to Brighton. My children are still talking about our day by the seaside.'

Jenny Lind was prompted to talk about her own children and of the difficulty of leaving them – now that she and her husband had settled in England – when she had engagements in various parts of the country. One of the reasons she'd had no qualms about ending her operatic career was that she wished to spend time with her family. Colbeck suspected that she also found the concert platform more congenial and less exhausting. Once started on the subject of parenthood, Jenny and her husband talked at length and Leeming compared his own situation as a father with the problems they faced.

It was a paradox. In seeking to draw the sergeant into the

conversation, Colbeck had effectively excluded himself because he and Madeleine had no children as yet and he could not therefore join in the discussion. He did not mind in the least. Even if she were not singing, it was a joy to hear Jenny Lind's voice and he was pleased that Leeming was relishing a train journey for once instead of complaining about it. Ostensibly, the detectives were there to act as bodyguards but Colbeck couldn't believe that anyone would wish to inflict harm on such a remarkable lady as the one sitting opposite him. Keeping an eye on her was the most rewarding assignment that he'd ever had.

As soon as they arrived at the station in Birmingham, it was clear that a veil would be unable to act as an effective disguise for the singer. Word of her arrival had spread and a large crowd of well-wishers had gathered for a glimpse of her. Reporters from local newspapers were there, autograph hunters were poised and someone had set up a camera on a tripod. Among those waiting to welcome her was Charles Rosen, the impresario who had persuaded Jenny Lind to perform in the city. He was a big, stout, flamboyantly dressed man in his fifties with a cigar in his mouth. When the train steamed into the station, he raised his top hat in triumph. She had arrived.

Jenny stepped onto the platform amid cheers and thunderous applause. Rosen had to bullock his way towards her, removing his cigar to greet her then pumping her husband's hand. As they headed for the exit, Colbeck and Leeming stayed close to the singer to prevent her from being jostled. They came out into the street and moved towards a waiting carriage but they never reached it. A shot suddenly rang out and the crowd flew into a panic. Colbeck's first instinct was to stand protectively in front of the singer. Leeming moved in the direction from which the shot had come. Rosen urged Jenny and her husband to get into the carriage so that they could be driven away. Reaching the vehicle, however, proved to be almost impossible in the swirling crowd. Colbeck was tripped up, Goldschmidt was thrust aside and Rosen was distracted by a second shot. Hysteria now gripped the throng and they began to run in all directions. Rosen stood beside the carriage, holding the door wide open but the only people who reached him were Colbeck and Goldschmidt. All three looked around in consternation.

'Where's my wife?' demanded Goldschmidt.

Colbeck squirmed with guilt. He and Leeming had failed signally to protect Jenny Lind. Assessing the situation, he reached a grim conclusion.

'I'm afraid that she's been kidnapped, sir.'

It was mystifying. Hundreds of people had been milling around yet not one of them could say with certainty what had happened. Jenny had somehow been hustled away in one of the many cabs that flitted around but nobody knew in which direction it had gone. Convinced that someone had tried to kill his wife, Goldschmidt railed at the detectives for their incompetence. Rosen added his condemnation, fearing that he would lose all the money he'd spent promoting the concert and laying the blame squarely on the shoulders of Colbeck and Leeming. All four of them adjourned quickly to the police station in Digbeth to alert the local constabulary and to institute a hunt for the missing singer. When he'd calmed the two men down, Colbeck began with an apology.

'The sergeant and I accept the blame unreservedly,' he said. 'We were given a task that we failed to fulfil. It's futile to claim that we could not have foreseen such an eventuality but one thing is clear, Mr Goldschmidt,' he went on, eager to reassure him. 'Your wife is not the victim of an assassination attempt.'

'You heard those shots, man!' wailed Goldschmidt.

'They were some distance away, sir.'

'It's true,' confirmed Leeming. 'In fact, the second shot was further away than the first. Someone was just trying to spread alarm.'

'Well, he succeeded,' said Rosen.

'But that's all he was there to do,' argued Colbeck. 'If an armed man really had designs on Miss Lind, he would have got within range of her and made one shot count. We're not looking for an enemy here. We're after a . . . well, I suppose you might call him a friend of sorts.'

'A friend!' howled Goldschmidt. 'Firing a gun and abducting my wife is a strange way to show friendship.'

'Let me explain. Jenny Lind is one of the greatest singers in the world.'

'She is *the* greatest,' asserted Rosen. 'It says so in all my advertisements.'

'I'm inclined to agree, sir, and so does the kidnapper. My feeling is that he's an ardent admirer who has let his admiration grow into an obsession. Knowing that she was coming here, he devised a plan to whisk her away so that he could hear her sing in private.'

'My wife won't be able to sing a note,' said Goldschmidt. 'Jenny will be terrified – and it's all the fault of you and your sergeant.'

'We will do our best to rectify our mistake.'

'And how do we do that, pray?'

'By drawing up a list of suspects,' said Colbeck.

'What's the point of that?' asked Rosen with a wild laugh. 'This is a city with a population of 200,000 or more. Every one of them is a suspect.'

'No, they're not,' said Leeming. 'We can eliminate women and children for a start. People in the lower classes might know the name of Jenny Lind but none of them could ever afford to hear her sing. They, too, can be forgotten. I think that the inspector is right. The abduction was carefully set up so that she was snatched under our noses without coming to any harm.'

'A number of accomplices were involved,' Colbeck reminded them. 'Apart from the person who fired the pistol, there were the ones who shoved us aside and those who actually spirited her away. We are searching for a rich man, gentlemen. He can afford to hire a number of reliable assistants. The vast majority of people at the railway station were devoted followers of Jenny Lind,' he said. 'One of them, alas, was rather too devoted. That isolates him at once. Only someone who worships her would go to such extraordinary lengths.' He distributed a smile among them. 'I fancy that our list of suspects will be very small.'

'But how can you possibly draw it up?' asked Goldschmidt.

'Oh, I'm not going to draw it up myself, sir. I will be calling on people who can do that much more accurately.

A love of music has driven this individual to such extreme action. And a love of music,' Colbeck declared, 'will be his downfall.'

Jenny Lind had been tricked. When the crowd scattered after the second shot, she was bumped into from all sides. A woman then took her by the arm and led her to a waiting cab where the driver was trying to control a horse frightened by the noise of gunfire. A strong young man almost lifted her into the cab, promising that her husband would join her soon and that they'd both be driven to their hotel. It was a ruse. Instead of waiting for Goldschmidt, he leapt in beside her and the cab set off. Jenny's cry for help was drowned out in the pandemonium. She was soon being driven through the streets of Birmingham as fast as the traffic would allow.

'Where are you taking me?' she asked, trembling with apprehension.

'There's nothing to worry about,' he told her. 'You're among friends.'

'Is this how friends behave?'

'It was the only way he could persuade you to accede to his request.'

'Whose request are you talking about?'

'Wait and see, Miss Lind.'

'I have to give a concert this evening.'

He smiled. 'Oh, you'll be giving a concert, have no fear.'

The cab rolled on until the road widened and the traffic began to thin out. Birmingham was a major industrial city with a permanent haze over its factories but there was no sign of its manufacturing aspect now. They were in an exclusive part of Edgbaston where houses grew bigger and the air became clearer. When they turned into the drive of a mansion, she saw that it was screened from the road by a high wall. It made her feel more like a captive than ever.

'At least tell me what's going on,' she begged.

'He will do that,' said the young man.

The cab stopped and he got out first then helped her to alight. The front door of the house was suddenly flung open and a tall, stooping man of middle years came out. He had gleaming eyes set in a cadaverous face and grey hair trailing carelessly to his shoulders.

'At last,' he cried with joy. 'Jenny has come to sing to me.'

Colbeck had sprung into action. Since no witnesses to the abduction could be found, he concentrated on trying to identify the man behind what had been a well-conceived plan. To do that, he believed, he needed the assistance of a special group of people. Even in a city as large as Birmingham, there would not be an excessive number of them. Policemen were dispatched to round them up as quickly as they could. Colbeck and Leeming had been given the use of a room at the police station. Goldschmidt and Rosen insisted on being present. Both were sceptical.

'This is hopeless, Inspector,' said Rosen. 'You are chasing moonbeams.'

'I am in search of a star,' replied Colbeck, 'and her name is Jenny Lind.'

'Then why aren't you out there looking for her?'

'The inspector knows what he's doing,' said Leeming, loyally.

'Patently,' snarled Goldschmidt, 'he does not.'

'Your lack of confidence in me is understandable, sir,' said Colbeck, 'but I ask you to reserve judgement until this whole matter has been resolved.'

'What will happen to my concert?' moaned Rosen. 'I'll lose thousands.'

'With respect, Mr Rosen, the safety of Miss Lind is far more important than any losses you may incur. Try to put self-interest aside for a moment.'

'I may be ruined!'

'Our sympathy is elsewhere at the moment, sir.'

'Indeed, it is,' said Goldschmidt. 'My wife will be in an appalling state.'

'I'm not so sure of that,' said Colbeck, thoughtfully. 'Once she realises that she's not in danger, she will cope well with the situation into which she's been thrust. After all, she has travelled the world in the course of her career and adapted to conditions in a whole variety of countries. I believe that Birmingham will hold no terrors for her.'

'It's easy for you to say that, man. Find her, damn you – *find* her!'

There was a knock on the door. 'The search is about to begin.'

The door opened and an elderly man came in, tapping his way forward with the aid of a white stick. Goldschmidt and Rosen were horrified.

'Heavens!' exclaimed Rosen. 'It's a case of the blind leading the blind.'

* * *

Jenny Lind was conducted into a spacious room at the rear of the house. Pride of place went to the piano but there were other musical instruments as well. She saw a framed print of herself hanging on the wall. On the top of the piano was a pile of old programmes. The woman who'd shepherded her away from the crowd came in after her. She waved their guest to a chair.

'We intend no harm to you, Miss Lind,' she said, softly, 'but it was an opportunity we could not afford to miss. My name is Eleanor Whittingham and this,' she added, indicating the man who'd brought her into the house, 'is my father, Caspar. He's a composer and your most fervent admirer.'

Caspar Whittingham tried to offer a respectful bow but the effort taxed him and he staggered slightly. His daughter rushed to assist him, helping him across to the piano stool. He lowered himself onto it with a mixture of care and anticipatory pleasure. Feeling less threatened, Jenny was able to take stock of her surroundings and to look more closely at her hosts. Eleanor was a pleasant, fresh-faced woman in her late twenties who exuded a sense of good health. Caspar, by contrast, was clearly a sick man, wasted by some sort of disease and haunted by the prospect of death. In feeling sorry for him, Jenny lost any concern for her own safety. Neither the father nor the daughter posed any physical threat to her.

'They're all here,' said Whittingham, pointing to the programmes. 'I saw every opera in which you appeared in this country and attended every concert. You are inimitable, Miss Lind. When I last heard you sing, I was blessed with the chance to secure your autograph. Show it to her, Eleanor.'

Taking the programme from the piano, his daughter passed it to Jenny.

'We'd have preferred to invite you here,' continued Whittingham, 'but there would have been no hope of your coming. Eleanor is a soprano and I am a composer but neither of us could ever ascend to the heights that you and your husband have reached. We are mere apprentices while you are masters of music.'

'My father is being characteristically modest,' said Eleanor with a fond smile. 'He is no apprentice but a fine musician and a gifted composer. His greatest wish is that Jenny Lind would get to sing one of his songs.'

'Then why not send it to me?' asked Jenny. 'I'd have considered it.'

'You must get deluged with songs,' said Whittingham, sadly. 'Everyone who can compose a tune wants it sung by you. Preference is bound to go to operatic arias and favourite airs. Also, of course, you are married to a composer who can write songs for you.'

Jenny was beginning to understand why she was there. It was not a whim of an eccentric gentleman. It was a final opportunity for someone with only a short time to live. Whittingham was ravaged by illness. What had kept him alive, in part, was the overwhelming desire to hear her sing in private. Cost meant nothing to him. He was obviously a wealthy man. Nor did fear of consequences hold him back. He and his daughter were ready to brave the strictures of the law if they could achieve their objective. Whittingham would never live long enough to suffer imprisonment. Jenny was there to sing his requiem.

'We can't apologise enough for what happened,' said Eleanor with a hand on her father's shoulder. 'We took great care that you were not hurt in any way. You must be very angry with us. Who would not be in your position? If you feel that we have abused you too much, you are free to leave at once. We can summon a cab.'

Wanting to accept the offer, Jenny somehow held back. She was confused. It had been very wrong of them to kidnap and frighten her in the way that they did. Part of her wanted them both punished along with their many accomplices. They had put her through a chilling ordeal. But another part of her urged clemency. She was there at the behest of a dying man with a last frail wish. Eleanor and Whittingham were musicians, dedicated to their art. They inhabited the same world as Jenny. Nothing mattered more to them than music. They were kindred spirits.

'Play one of your songs,' she told the composer. 'Eleanor can sing it.'

Pursuit began with a series of false starts. Colbeck and Leeming raced around the city in a cab that called at four addresses in vain. They were turned away empty-handed each time. The fifth address took them to the leafy district of Edgbaston.

'Look at the size of some of these places,' said Leeming, marvelling at them. 'They're ten times bigger than our little house.'

'I did sense that the kidnapper was not short of money.'

'Does he know what the sentence is for abducting someone?'

'I doubt it, Victor, but he'll soon find out.'

'I do hope we're on the right track at last.'

'I'm sure we are,' said Colbeck as they turned into a wide road lined with trees. 'I can almost *feel* that we're getting closer.'

Halfway down the road, the cab rolled to a halt and the detectives got out. Colbeck asked the driver to wait then led the way up the drive. Its dimensions might be striking but the mansion had an air of neglect. Slates were missing on the roof, walls were overgrown with ivy and chunks of plaster had come off the pillars supporting the portico.

'Go round the back,' said Colbeck.

'Yes, sir.'

'But don't try to get into the house. We mustn't frighten them into impulsive action. People can get hurt that way.'

'We don't even know if it's the right place, sir.'

'Oh, it's the right place. I'm certain of it.'

Waiting until Leeming had gone, Colbeck went to the front door and rang the bell. There was a long delay before it was opened by a young man with an impassive face. Colbeck introduced himself and asked if he might see Caspar Whittingham.

'The master is away at the moment,' said the servant, crisply.

'Is any other member of the family here?'

'I'm afraid not, Inspector.'

'When will Mr Whittingham return?'

'I can't answer that question. He told me that they might be away for a day or two. Would you like to leave a message?'

Colbeck knew that he was lying. The man's voice was calm but his eyes gave him away. He kept blinking. Evidently, he was obeying his master's orders and pretending that he was not there. Colbeck removed his hat and stepped forward.

'In that case, I'll wait until he returns.'

He servant was flustered. 'You can't come in,' he protested.

'I can acquire a search warrant, if you prefer.'

'Look, Inspector, I give you my word that nobody from the family is here.'

Hand on his hat, Leeming came running around to the front of the house.

'You'll never guess what I just saw, sir,' he said.

'I fancy that you saw Mr Caspar Whittingham,' suggested Colbeck.

'Is that his name? He was playing the piano and someone was singing to him. I couldn't believe my eyes,' he said with a hollow laugh. 'It was Jenny Lind.'

Colbeck swung round to confront the servant. 'Are you still going to insist that nobody is at home?'

The man wilted visibly.

When his wife was returned unharmed to him, Goldschmidt showered the detectives with apologies for doubting them. He was sorry for his earlier harsh criticism of them and promised to write to the superintendent in praise of them. Rosen's apology was delivered with reluctance until he realised that the concert would go ahead, after all. He was so excited that he thrust a grateful cigar at each of the detectives. After the initial horror of being kidnapped, Jenny had become reconciled to what was a heartfelt plea from Caspar Whittingham. His songs had definite merit though not enough to tempt her to include any of them in her programme that evening. Jenny declined to press charges against him or his daughter. She preferred to dismiss the whole thing as a rather bizarre adventure.

From the point of view of the detectives, their reputation

had been vindicated. What pleased them most was that they were given free tickets to attend the concert at Town Hall, an imposing neoclassical structure at the heart of the city. Leeming was astonished when Colbeck told him that Joseph Hansom, the man who'd designed it, had also given his name to the cab that took them there. Resplendent in their finest attire, the concert-goers of Birmingham came in large numbers and there was a buzz of excitement. When Jenny Lind first appeared onstage, the ovation went on for minutes. The performance was a continuous source of pleasure for Colbeck but for Victor Leeming it was a revelation. Jenny Lind's voice held him spellbound. He had never heard anything so melodious and yet so apparently effortless. When the first half of the concert ended, he clapped as enthusiastically as anyone.

'I'm so glad that we were able to rescue her, sir,' he said.

'You were the one who spotted her through the window, Victor.'

'Yes, but it was you who eventually got us to the right house.'

'I was sure that we were looking for a wealthy man with a passion for music,' explained Colbeck. 'That meant he would certainly have a piano in the house and make sure that it was looked after properly. I simply had to make a list of gentlemen in the city who fitted that description. That's why I called on expert advice.'

'It was a stroke of genius, sir,' said Leeming. 'We may get the credit but this was the first case I know that was really solved by a blind piano tuner.'

SUFFER LITTLE CHILDREN

Ben Grosvenor was a lugubrious man with such a jaundiced view of the human condition that his colleagues either mocked him or avoided his mournful diatribes. At the end of the week, however, Grosvenor acquired an instant popularity because he was one of the pay clerks for the London and North Western Railway. As he went on his rounds, doling out money from his leather bag, he was always welcomed with a cheer. That morning was no exception. When he approached a group of cleaners in the carriage shed, he set off a chorus of approval. They stopped working at once and rubbed their hands. Grosvenor was a skinny beanpole of a man in his fifties with a beaky nose on which a pair of wire-framed spectacles was perched. A stickler for the rule book, he kept a pencil behind his ear and used it to record every penny that was handed over. He put his bag down on the ground.

'Is it true that we have double wages this week, Ben?' joked someone.

'That'll be the day!' moaned Grosvenor.

'Can't you slip us a bit extra out of the kindness of your heart?'

'*What* heart?' asked another man. Everyone laughed.

'If you're going to poke fun,' warned Grosvenor, 'I can leave you all to the end of my round so you'll have to wait a couple of hours before you see your money.'

'We want it now,' said a big man with bulging forearms, 'and we're not poking fun at you, Ben. We love you, really. Isn't that so?'

Everyone agreed wholeheartedly. One man even embraced the pay clerk.

Opening his bag and checking everything against his ledger, he paid them one by one before snapping his bag shut. The men had to listen to his doom-laden prophecies about the dire future of mankind for a few minutes but, with money in their pockets, they were happy to do so. When he picked up his bag and walked away, they gave him a rousing cheer.

Grosvenor's next stop was some distance away. He had to pay men at work repairing the track. They, too, gave him a cordial welcome and lined up eagerly to get their wages. Grosvenor kept them waiting so that he could unload some of his sour opinions of life on them. He then opened his bag and reached in it for his ledger.

To his horror, it was not there and neither was the money. He was staring at a small pile of ballast. Lifting up the bag, he examined it more closely. Though similar in every way, it was not his. He clutched at his throat.

'Come on, Ben,' urged someone. 'Give us our wages.'

'I can't,' said Grosvenor in despair. 'I've been robbed.'

Since their husbands worked so closely together, Madeleine Colbeck had become friendly with Estelle Leeming. They saw each other infrequently but, when they did get together, it was always a pleasurable occasion. It was Caleb Andrews who suggested a possible outing and Madeleine was at once grateful for the offer yet wary of accepting it.

'I'm in two minds,' she admitted.

'But you love going to the engine shed, Maddy. When you first took up painting, you badgered me to take you there whenever I could.'

'I know, Father. It's an inspiration to me. I've had some of my best ideas in that shed. It's not me that I'm worried about. It's the two boys.'

'They'll be thrilled. All boys of their age want to be an engine driver.'

'Don't exaggerate.'

'They do,' he said. 'If they knew what it was really like, of course, they might not be so keen. They're too young to realise the dangers involved, not to mention the effort it takes. Long days on the footplate are very tiring and you come home filthy.'

'You don't need to tell me that, Father,' she reminded him. 'When I was living at home, I saw the state of your clothes. As for the outing, my only concern is that David and Albert can be boisterous. Estelle says they sometimes run her ragged.'

'They just need a strong hand.'

'They get that when their father is there but, like Robert, he's often away for extended periods. Estelle struggles to cope without Victor there.' She paused to think it over. Reaching a decision, she gave an affirmative nod. 'We'll take them. It's unkind to deprive them of a treat like this and Estelle will have us to help look after them. They're good boys at heart. They just lack discipline.'

'Not when I'm around, they won't,' said Andrews, tapping his chest. 'I'll keep them on a short leash. I'll have to, Maddy. When I asked for permission to take them there, the manager insisted that the lads behaved themselves.'

'Let's hope that they do,' said Madeleine.

But she had lurking doubts.

When Estelle turned up at the house with her sons, it was clear that they were on their best behaviour. Smartly dressed and with gleaming faces, they spoke respectfully as they thanked Andrews for arranging the outing. David Leeming was the elder of the two brothers, a chunky ten-year old with an unmistakable resemblance to his father. Albert Leeming was small and stringy with a mischievous glint in his eye. Madeleine knew that he was the potential troublemaker. Estelle herself was a pretty woman in her early thirties with a slim body, a freckled face and auburn hair peeping out from beneath her hat. Madeleine was delighted to see her again.

It was a relatively short walk. As soon as the five of them set off from his house in Camden, Andrews started his lecture.

'It was built over ten years ago,' he began. 'What made it so unusual was that it was round. Other companies have copied the design. Some people call it the Great Circular Engine House but there's a much simpler name.'

'What is it, Mr Andrews?' David piped up.

'It's the Roundhouse, son.'

When the building came in sight, Andrews called them to a halt so that they could appreciate its size and distinctive shape. Constructed of yellow brick, it had a conical roof with a central smoke louvre.

'It looks enormous,' said Estelle, gazing up at it.

'Its diameter is well over fifty yards,' said Andrews, before explaining to the boys what a diameter was. 'The problem is that it's not really big enough.'

'Why not?' asked David.

'I know the answer to that,' said Albert, nudging him aside.

'Trust you!'

'Shut up, David.'

'You're just stupid.'

'Now, now,' cautioned Estelle. 'We'll have no arguments.'

'So what *is* the reason, Albert?' asked Madeleine.

'Engines are getting longer,' the boy replied. 'Everyone knows that – except my brother, that is.' He collected a sharp dig in the ribs from David. 'Aouw!'

'Behave yourselves, both of you,' said Estelle, sternly.

'Albert is quite right,' Andrews went on. 'The earliest locomotives were very short but they slowly got bigger and longer. The shed can house fewer and fewer of them so it will probably be closed before too long. It's a great pity,' he sighed. 'I have fond memories of it. Come on – let's look inside, shall we?'

As the five of them strolled towards the building, Madeleine could feel the boys' excitement. It was a visit about which they could boast to their friends. She took great pleasure from their obvious enjoyment. Madeleine was also pleased to liberate their mother from the task of managing them on her own. Estelle was deeply grateful. Andrews was in his element, taking charge and basking in reminiscences of his years as a railwayman.

'What do you want to be when you grow up, David?' he asked.

'An engine driver,' replied the boy.

'There you are, Maddy. That's exactly what I told you.' He put a hand on the smaller boy's shoulder. 'What about you, Albert?'

Albert grinned. 'I'm going to be a *better* engine driver than my brother.'

Superintendent Tallis picked the letter up from his desk and handed it to Colbeck.

'That will tell you all you need to know, Inspector.'

'Thank you, sir.'

'They should have called us in earlier. A theft of this magnitude is a serious crime. They were foolish to imagine they could solve it themselves.'

'How much was taken?' asked Colbeck, scanning the letter.

'A substantial amount,' replied Tallis. 'They were too embarrassed to tell me the exact figure. The pay clerk had just begun his rounds so the bag was filled with money.'

'That means we're looking for an employee of the company

who is aware of the routine on payday. In fact, we may be after two of them.'

'Why do you say that?'

'It would be much easier to steal and replace that bag if the pay clerk is momentarily distracted. What's his story?'

'That's for you to find out – he's been suspended.'

Colbeck was surprised. 'He's not a suspect, surely.'

'It seems that he is.'

'Men rarely get to become pay clerks unless they're extremely trustworthy. According to the letter, this fellow – Ben Grosvenor – has been with the LNWR since it came into being over ten years ago. If he had any inclination to steal from it,' said Colbeck, 'I don't think he'd have waited a whole decade.'

'Take the sergeant and speak to Grosvenor.'

'I will, sir, and then we'll visit the exact spot where the switch occurred.'

'You'll find the place crawling with railway policemen.'

Colbeck rolled his eyes. 'Where were they when the crime was actually committed?'

'A good question,' said Tallis, who shared Colbeck's reservations about the railway police. 'A pay clerk should have been given some sort of protection.'

'He was doubtless relying on his long experience, sir. Thefts of this kind are highly unusual. I'm sure that the clerk never believed he was in any danger.'

'Well, he was. You're after a cunning devil, Inspector – smoke him out.'

Colbeck put the letter in his pocket. 'Even the most cunning criminals have a habit of making a mistake, Superintendent,' he said, confidently. 'All that we have to do is to find out what it was in this case.'

When they stepped into the engine shed, the boys were overawed. It was like the interior of a cathedral with twenty-four Doric columns made of steel supporting a metal fretwork that held up the roof. At the centre of the shed was the turntable. Tracks ran into bays between the columns. There were locomotives galore. Some were in service, others were waiting until they were needed and others again were being examined to see what repairs were necessary. Noise was amplified in the huge cavern. Madeleine and Estelle took a few moments to adjust to it but Andrews and the two boys were instantly at ease. With Andrews as their guide, David and Albert went from one locomotive to another, having the salient points of each pointed out to them then climbing up onto the footplate. Both boys were enthralled.

The women watched from a safe position. Estelle was mesmerised.

'Is this where you come to paint, Madeleine?'

'It's where I come for ideas,' replied the other. 'I make sketches of a particular engine here but the real work takes place back in the studio.'

'I wish that I could do something like that,' said Estelle. 'Victor is always telling me to take up an interest but my hands are full at the moment. Running the house keeps me busy and you know what a problem the boys can be.'

'They're no trouble at all this morning, Estelle.'

'That's because they're interested in something. It's when

they get bored that they start arguing and fighting. Because he's the youngest, I usually have to take Albert's side but he's very often the person who causes the upset.'

'Bringing up children is never easy.'

'No,' said Estelle with a mirthless laugh. 'You'll find that out one day.'

It was a casual remark but it struck home with Madeleine. Though the two boys could be a nuisance, there was no real harm in them. As she watched them, she experienced a sudden envy. Andrews was both educating and entertaining them. It occurred to Madeleine that he would make a wonderful grandfather.

Andrews lifted the boys onto the footplate of another locomotive.

'They're having the time of their lives,' said Estelle.

'That's *Menai*,' observed Madeleine. 'It was designed by Alexander Allan. The LNWR had almost three hundred engines with an Allan design built at Crewe. Only my father could tell you why they were so popular. He drove some of Allan's goods and passenger engines.'

Estelle was impressed. 'You really love railways, don't you?'

'I have to – I'm married to Robert.'

Ben Grosvenor was a sorry sight. His misery was for once justified. Having been a faithful servant of the LNWR, he was the victim of a crime yet had been made to feel like its perpetrator. Being suspended from his post was a profound shock. At a stroke, his reputation and his confidence had been shattered. He sat in a chair in his living room and shuddered as he contemplated the future. Grosvenor was a bachelor so there was no comforting wife to help him through the crisis. He was alone and adrift.

'Tell us, in your own words, what happened,' said Colbeck, gently.

'I didn't do it, Inspector,' croaked Grosvenor. 'I *couldn't* do it.'

'We know that, sir. Your record of service is exemplary.'

'Why did they kick me out, then?'

'You haven't been dismissed,' said Leeming, 'only suspended.'

'It amounts to the same thing, Sergeant. They won't want me back after this.'

'You never know, sir.'

'I'll never get another job as a pay clerk.'

'Let's worry about the job that – technically – you still have,' said Colbeck.

The detectives had arrived at the little house to find him anguished. Although he lived alone, the place was spotless and they both noticed the full bookshelf in the alcove. Grosvenor was an avid reader. There was a crucifix on the mantelpiece and a sense of order in the room.

'We can't help until we know all the facts,' Colbeck pointed out.

'I understand, Inspector.'

Leeming had his notebook ready. 'Go on, sir.'

It was days since the incident but the details remained uncomfortably fresh in Grosvenor's mind. He began slowly, describing his routine and the way that he always kept rigidly to it. Devastated by the loss of the money, what hurt him even more was the theft of his ledger.

'That book tells the story of my life,' he bleated, 'and it's been a good, honest life with the LNWR. Being a pay clerk puts you in a very responsible position. I was always keenly aware of that.'

As they listened to his sad tale, Colbeck and Leeming were very sympathetic. Grosvenor made no excuses. A lapse on his part had led to the disappearance of a large amount of money. Angry scenes had occurred among men expecting him to pay them their weekly wage. The pay clerk had endured abuse and threats of violence. When the full account had been given, Colbeck had a first question.

'Do you have *any* idea who might have taken your bag, sir?'

'No, Inspector, I don't. They were all my friends – at least, I thought so.'

'What happened when you reported the theft?'

Grosvenor shuddered again. 'They looked at me as if it was *my* doing.'

'I'm asking what immediate steps the management took.'

'They got hold of every railway policeman they could and stationed them at all the exits. Nobody could have left the area with that bag of mine. As for the men I'd just paid *before* I was tricked,' said Grosvenor, 'they were all searched to make sure they didn't have more money on them than they were supposed to.'

Leeming studied his notebook. 'You say you were in the carriage shed.'

'That's right.'

'So it would have been easy for someone to sneak up behind the carriages.'

Grosvenor shrugged. 'I suppose so.'

'Tell us about the men you paid at that point,' said Colbeck. 'What did they do when they had their money?'

'They counted it. One of them accused me of short-changing him but I took no notice. Someone always does that. They like to have a laugh at me.'

'In other words, that group of men would have been distracted.'

'Once they had money in their hands,' said Grosvenor, 'they began talking about how they were going to spend it. Some of them owed money to others and there was one man who takes bets. I tried talking to them but nobody listened.' He snapped his fingers. '*That's* when it must have happened.'

'Thank you, sir. You've been very helpful. I must now ask you to take us to the place where the crime was committed.'

Grosvenor was aghast. 'But I've been suspended. They won't let me in.'

'They'll do what I tell them,' said Colbeck, firmly. 'If they want their money found, they'll have to.'

'Do you really think you'll ever get it back?' asked Grosvenor, a faint glimmer of hope making him stand to his feet. 'Do you?'

'Yes, I do. From what you've told us, nobody could have left the premises with a distinctive leather bag. What criminals usually do in such situations is to hide their booty somewhere, wait until the coast is clear then slip back to reclaim it. In short, sir,' Colbeck told him, 'the money and the ledger are still there. Our task is to find it before the thief or thieves come back to reclaim it.'

* * *

The best moment of their visit to the engine shed was when David and Albert were allowed to stand on the turntable when it was in action. It was a wonderful thrill for them. They could not believe that it only took two men to push a large, heavy, solid lump of metal in a complete circle. Having seen the locomotive drive headfirst onto the turntable, they watched it drive headfirst off. Andrews had been given a lot of help from old friends, who let the boys onto the footplates of their respective engines, but he was conscious that the manager was now looking askance at him. He therefore led his two young charges towards the exit. Madeleine and Estelle joined them.

'I can't thank you enough, Mr Andrews,' said Estelle.

'Yes,' chirped the boys in unison. 'Thank you, Mr Andrews.'

'Now you know what being an engine driver is like,' said Madeleine.

'We haven't finished yet,' said Andrews. 'There's the carriage shed to see next. We got a whole range of carriages in there, including some that are used by the royal family.'

'Father's had the privilege of driving the royal train,' recalled Madeleine. 'It was a real feather in his cap.'

'Do you still *have* the feather, Mr Andrews?' asked David, innocently.

She smiled. 'It wasn't a *real* feather, David. It's just an expression.'

'*I* knew that,' said Albert, scornfully.

The carriage shed was a large rectangular building with chutes – long ventilators – in the roof to carry smoke out of the shed from locomotives in steam. Carriages of all kinds abounded. Those reserved for the royal family commanded most interest and Estelle was as eager to see them as her sons. Andrews lifted the boys up one by one so that they could peer through the windows and see the luxurious interiors. The contrast with standard carriages – even those with the words First Class emblazoned on their doors – was stark.

After a while, however, the boys started to lose interest as they walked up and down the long parallel lines of rolling stock, all of it painted in the distinctive colours of the LNWR and bearing its insignia. Albert decided that it was time to have some fun. Pushing his brother in the back, he tore off in the opposite direction.

'Catch me!' he shouted.

David accepted the challenge and hared after him, ignoring his mother's plea to come back to her at once. The boys were completely out of control now, racing around what was a kind of enormous, gloomy labyrinth. High spirits suppressed until now suddenly had free rein. Albert ducked under couplings, climbed in and out of open carriages and somehow managed to keep ahead of his brother. Eventually, he ran out of breath and crawled under a carriage to hide. David walked up and down the avenues of rolling stock until he heard the telltale giggle of his younger brother.

Estelle was apologising profusely to the others for her children's naughty behaviour. Madeleine waved the apologies away but Andrews was annoyed, blaming himself for not having exerted enough authority over them. His voice reverberated around the building.

'Come back here this minute!' he bellowed.

There was a long pause then a contrite David finally appeared.

'We're sorry, Mr Andrews,' he said, penitently, 'but you have to come and see Albert right now. He's found something.'

When he heard what had happened, Victor Leeming was torn between anger and delight, feeling the need to admonish his sons for their bad behaviour while at the same time filled with paternal pride. Quite by accident, they had found the bag stolen from the pay clerk and hidden beneath a carriage. Restored to the manager, its contents were found to be intact. When he and Colbeck reported to the superintendent, Leeming was congratulated.

'Your sons are to be commended,' said Tallis. 'They did what a whole bevy of railway policemen failed to do.'

'Thank you, sir,' said Leeming with a grin.

'However, we can't rely on a pair of obstreperous lads to solve *all* our crimes for us. Coincidences like this rarely occur.'

'My sons are not really obstreperous, sir.'

'Boys will be boys,' said Colbeck, tolerantly.

'That's a matter of opinion,' said Tallis. 'There are times when boys should be *prevented* from being boys, if you take my meaning. Valuable as their contribution was, of course, all that they did was to find the stolen bag. The thief is still at liberty.'

'He won't be for long, sir.'

'What makes you say that, Inspector?'

'We hope to make an arrest tonight.'

'How can you be so specific? It may be days or even weeks before the thief returns to reclaim the bag from its hiding place.'

'That *would* have been the case, sir,' said Colbeck, 'had it been undiscovered. I suggested to the manager that the thief needed an incentive to come immediately.'

'I don't understand.'

'They're going to offer a reward,' explained Leeming.

'It's a very tempting reward,' added Colbeck, 'but, then, it will never have to be paid. What it will do is to convince the thief that he needs to change his plan. Instead of making off with all the money in the pay clerk's bag, he can get a large proportion of it by way of a reward and appear completely innocent of the crime. That will have an irresistible appeal to him.'

'What a clever idea, Colbeck!' said Tallis.

'I do have one from time to time, sir.'

Top hats and frock coats would have been an encumbrance in the carriage shed. The detectives had therefore chosen rough garb that allowed freedom of movement. There was poor light during the day. At night the shed was plunged into total darkness. They used a lantern to find their way to the right place then took up their positions nearby. It was several hours before anyone came and they were beginning to think that their vigil had been futile. Then they heard footsteps approaching stealthily and a lantern flashed in the darkness. Someone approached the hiding place and bent down to crawl under the carriage. Retrieving the leather bag, he came out again and stood up with a quiet chuckle. Colbeck spoilt his moment of triumph.

'Hello,' he said, letting his lantern spill out its light. 'We had a feeling that we might see you here tonight. It's my duty to place you under arrest, sir.'

Shocked for a moment, the man quickly recovered and tried to dart off but he ran straight into Leeming's shoulder and bounced backward. The sergeant grabbed him and held him tight. Colbeck held the light up to the man's face.

'The game is up, sir.'

'No, no,' gabbled the other, 'you don't understand. I didn't *steal* the bag. I stumbled on it earlier today and wanted to claim the reward.'

Colbeck took the bag from him and opened it wide. It was full of ballast.

'I doubt if you'll get much in the way of reward for this,' he said.

It was not until he came back from Scotland Yard the following day that Madeleine learnt the full story. Colbeck explained that the thief was an employee of the company who had stalked the pay clerk for weeks until his opportunity finally came. Ben Grosvenor had now been completely vindicated and restored to his post.

'When he saw that his ledger was unharmed,' said Colbeck, 'he was like a child on Christmas Day. He won't be robbed again. On my advice, he's going to fit a chain to the bag and attach it to his belt. The next time someone tries to steal his money, they'll have to take the pay clerk with it.'

'I'm so glad that it all worked out well in the end,' said Madeleine. 'Estelle was so upset when the boys went running off like that.'

'Victor has been very strict with them. They won't do it again, I fancy. But you'll be interested to know that their little adventure has had an unexpected result.'

'What's that, Robert?'

'They've changed their minds,' replied Colbeck. 'When they went into that carriage shed, they both wanted to be engine drivers. When they came out, David and Albert were determined to become detectives.'

'How does Victor feel about that?'

'He doesn't know whether to encourage their ambition or do his best to thwart it. I suggested that there was one simple way to test the strength of their resolve.'

'What's that?'

Colbeck's smile blossomed into a grin. 'Victor could introduce the boys to Superintendent Tallis.'

THE MISSIONARY

Friendships forged in battle had the strongest bonds of all. That, at least, was what Edward Tallis believed. When his closest army comrade had committed suicide in Yorkshire, Tallis had been shocked both by his death and by the bizarre circumstances surrounding it. He had led an investigation into the case and been grateful when Colbeck had exposed a startling family secret that explained the gruesome event. As he boarded the train at Dover, Tallis recalled the incident. It was a paradox. Having gone to a funeral on the coast of Kent, he came away thinking about one in Yorkshire. He'd just paid his respects at the grave of his cousin, Raymond Tallis, who'd held a senior position in the port until his retirement. Tallis remembered playing with him when they were boys and enjoying his company. Yet they'd drifted apart as adults and had not seen each other for twenty years or more. Tallis was keenly aware of the fact. He kept asking himself why he felt no real sense of bereavement at the passing of a blood relative yet was still haunted by the death of an old army friend.

Having found an empty first-class compartment, he settled back in his seat. So preoccupied was he that he didn't hear the door opening and shutting or realise that he now had company. Nor was he aware of the din of departure and the sudden lurch forward. It was only when he felt a consoling hand on his arm that he noticed the man opposite.

'Please accept my sincere condolences,' said the stranger.

Tallis blinked. 'Oh – thank you, sir.'

'I can see that you're troubled and won't intrude further.'

'No, no, it's not an intrusion, I assure you.'

'You are in mourning,' said the man. 'I merely wanted to offer a word of comfort.'

'It is most welcome.'

Tallis's companion was an elderly clergyman with sparkling eyes set in a wrinkled face and a well-trimmed white beard. His voice was low, melodious and soothing. He exuded kindness and understanding. Tallis's spirits lifted a little.

'I'm the Reverend Paul Youngman,' said the clergyman, smiling benignly, 'though it's a misnomer for someone as old as me.'

Tallis shook the hand offered to him. 'Edward Tallis, at your service.'

'Dover is an unlovely town. Seaports often are. What took you there?'

'I attended a funeral.'

'They can be harrowing events. In the course of my ministry, I've had the misfortune to attend hundreds. Grief can eat away at the strongest of us. I've seen it destroy some people.' He settled back in his seat. 'Was it a family member?'

'No,' Tallis heard himself saying. 'It was a friend from my army days.'

'I had a feeling you'd served Queen and Country. Military life does tend to leave its mark on a man.'

'I was proud to wear a uniform – and so was Colonel Tarleton.'

Youngman was impressed. 'So he was a colonel, no less!'

'He was an example to us all.'

And before he could stop himself, Tallis began to talk about the respect and affection in which he held his former army colleague. Colonel Aubrey Tarleton was exhumed from his grave in Yorkshire and reburied in Dover in place of a dead cousin. Grief that had lain dormant for years now bubbled up inside him. He at last felt able to let it out. Living quite alone, he'd had nobody with whom he could share his sorrow and had therefore bottled up his emotions. In the presence of the Reverend Youngman, they were uncorked. There was something about the clergyman that enabled Tallis to talk freely and unselfconsciously about the loss of his friend. What he didn't do, however, was to describe the way in which the colonel had died. A death was a death. Youngman didn't need to be told that Tarleton had deliberately walked along a railway track so that he could be killed by a train.

It was a lengthy recitation. When Tallis finally stopped, he was overcome by a sense of gratitude. A complete stranger had helped him to pour out his heart and achieve a measure of relief. The pain inflicted by his friend's death was no longer so sharp.

'I can't thank you enough,' he said.

'All that I did was to listen.'

'A sympathetic ear was exactly what I needed.'

'Then I'm glad to be of service,' said Youngman with a supportive smile. 'It's the only ministry I can offer at my age, you see. I'm too old to tend a flock so I look for people who might be helped by what meagre gifts I possess. It was not accident that brought me into this compartment, Mr Tallis. I saw you standing on the platform at Dover in a state of unmistakable anguish.'

'Was it so obvious?'

'It was to me, sir, because I am well acquainted with the signs.'

'And is this what you do on the railway?'

'It's what I endeavour to do,' replied Youngman. 'You might call it my mission in life. Since my wife died, I've been liberated from domestic concerns so I can dedicate myself to the service of people I encounter on trains. It's not just those in mourning who catch my attention. Sometimes I give help of a more practical nature. When a woman is travelling with more children than she can easily control, I lighten her load by diverting and entertaining them. Then again, I do offer medical help of sorts. Unlike our Lord Jesus,' he went on, modestly, 'I'm no miracle worker but I do know how to stem the bleeding on a wound or put salve on a bruise.' He tapped the valise by his side. 'I always carry bandages, ointments and a small bottle of brandy. May I offer you a tot, Mr Tallis?'

'No, thank you.' Tallis raised a hand. 'You provide a comprehensive service,' he said, admiringly. 'I wonder that you can afford to travel so often by train. If you do so a great deal, you must incur appreciable costs.'

'I do, Mr Tallis. Fortunately, one or two railway companies have recognised the value of my work and allowed me to travel on their lines without charge. Also, passengers I've been able to help have contributed to my mission. No, no,' he protested as Tallis reached for his wallet. 'That was not a plea for money. My service is free to all. You are under no obligation whatsoever.'

'Even missionaries must eat.'

'Unhappily, that's true.'

'Go on,' urged Tallis, offering him a five-pound note. 'Take it.'

'Your generosity is overwhelming.'

'I could never repay what you did for me, Reverend.'

'Thank you very much,' said Youngman, taking the money. 'This will buy me a lot of train tickets to continue my ministry on the railways of England.' He looked up as the train began to slow. 'Ah, this must be Ashford station. I'm getting off here to visit the former archdeacon of my diocese. Because he's crippled with arthritis, he's largely immobile but he does help to fund my work.'

'I wish you every success,' said Tallis, shaking his hand again.

'Bless you!'

The train slowed to a halt as it came into the station and Youngman got out. Tallis was amazed at how much better he felt after the conversation. The missionary had not only softened his pain, he'd left him much more reconciled to the death of his friend. Five pounds, Tallis felt, had bought him a peace of mind that was priceless.

* * *

There was no peace of mind for Robert Colbeck. During the two days that Tallis was away in Kent, the inspector had become acting superintendent. There had been times in the past when Colbeck had been ambitious enough to want a promotion but having finally achieved it – albeit for a short time – he realised that it gave him nothing like the satisfaction of being closely involved in the hunt for criminals. He was fettered to a desk in the superintendent's office, filtering reports, issuing orders, monitoring investigations already in motion and answering directly to the commissioner. Increased power bought greater responsibility and cut him off from the relative freedom he enjoyed as an inspector. After one hour as a superintendent, his respect for Tallis had shot up.

Victor Leeming had a parallel experience because he was temporarily the replacement for Colbeck as inspector. Contented as a sergeant, he felt hopelessly at sea when taking charge of an investigation. When he had a free moment, he seized the opportunity for a meeting with Colbeck.

'I was never destined to be an inspector, sir,' he admitted.

'You may well be promoted one day, Victor.'

'I know my limitations.'

'They can't be any worse than mine,' said Colbeck. 'A different case comes through that door every twenty minutes or so and I have to separate the wheat from the chaff. How the superintendent copes with the pressure of work, I can only guess. He must have the most remarkable constitution.'

'I don't think it can compare with yours, Inspector. Oh, I'm sorry, sir,' said Leeming, quickly. 'You're a superintendent now.'

Colbeck's laugh was mirthless. 'I feel more comfortable as an inspector.'

'And – if truth be told – I feel better as a sergeant.'

'This charade will not continue for much longer.'

In fact, it was already over. Tallis had returned to Scotland Yard, made the commissioner aware of his presence then headed for his office. When he opened the door, he was annoyed to see Leeming loitering there and Colbeck seated behind his desk. The familiar rasping tone came into his voice.

'What the devil are you doing in here?' he demanded.

'I was just going, sir,' said Leeming.

'Then go!'

'We are glad to see you back, Superintendent.'

'Well, I'm not glad to see you masquerading as an inspector when you are so ill-fitted for the post. Now get out and return to a rank more suited to your scant abilities as a detective.' Leeming fled and closed the door behind him. 'The same goes for you, Colbeck.'

'You are unfair on the sergeant, sir,' said Colbeck, vacating the chair, 'and, by the same token, I was unfair to you. I underrated the amount of work you are forced to do and can only admire the skill with which you habitually do it.'

'Thank you,' said Tallis, savouring the compliment.

'Your return has brought nothing but relief to the sergeant and me.'

'I had a feeling that you'd bitten off more than you could chew.'

'The promotion was not sought, Superintendent.'

'Nor was it deserved in my view,' said Tallis, airily. 'What were you doing before you tried to replace me?'

'I was leading the investigation into that forgery.'

'Then please wrest control of it from Leeming. If he's in charge, we'd have to wait until Christmas for an arrest.'

'That's where you're wrong, sir,' said Colbeck, smoothly. 'Victor has already made two arrests in connection with the case. By the end of the week, he and I will have brought the investigation to a conclusion.' He opened the door then turned round. 'Welcome back, Superintendent.'

It was ten days before the first report came in. Tallis hardly looked at it, feeling that it was too trivial a matter for the Detective Department. When there were major crimes in the capital, he could not deploy men to look into an alleged fraud committed on a train near Brighton. The second report was also ignored. If someone was foolish enough to be taken in by a confidence trickster on an excursion train to Portsmouth, it was their own fault. Tallis had far more important matters to occupy his time. It was the third report that made him sit up. Someone complained that he had been inveigled into giving money to a retired clergyman for a project that turned out to be a fake.

Tallis refused to believe that it could have been the Reverend Paul Youngman. That man had glowed with sincerity. Attuned to pick out criminals, Tallis had heard no warning bells during his time on the train from Dover. Another person, posing as a clergyman, must have been responsible for the crime. Youngman was above reproach and he remained so until someone filed a complaint that actually named the old clergyman who'd talked him into contributing to a restoration fund for the tower at a church which – on investigation – turned out never to have existed.

There was no denying the fact. Tallis had been the victim of deceit. The five pounds he handed over suddenly seemed like five hundred pounds and he felt robbed. The Reverend Paul Youngman's mission was to line his own pockets under the guise of helping others. It pushed Tallis's blood close to boiling point. Though his instinct was to send his detectives in search of the man, he feared that it would expose him to scorn. Of all people, a detective superintendent should not have been taken in by a plausible rogue in a dog collar. He could imagine the sniggers he'd have to endure. There was only one way to appease his fury and that was to pursue the man himself. Tallis was determined. His mission was to catch the bogus missionary.

Madeleine Colbeck had a pleasant surprise when her husband arrived home earlier than she'd expected. Abandoning work in her studio, she hurried downstairs to greet him with a kiss then ushered him into the drawing room.

'The superintendent has let you leave early for a change,' she said.

'He's quite unaware of what I did, Madeleine, because he hasn't been at Scotland Yard today. In fact, we've seen very little of him since last weekend. It's meant that Victor and I could get on with our work unimpeded.'

'Where has Mr Tallis gone?'

'Nobody seems to know.'

'A building full of detectives and not one of you has any

idea of his whereabouts?' she teased. 'What does that say about Scotland Yard?'

'It says that we don't question his absence – we simply relish it.'

'Have you been taking on the superintendent's mantle again?'

'No, Madeleine,' he said with a self-effacing laugh. 'I learnt my lesson. I already have the job that I covet. Trying to rise higher would be a form of setback.'

'That doesn't make sense, Robert.'

'Put bluntly, Edward Tallis is better at the job than I could ever be.'

'But you've just said that he's deserted his post this week. Why?'

He took her into his arms. 'It is a mystery, my love.' He kissed her on the lips. 'And I don't propose to let it come between me and my dinner.'

Tallis became more and more frustrated. He made such little progress that he began to doubt his abilities as a detective. Time away from Scotland Yard meant that unread reports piled up on his desk. More to the point, requests from the commissioner were ignored. That was unforgivable. When he finally did turn up, he was summoned by the commissioner to explain himself and had to resort to a series of unconvincing white lies. Once he'd survived a withering reprimand, he went to his office and worked hard to clear the accumulated reports and correspondence. He then sent for Robert Colbeck.

When the inspector knocked on his door, Tallis snatched it

open and drew him in. Closing the door, he eased his visitor into the middle of the room.

'I have an important assignment for you, Colbeck.'

'Would you like me to fetch Sergeant Leeming?'

'No,' said Tallis with emphasis. 'What I have to tell you is for your ears only and I won't proceed until you give me your word that you will be utterly discreet.'

'I give it freely, Superintendent.'

'Thank you – take a seat.'

While Colbeck sat on an upright chair, Tallis went behind his desk, took out a cigar from the box and bit a piece of it off before lighting it. The first few clouds of smoke climbed up to the ceiling.

Colbeck was intrigued. 'What seems to be the problem, sir?'

'Don't you dare have a laugh at my expense,' warned Tallis.

'I had no intention of doing so.'

'Then be quiet and listen.'

Tallis was succinct. He explained his dilemma and made no excuses for lowering his guard in the wake of the funeral. He showed Colbeck the reports of crimes committed by the same man.

'I felt humiliated,' he confessed. 'I am supposed to be leading the fight against crime yet I was a hapless victim of it in a railway carriage. I don't know how I could be so gullible.'

'You were in mourning, sir,' Colbeck pointed out. 'That made you vulnerable. The one person you would not suspect of dissembling was a clergyman.'

'It was his voice, Inspector. It was so convincing.'

'Then he might at one time have actually been in holy orders.'

'No,' said Tallis. 'That much is certain. When I foolishly imagined that I could track him down, the first place I went was to Lambeth Palace. They had no record of a Reverend Paul Youngman in the Anglican Church. The man is a fraud.'

'What else did your researches reveal?'

'In essence, I discovered that everything he told me was a downright lie. As you can see from those reports, his activities seem to be limited to the south of England. I checked with every railway company operating in the region and not one of them was granting free travel to a self-appointed missionary.'

'Also, of course,' said Colbeck, 'he is not always operating in the guise of a clergyman. In the case near Brighton, he claimed to be a retired bank manager who'd grown rich by making astute investments. As for the excursion train to Portsmouth,' he continued, glancing at the report, 'he posed as a jeweller and managed to extract a deposit out of someone for a necklace that never existed.'

'Yet it's the same man every time,' said Tallis. 'I'm certain of it. In each case, the description of him tallies.'

'And these are the only instances of fraud that have come to light, sir. There are doubtless other victims who feel too ashamed to come forward and admit what happened.'

'I'm one of them. I feel so embarrassed that he chanced on me.'

'Oh, I don't think that it was entirely a case of chance, sir. A man like that would comb the obituary columns for details of funerals. In the case of the one in Dover, it's a reasonable supposition that some of those attending would come by train. He waited on the platform for someone in mourning apparel to turn up.'

'I'm a detective superintendent,' roared Tallis. 'Couldn't he *see* that?'

'What he saw was a man in distress, sir. You were defenceless.'

'Catch him, Colbeck.'

'I'll do my best, sir.'

'And say nothing of what I've told you to Leeming.'

'All that the sergeant needs to know is that we are after a confidence trickster.'

'Where will you start?'

Colbeck smiled to himself. 'I believe that I know just the place.'

As he enjoyed a glass of whisky in his lodging, he ran his eye down the obituary column and used a pencil to circle the details of two funerals in Brighton. Since they were on the same day, he had to choose between them and opted for the one that concerned the death of a former Member of Parliament. It would be an event of some significance with many visitors coming and leaving by train. Grief-stricken and off guard, they would be susceptible to his unique gifts of persuasion. After finishing the whisky with a last gulp, he crossed to the wardrobe and opened the door.

'I think it's time for the Reverend Youngman to make another appearance,' he said with a chuckle. 'Or perhaps I should elevate him. Yes,' he decided, 'Paul, former Bishop of

Chichester, has a pleasing ring to it. Having retired as a prelate, I'll garner praise for taking on the humbler duties of a railway missionary.'

Victor Leeming was given a task he enjoyed least, that of travelling on trains to a series of destinations. He went to a number of towns along the south coast, talking to station employees and giving them a description of the man known as the Reverend Youngman. In most cases, he came away empty-handed. Such were the crowds that thronged the platforms, it was impossible to pick out individuals. He had more success at Dover and Brighton. A stationmaster at one and a porter at the other remembered the clergyman clearly. They said that he always carried a valise and travelled first class. Enquiries at police stations in both places yielded no additional information. The confidence trickster was not known to the police either in Dover or Brighton. Yet he was patently in the area. Having established where the man's primary territory was, Leeming felt able to catch a train back to London.

Colbeck's search also involved a number of blind alleys. Though the man he sought was reportedly in the capital, it took him the best part of the day to track him down. When he finally did so, he discovered that Nigel Buckmaster was holding a private rehearsal with a beautiful young actress in a room at an exclusive hotel. It was not Colbeck's business to probe too deeply into the nature of the instruction that she had received but he knew from experience that the actor-manager always mingled work and pleasure in a way that made them indistinguishable.

When they met in the bar, Buckmaster was as flamboyant as ever.

'Well met, Inspector,' he said, pumping Colbeck's hand. 'I'm glad to see you again. Life has been good to me since our first encounter.'

'I have followed your career with interest.'

'Then you will know that I now dominate the London stage like a Titan. I am at the pinnacle of my profession. Gone are the days when I had to peddle my talent around dingy theatres in the provinces.'

'Your success is well deserved, Mr Buckmaster.'

Colbeck knew that a combination of flattery and a free drink always made the actor more amenable. They had first met years earlier in Cardiff when the inspector was investigating a murder and when the actor was playing the title role in *Macbeth*. Events had thrown them close together and – because he was a genuine admirer of Buckmaster's work – Colbeck and he had become friends.

Over a drink in the bar, the conversation began with the theatre.

'Your Hamlet was without compare.'

'Thank you, Inspector. I intend to revive my production. The young lady you saw leaving just now has made an excellent impression on me. I auditioned her for the role of Ophelia.'

'I hope that you will soon revive your Othello as well.'

'The public clamour for it is very heartening.'

Buckmaster was a tall, lean man with a face that was at once handsome and sinister and long dark hair that fell to his shoulders. Noted for his dandyism, Colbeck felt invisible beside his friend's ostentatious attire.

'I am looking for an actor,' he said.

'One sits before you, sir,' said Buckmaster, arms spread wide.

'This gentleman's performances are of a more criminal nature. In short, he preys on gullible people in various guises and draws money out of them. What every victim has commented on is his voice. It is low and beguiling. My belief is that the fellow must have had training on the stage.'

'That's a reasonable assumption.'

'We need to catch him before others fall into his clutches.'

'In what guises does he appear?'

'Well,' said Colbeck, 'his favourite seems to be that of a clergyman. He claims to be a missionary on the railways and is, by all accounts, highly plausible.'

'The world is full of actors who've fallen on hard times and turned to crime. It will be difficult for me to pluck one out of the hundreds with whom I worked.'

'In this case, we have a name.'

'Then it's certainly a false one. We thespians love to hide our true selves.'

'That's why I came to you, Mr Buckmaster. When I first heard the name, I was ready to dismiss it as an invention but it has tickled something in my memory. I have heard it before somewhere but I cannot, for the life of me, remember where. Actors – I need hardly tell you – are superstitious creatures. I begin to wonder,' said Colbeck, thoughtfully, 'whether the man I seek has perhaps fastened on the name of a character he once played on the boards.'

'That would not surprise me in the least,' said Buckmaster. 'I have met several actors who have stolen names from elsewhere. In my own company, for instance, I have a Romeo Armstrong and a Mark Antony Williamson. Unfortunately, in both cases, their ambition far outruns their talents and neither will ever play the parts in which they cast themselves. What is the name of the villain you are after?'

'He calls himself the Reverend Paul Youngman.'

Buckmaster slapped his thigh. 'Then he gives himself away.'

'You know the name?'

'I know the part and I know the rogue who played it. I was unlucky enough to engage him. The Reverend Youngman appears in a trifling comedy by Tom Taylor called *A Love Denied*, an early work rarely performed now. I had the misfortune to take the lead and play opposite one of the greatest scoundrels ever to infect our profession. Hell's teeth!' exclaimed Buckmaster. 'He had the nerve to steal a scene from me. And his thievery did not end there. When I dismissed him from the company, he robbed the rest of the cast and made off with my valise.'

Colbeck was delighted. 'Who played the Reverend Paul Youngman?'

'His real name is Douglas Aird.'

'I owe you a thousand thanks, Mr Buckmaster. When I run him down, I'll see if I can't retrieve your valise.'

'He is a disgrace to the profession.'

Buckmaster emptied his glass then rose to his feet. Colbeck offered to buy him another drink but the actor dismissed the offer with a lordly wave.

'Alas, I may not tarry,' he said. 'Another young hopeful is to audition for the part of Ophelia. She may well be tapping on the door of my room right now.'

Armed with a name, the detectives found it much easier to pick up the scent. Having first tried Dover, they moved to Brighton and, by dint of making an endless series of enquiries, finally got an address on the seafront. Appropriately, Aird's lodging was only four doors away from a costume-hire shop. Before they reached the place, the man himself stepped into view disguised as a bishop with a large pectoral cross dangling on his chest. In his hand, he was carrying a valise. He fitted the detailed description that Tallis had provided. Colbeck and Leeming followed him all the way to the railway station. When he stood alone on the platform, the detectives moved in.

'Are you the Reverend Paul Youngman?' asked Colbeck, politely.

'I *was*,' replied Aird, loftily. 'In its wisdom, the Anglican Church saw fit to transform me into the Bishop of Chichester.'

'And do you intend to continue missionary work on the railways?'

Aird was unruffled. 'God will not be mocked, sir. I'd be grateful if you and your friend will leave me alone or I will have to summon a policeman.'

'*I'm* a policeman,' said Leeming, stepping forward. 'I'm Detective Sergeant Leeming of Scotland Yard and this gentleman is Inspector Colbeck.' Aird was very ruffled now. 'Our superintendent would value a word with you, sir. I believe you owe him five pounds.'

'When you've returned that,' said Colbeck with a steely smile, 'you can hand back the valise you stole from Nigel Buckmaster. It's my sad duty to report that he does not speak well of you. And, while we're on the subject of reparation, I daresay that Tom Taylor, the playwright, would like you to surrender the name of the clergyman you purloined from *A Love Denied*.' He put a hand on the man's shoulder. 'Not to put too fine a point upon it, sir, you and your false identity are both under arrest.'

Douglas Aird gave a carefree laugh and tried to bluff his way out of the situation. When his charm failed, and when Colbeck produced a pair of handcuffs, the Bishop of Chichester swung the valise like an incense burner and knocked the inspector aside. He then lifted his cassock and took to his heels, sprinting along the platform as if the hounds of Hell were on his tail. In fact, it was Leeming who went in pursuit and who caught him without undue difficulty. Diving on Aird's back, he brought him crashing down. As he hit the hard stone, Aird yelled out in pain.

'If you think *that* hurt,' said Leeming with a wolfish grin, 'wait until you meet Superintendent Tallis again.'

ON GUARD

Jake Fullard had always wanted to be a guard. It gave him a wonderful sense of authority because he was in charge of a train. The engine driver and the fireman were subservient to him. If a train stopped for any reason other than at a signal, it was Fullard's job to apply the brake in the brake van then walk back down the line to warn oncoming trains that there was a blockage ahead. By his count – and he was a pedantic mathematician – he had prevented fourteen potential collisions by his prompt action. Fullard was a slight man in his forties with a long neck and narrow shoulders. He had a full beard, bushy eyebrows and protruding ears. Highly efficient at his job, he was also known for the care he took in his appearance. He'd never venture outside the house unless his uniform was brushed clean and his boots polished. His preference was for acting as guard on passenger trains so he was irked when he found himself assigned to a livestock train. His wife, Hannah, bore the brunt of his annoyance.

'I'm too good to be wasted on animals,' he protested.

'Yes, Jake, I'm sure you are.'

'The noise is always deafening and you wouldn't believe the stink.'

'Yes, I would,' she said. 'It gets into your clothes sometimes.'

'It's ridiculous,' he went on. 'I'm the best guard in the whole company and they make me look after pigs, cattle, sheep and horses. I should be above that kind of thing. Apart from anything else, I hate farm animals. Whenever I get anywhere near one, I start coughing and wheezing.'

'It's not fair on you, Jake.'

Hannah was a full-bodied woman in her forties with a pleasant face framed by a mass of dark curls. Fiercely loyal to her husband, she always oozed sympathy when she felt he'd been slighted.

He gave her a token peck on the cheek before setting off for work. It was a dull morning with persistent drizzle falling from a leaden sky. Fullard walked the half-mile to the station at a brisk pace. On arriving there, he saw that the stock wagons had already been loaded and that the animals were protesting noisily at being penned up. When he was guard on a passenger train, he travelled inside the brake van and was protected from the elements. On a livestock train, however, he sat high up at the rear of the wagons so that he could keep an eye on them in transit.

Fullard went first to the engine. The driver was puffing on his pipe while the fireman was complaining about the drizzle. After moaning about the animals, Fullard chatted with them for a few minutes then walked the length of the train towards the brake van. There were thirty wagons in all, each producing its individual cacophony and giving off its distinctive reek. Fullard checked each wagon to make certain that it was secure. He found the stink of the pigs particularly offensive and held his nose when close to them. When he reached the brake van, he was about to climb up on top of it when something hit him so viciously on the back of the head that his skull split open and his career as a guard came to a premature end.

There were two things that Victor Leeming remembered about Devon. It was a long way from London and it was the scene of a hideous murder that he and Robert Colbeck had once investigated in Exeter. The county town was again involved because the death of Jake Fullard had occurred at Cullompton beside a train that was taking animals to market in Exeter. The detectives had been summoned from Scotland Yard by telegraph. Leeming was, as usual, afraid that they might be kept away from London for days. Colbeck was more sanguine.

'Cullompton is a small town, Victor,' he said. 'People tend to know each other in places like that. It's not like London where strangers can go unnoticed in a huge population. If anything out of the ordinary happened in Cullompton, somebody will have been aware of it.'

'All we know is that the guard was trampled to death.'

'Foul play is suspected.'

'It could have been an accident. They happen all the time.'

'This one is different – at least that's what the railway company thinks.'

'Where will you start, Inspector?'

'I'll view the body, examine the scene of the crime then speak to the driver and the fireman.'

'What about me?'

'Do you really need to ask?' teased Colbeck. 'You'll be taking statements from the animals. They'll have lots to tell you, I'm sure.'

The town was a hundred and eighty miles from London but the express train got them there speedily. They found Cullompton station in turmoil. Farmers were demanding to know why their animals were still stuck in a siding and threatening to sue the company if they weren't on sale in Exeter market on the following morning. Passengers awaiting trains had drifted over to a position from which they could see the actual spot where the dead body had been found. Word had spread quickly in the town and dozens of people had congregated out of curiosity. Martin Rimmer, the tubby stationmaster with a walrus moustache, was besieged.

'Thank God you've come,' he said when the detectives introduced themselves. 'It's been like a madhouse here.'

'What exactly happened?' asked Colbeck.

'We don't rightly know, Inspector. Jake Fullard is an experienced guard who prides himself on the way he does his job. Yet he got trampled by a wagonload of bullocks. The driver and fireman only realised that something was amiss when a couple of the animals went galloping past them. Others charged off in another direction and three of them mounted the platform and caused mayhem among the passengers. Dan Ferris, the farmer who owns them, has only just finished rounding them up. I'm not looking forward to meeting him,' said Rimmer, grimacing. 'Dan's language is ripe at the best of times.'

'Were there any witnesses?'

'None have come forward.'

'Has there been any attempt to find them?'

'One of the local constables has been doing the rounds in search of anyone who might be able to shed light on what happened.'

'Where's the guard now?' asked Leeming.

'He's in my office, Sergeant. I wasn't sure whether to leave him here or have him moved by the undertaker. In the end, I decided to keep him.'

'Good,' said Colbeck. 'Has the family been informed?'

'Yes,' replied Rimmer, nervously. 'Hannah Fullard and her daughter both know that Jake is dead. What they haven't been told, however, is whether or not he was murdered. We're hoping that you could confirm that.'

'Let's go and see him.'

The appearance of the detectives had aroused a lot of interest and there was a heavy murmur all round them as they walked towards the stationmaster's office. Two uniformed railway policemen were standing outside to keep people at bay. When they realised who the newcomers were, they stepped aside. Rimmer unlocked the door to let the detectives into the office then he locked it behind them. Curtains had been drawn to keep out prying eyes, so there was diminished light.

The body of Jake Fullard was stretched out on a trestle table and covered with a blanket. Though the faces of the dead were an all too common sight to Colbeck and Leeming, both of them recoiled slightly when the blanket was peeled back. Fullard's face had been smashed in by the impact of several hooves. Covered in gore, it lacked eyes and a nose. The black beard was now a dark red. Colbeck drew the blanket back so that the whole body was revealed. In their escape from the wagon, the bullocks had left muddy hoof marks all over the guard and had doubtless broken many of his bones in the process.

'What makes you think he was murdered, Mr Rimmer?' asked Colbeck.

'It's the wound on the back of his head, Inspector. It's far worse than anything else. Yet he was lying on his back in the grass beside the track,' explained Rimmer. 'It was wet from the rain we had this morning and quite soft. As you can see, the bullocks did the damage to the face and the front of his body. How did he get that horrible gash in the back of his head?'

Colbeck removed a handkerchief from his pocket and wrapped it round his hand before gently lifting up the guard's head. He and Leeming could see that the skull had taken a fearful blow that could not have been the work of scampering hooves.

'Were you called to the scene, Mr Rimmer?'

'Yes, I was, Inspector.'

'And what did you see?'

'Well,' said the stationmaster, 'I saw Jake on his back and the wagon empty. What made it worse, you see, was that they'd all jumped on top of him. When they're unloaded, a ramp is used so that they can come down it one at a time. In this case, the bullocks each leapt three feet before they landed on top of poor Jake.'

'I don't think he would have felt a thing,' said Colbeck,

sadly. 'My guess is that he was dead before the first bullock hit him. That blow to the head was lethal.' He eased the head back down again. 'Have you searched his pockets?'

'No, I didn't think it was my place to do so.'

Colbeck conducted a quick search of the dead man. Apart from a spotted handkerchief, a notebook, a pencil and a small box of lozenges, the pockets were empty. He pulled the blanket over the corpse.

'His wallet is missing. That gives us a possible motive for murder. Also,' said Colbeck, 'someone has taken his watch.'

'We don't know that he had a watch,' said Leeming.

'I can see that you don't work on the railway, Sergeant. Everything is covered by time. A guard would be certain to have a pocket watch.'

'Perhaps it came off when the bullocks jumped on him.'

'Then it would have been found beside him,' said Rimmer, 'and it wasn't.'

'Right,' decided Colbeck. 'Contact the undertaker. Mr Fullard can be moved.'

'Thank you,' said Rimmer with a sigh of relief. 'I'm not squeamish as a rule but having him here is . . . well, unsettling. I knew Jake Fullard. He was a first-rate guard. Seeing him like this is really upsetting.'

'Where will we find the driver and the fireman?' asked Leeming.

'Olly had to go home – that's Oliver Dann, the driver. He and Jake were good friends. They used to play cribbage together. Olly was so distressed when he saw what had happened that he passed out.'

'What about the fireman?'

'That's Luke Upton,' said Rimmer. 'He's younger and has got a stronger stomach. When he and Olly were laid off for the day, Luke went straight to the White Hart.'

'Then that's where you'll find him, Sergeant,' said Colbeck, nodding towards the door. 'See what he has to say then meet me at the police station.'

'Yes, Inspector,' said Leeming.

The stationmaster unlocked the door and let him out. 'Olly Dann lives only a stone's throw away, Inspector,' he said. 'I'll give you the address.'

'First things first, sir,' said Colbeck. 'Since the train has been kept in the siding, I'd like to take a closer look at it.' He stilled Rimmer's protest with a gesture. 'Don't worry. I won't take you away from your duties here. I'll find my own way.'

'Thank you. The wagon you want is the fifth one along from the brake van.'

Colbeck was about to leave when a thought detained him. Lifting up the other end of the blanket, he studied the guard's boots before lifting one of the feet up to look at the heel. The stationmaster was baffled. Without a word, Colbeck lowered the foot down and covered it with the blanket. Then he opened the door and went out.

Victor Leeming had no trouble finding him. Luke Upton was sitting on a bar stool at the White Hart with a half-empty tankard of cider in front of him. As soon as the fireman spoke to him, Leeming could hear that he'd already had several drinks because he slurred his words. After explaining who he was, he bought a pint of beer for himself then took Upton to a table in a quiet corner. The fireman was a hulking man in his early thirties with an open face now darkened by the tragedy. When he was invited to make a statement, he first took a long sip from his tankard.

'Let me be honest, Sergeant . . .' he began.

'I hope you weren't planning to be *dis*honest, sir.'

'I never liked Jake Fullard. He was Olly's friend, not mine. I always found him too bossy. Fair's fair,' he went on, 'he was good at his job. I don't know a better guard in the whole county. But . . . well, I don't like being given orders.'

'None of us enjoys that,' said Leeming.

'We never had any trouble with Jake. When he was on board, we knew that we were in safe hands. Not all guards are like that.'

'How much of him did you see today?'

'We saw very little, really,' said Upton. 'As soon as he came on duty, Jake came over to see us. He couldn't have spent more than a couple of minutes by the engine. As he walked off, we thought he was just going to the brake van. Instead, he was walking to his death. When Olly saw him, he fainted and I almost spewed up my breakfast.'

'You have my sympathy, Mr Upton,' said Leeming. 'We viewed the body but we'd been warned in advance what to expect. You and the driver hadn't.'

'The bullocks stampeded all over him. It was only when two of them charged past us that we realised something was up.'

Leeming took out his notebook and wrote something in it.

Then he tasted his beer and gave an appreciative sigh. Upton also had another drink.

'Did the guard have any enemies?' asked Leeming.

'Well, he was never going to be popular, Sergeant.'

'Was that because he was bossy?'

'It was because he was a guard. His job is to ensure the safety of the train and, when it's a goods train, there are special problems. You get people climbing into the wagons for a free ride, or kids playing on the line or thieves trying to steal whatever you're carrying. Someone made off with a pig under his arm once. They'll take anything they can get their hands on.'

'Isn't it the guard's job to scare them off?'

'Yes,' said Upton, 'and Jake was good at doing that. The only real trouble he'd had was with that Irishman he caught sleeping in an empty wagon.'

'When was this?'

'Oh, it was a week ago. Jake was thorough. He always checked each load before we set off to make sure that it was safe to travel. Anyway, he climbed up on this wagon full of sand and found this man fast asleep in it. That kind of thing made Jake furious,' said Upton. 'He not only kicked him awake, he began to yell at him. The man – he was Irish, remember – turned violent. If Jake hadn't called a couple of railway policeman, there'd have been a fight. The man was led off.'

'Did he make any threats to the guard?'

Upton gave a grim laugh. 'He never stopped, Sergeant. He said he'd come back one day and get even with Jake.'

'How did Mr Fullard react to that?'

'He just shrugged his shoulders and got on with his job.

That was the kind of man he was. Jake was fearless. He's had hundreds of threats over the years and always ignored them. Why should he worry any more about this one?'

Colbeck got to the train just in time because it was due to leave fairly soon. The escaped bullocks had been caught and put back in their wagon. As he walked past the brake van, he saw that the first four wagons contained sheep, smaller animals who would have done far less damage to the guard had they jumped on top of him. Evidently, he was placed beside the bullocks so that his death could be seen as the result of an accident. Yet when he examined the narrow wooden gate that held the animals in, Colbeck saw that it was sound. The bullocks had been deliberately let out by someone. The ground was covered with the imprint of their hooves but it was something else that claimed his interest. Colbeck could see two runnels in the mud, going all the way back to the brake van. He thought about the heels on the boots of the murder victim.

Having identified a potential suspect, Leeming went straight to the little police station and asked if anyone had been aware of an Irish visitor to the town. Sergeant Rogers, a hefty, pockmarked individual, recalled the man immediately because he had hauled him out of the White Hart for causing an affray. His name, it transpired, was Gerard Devlin and he'd spent the night in custody.

'Has he been hanging around the area?' asked Leeming.

'Yes,' replied the other, 'but he's been keeping out of my way. Someone spotted him in Hele, only four miles away, and we had reports of an intruder who slept in a barn near here – that might well have been Devlin.'

'We need to find him.'

Rogers gave a wry chuckle. 'Then I need more men,' he said. 'There are over three thousand people in this town, Sergeant, and I have only two constables to help me uphold the law here. I can't spare either of them to conduct a manhunt. What I can do is to ask them to keep their eyes peeled for any sign of Devlin.'

'Do you think he's likely to come back?'

'That's what he threatened to do. When I gave him a black eye, he swore that he'd be back to settle a score with me. I told him he was welcome. It would give me a chance to black the other eye for him.'

He let out a peal of laughter and exposed a row of tiny blackened teeth.

'Do you have much trouble here?' asked Leeming.

'It's mostly petty crime. You know the sort of thing – thieves who steal an apple or two on market day, youths who get into a fight over a girl and noisy drunks who piss in people's gardens. Oh, and we had a spate of breaking windows by some children with nothing better to do on a Saturday night. We never have anything really serious,' said the sergeant, complacently. 'I make sure of that.'

'Then it's a pity you weren't at the railway station this morning,' said Leeming, pointedly, 'or you might have stopped a guard from being murdered.'

Oliver Dann was still stunned by what he'd seen. When his wife admitted the visitor, Colbeck found the engine driver, still in his working clothes, perched on the edge of an armchair and staring gloomily into the empty fireplace. It was a full minute before he came out of his reverie to be introduced to the detective. Colbeck refused the offer from Margery Dann of refreshment and she left the room so that he could talk alone with her husband. Dann took time to collect his thoughts.

'You have my sympathy, sir,' said Colbeck, sitting opposite him. 'I gather that you and Mr Fullard were close friends.'

'Jake was good company, Inspector. Most people found him a bit dry but they didn't know him as well as I did. We played cribbage together two or three times a week. I'll miss him terribly.'

'I'm told that he was an outstanding guard.'

'I've never met one better,' said Dann. 'For this to happen to Jake of all people – well, it's cruel. I mean, he was always so careful. He'd have checked every wagon to see that the livestock was securely penned in.'

'It was, Mr Dann.'

'Obviously not – those bullocks got loose.'

'That wasn't what happened, sir,' said Colbeck, softly. 'They didn't get loose of their own volition, I'm afraid. Somebody opened the gate so that the animals could leap out on top of Mr Fullard.' Dann drew back in horror as if from a blow. 'My belief is that he was killed by the brake van then dragged alongside that wagon.'

'*Killed?*' The engine driver looked as if he was about to pass out again. 'Are you saying that Jake was *murdered?*'

'I'd stake my reputation on it.'

'I thought that . . .'

Eyes moist and mouth agape, Dann went off into another

reverie. When he finally came out of it, his voice was solemn and serious.

'The truth is that I *didn't* think,' he confessed. 'I saw him on the ground and everything went blank. If I *had* thought about it, I'd have known that it couldn't have been an accident.'

'I came to the same conclusion, sir,' said Colbeck. 'I stood beside that wagon earlier on. If the gate had suddenly opened and a bullock had jumped out, I'd have leapt instinctively to the side. One animal might have caught me a glancing blow but not the dozen or more I saw penned up. Mr Fullard was placed there like a sacrifice.'

Dann was roused. 'Then I'd like to get my hands on the bastard who put him there,' he shouted. 'I'd tie him to the rails and drive the engine over him again and again. Yes, then I'd feed the pieces to the pigs.'

'I can understand how you feel, Mr Dann,' said Colbeck, trying to calm him with upraised palms 'You've a right to feel angry but anger won't help us to bring the villain to justice. That takes cool, clear, logical deduction. What I'd like you to do, please, is to help us. You were fond of Mr Fullard but his job might have made him enemies. Can you think of anyone – anyone at all – whom he might have upset sufficiently for them to want revenge?'

As he tried to master his emotions, Oliver Dann sat back into his chair and looked up at the ceiling. Colbeck could hear the man's teeth grinding. There was a long wait but it was productive. When he finally came out of his trance, Dann was cold and decisive.

'Yes, Inspector,' he said. 'I can suggest two or three people.'

* * *

Sergeant Rogers had been sobered by the information that a murder had occurred in Cullompton. Never having had to deal with a heinous crime, he had no idea how to react. His main concern was how he would be portrayed in the newspapers. Once the word got out, reporters from Exeter – perhaps even from London – would converge on the town. What sort of role should the sergeant pretend that he'd played? He was still trying to decide when Colbeck arrived. Leeming introduced him to the sergeant then told him about Gerard Devlin.

'He's still in the area, sir,' said Leeming. 'I think he's our man.'

'That depends how strong he is,' argued Colbeck.

'I can tell you that, Inspector,' said Rogers, trying to ingratiate himself. 'He's as strong as an ox. I had to take some hard punches from him before I knocked him out. Devlin is your killer, no doubt about that. I'm glad that I'm the one who pointed you in his direction.'

'That's not strictly true,' observed Leeming. 'It was Luke Upton who first mentioned the Irishman.'

'It doesn't matter who it was,' said Colbeck, 'because Mr Devlin is not the killer. Jake Fullard was dragged along the ground by someone who was not strong enough to lift him. That rules out the Irishman. Besides,' he continued, 'Devlin lives on his wits, by the sound of it. He's used to dodging policemen and taking his chances where he finds them. He's a petty criminal by nature. The person we're after is an amateur. He actually *believed* that we'd be fooled by the scene he set up beside that wagon. If we accepted that it had been a grotesque accident, then he'd be in the clear.' Colbeck smiled thinly. 'As it happens, he is not.'

Leeming was excited. 'You know who he is, sir?'

'I can make an educated guess who *they* are, Sergeant, because an accomplice was involved. Something troubled me from the outset, you see. When the gate was opened on that wagon,' said Colbeck, 'why did the bullocks charge out? They'd have shown curiosity, of course, but would the first one have jumped down three feet unless he'd have cause to do so? A gunshot would have frightened them into a panic-stricken escape but that would have given the game away. They must have used something else – a stone, for instance. If it hit an animal hard enough, it would make it burst into life.'

'Those children on the line,' said Leeming, as the truth dawned on him. 'Upton told me about them.'

'Go on.'

'Well, they were a real nuisance, apparently. No matter what the guard did, they kept coming back. Then he caught one of them and gave him a hiding.'

'Jed Lavery,' declared Rogers.

'Who's he?' asked Leeming.

'He and his brother, Harry, are thorns in my flesh. They're always causing trouble. I'm fairly certain they were the ones responsible for breaking those windows and it only stopped when I took them aside and boxed their ears.'

'How old are they?' wondered Colbeck.

'Jed is twelve or so and he's the nasty one. Harry is a year or two younger and does what his brother tells him. They're rotten to the core, Inspector.'

'How did they break windows?'

'Oh, they were very clever,' said Rogers. 'They did it from a distance so they could run away without being seen. They used catapults.'

The brothers lived with their widowed mother in a smallholding on the outskirts of the town. The detectives hired a trap to drive there. Leeming was shocked by what they'd discovered. He still found it beyond belief.

'Can children of that age really be *killers*, sir?'

'I'm afraid so, Victor.'

'But they're not much older than my two boys. David and Albert would never do anything like that.'

'That's because you've brought them up properly,' said Colbeck. 'Yet even at their age, they're physically capable of murder. If you put a hammer or an axe in their hands, they'd be strong enough to knock someone out if not able to lift them up afterwards. In any case,' he added, 'we don't know that murder was intended here. It's conceivable that the guard was supposed to be wounded in payment for the hiding he gave the two boys. When he was hit hard, he died unexpectedly so that his killer had to drag his body beside that wagon. He and his brother – if they really are the culprits – then used their catapults to scare the bullocks into life.'

Leeming was saddened. 'We've never arrested anyone so young before.'

'Criminals have to answer for their crimes.'

When they reached the little cottage, they saw that it had an air of neglect about it. The fence outside it was also in need of repair. Chickens squawked and fled out of the way as the wheels of the trap rolled towards them. After giving Leeming his orders, Colbeck went to the front door and knocked. It was opened by a thin, hard-faced woman in her forties. She put her hand on her hips.

'What do you want?' she asked, pugnaciously.

'Are you Mrs Lavery?'

'Who wants to know?'

'My name is Detective Inspector Colbeck and I'd like to speak to your sons, if I may. I will, of course, only do so with you there.'

Her truculence vanished at once and she became more respectful.

'Don't believe what people tell you about Jed and Harry,' she said. 'They've been wonderful to me since my husband died. Without them to help, this place would have been impossible to keep on. My sons are my salvation.'

Colbeck felt a fleeting sympathy for her. The loss of her husband had clearly thrown her into a dire predicament. It had also had a visible effect on her health. She was pale and utterly exhausted. Yet he couldn't let compassion get in the way of duty.

'Where are your sons now, Mrs Lavery?'

'They're feeding the horses,' she replied.

'Then I'd like to talk to them, please.'

She was defensive. 'Is it about those windows that were smashed?'

'Yes,' he said. 'In one way, I suppose that it is.'

'It wasn't them. I'd take my oath on it. Jed and Harry were here all the time.'

Colbeck pretended to accept her word. 'I'm sure that they were.'

He was invited into the kitchen, a small, bare, cheerless place with a rickety table and whitewashed walls. The paved floor had undulations. An unpleasant smell hovered. She waved him to a chair but he preferred to stand. Because she went out for several minutes, Colbeck decided that she was rehearsing what she wanted her sons to say. When they came in with bowed heads, they looked meek and obedient. Jed Lavery was a wiry lad in rough clothes in desperate need of washing. Harry was shorter and even skinnier, wearing a pair of trousers that were too big for him and which had obviously been handed down to him by his brother. There were patches badly sewn on both knees.

Colbeck got both of them to sit down before he fired his question at them.

'Which one of you has the catapult?'

Caught unawares by what amounted to an accusation, they looked guiltily at each other. It was their mother who provided the answer.

'They both have one, Inspector. They use them to kill pigeons.'

'I think they used them for something else today, Mrs Lavery.' He stood over the two boys. 'Isn't that true?'

They avoided his searching eyes and were patently discomfited. For once in their lives, Jed and Harry were out of their depth. Defying the local police had been easy and they'd baited a railway guard without fear. Colbeck represented a different problem altogether. His status, height, authoritative manner and impeccable tailoring combined to unnerve them completely. He pressed home his advantage.

'Now that we know you both have catapults,' he said, quietly, 'which one of you stole Mr Fullard's watch?'

The sheer directness of the question made the pair of them twitch noticeably. Harry's eyes flicked to and fro but it was his brother, Jed, who was under the most intense pressure. He began to fidget. After trying and failing to concoct a lie, Jed gave up and jumped to his feet. To his mother's horror, he pushed Colbeck aside and ran to the back door, hurtling through it in a frantic bid to get away. All that he managed to do, however, was to bounce off the formidable frame of Victor Leeming who, at Colbeck's suggestion, had worked his way round to the rear of the cottage so that he could block a potential escape route.

The force of the collision knocked something out of the boy's pocket and it fell to the ground. Holding him firmly by his collar, Leeming bent down to retrieve a large pocket watch. He flicked it open to look at the dial.

'I think your time is up, son,' he said.

THE BARBER OF RAVENGLASS

'Why are we in such a rush, Inspector?' asked Leeming in bewilderment.

'We have a train to catch, Victor.'

'Where are we going?'

'Ravenglass.'

'Is it far away?'

'It's far enough,' said Colbeck. 'That's why I advised you to bring the change of clothing you keep at Scotland Yard.'

'Estelle will worry when I don't come home tonight.'

'Madeleine will be anxious for the same reason. Since they were misguided enough to marry detectives, however, they must learn to expect sudden departures.'

'We've never had one as sudden as this, Inspector.'

They were in a cab that was taking them to Euston station. All that Leeming could think about was being apart from his wife and two sons. Colbeck gave him a friendly pat on the knee.

'I'm not that hard-hearted, Victor,' he said. 'I considered

the ladies and sent word of our movements to Estelle and to Madeleine. They'll still fret in our absence but at least they'll know where we are.'

'That's more than I will, sir. Where *is* Ravenglass?'

'It's in the county of Cumberland.'

'That's way up north!' protested Leeming.

'Your knowledge of geography cannot be faulted.'

'What did the telegraph say?'

'It merely said that a crisis had occurred. We are responding to it.'

'Why does it always have to be us?'

'A challenge has been set,' explained Colbeck. 'We must not shirk it simply because we enjoy the comforts of home life. Ravenglass needs our help.'

'What sort of place is it?'

'It's a very small one. We are escaping the bedlam here and going to the coast where the air will be clean, and where fresh fish will be served to delight the palate.'

'I'd still rather stay here.'

'Even if it means that a killer goes unpunished?'

Leeming frowned. 'I thought the superintendent said something about a burning railway carriage.'

'Indeed, he did,' agreed Colbeck. 'What he omitted to tell you was that someone was *inside* the carriage when it was set ablaze.'

The journey was long, tiresome and involved a change of trains. When they finally reached their destination, they discovered that the station was a quarter of a mile away from the little market town. The enforcement of law and order rested in the nervous hands of Clifford Baines, a tall, gangly, young constable with a prominent Adam's apple and a pair of bulging eyes. He had been walking up and down the platform for hours, praying for help and trying to keep people away from the wreckage. Relieved at the arrival of the detectives, he let out a cry of joy and fell on them with a gratitude verging on desperation.

'Thank heaven you've both come!' he said.

'Thank heaven we actually got here!' murmured Leeming.

Colbeck introduced them then asked to see the murder scene. It was over thirty yards away. A disused railway carriage had been shunted into a siding and left there until someone could decide what to do with it. During the night, it had been set alight and had burnt so fiercely that the glare could be seen for miles. All that remained was the shell of the carriage and the charred body of the victim. To give it a degree of dignity, Baines had draped some sacking over it.

'It's been dreadful,' he complained. 'Everybody has come here to stand and stare. It's like having a beached whale. The ghouls turn out in force.'

'A beached whale can sometimes be saved,' observed Colbeck as he drew back the sacking. 'This unfortunate person is way beyond salvation.'

The detectives were horrified to see what fire could do to the human body. Clothes and hair had been burnt off what was patently the shrivelled body of a woman. Leeming felt embarrassed to look at the naked black torso. He was also ashamed at his reluctance to come to Ravenglass. A grotesque crime had obviously occurred and it was their duty to find the culprit. He shook off his exhaustion at once.

'Do you know who it is?' he asked.

'No, Sergeant,' said Baines. 'And nobody else does either. The truth is that we had no idea that someone was inside the carriage.'

'The killer obviously did.'

'I'm not entirely sure there *was* a killer.' They shot him a sceptical glance. 'It might just be that someone wanted to get rid of the carriage. Quite a few people have complained about it.'

'Arson is a crime,' said Colbeck. 'When it's also a form of murder, it's even more heinous. If you hold your finger over a match, it's painful. Don't you think that somebody inside that carriage would have got out quickly the moment they felt the heat and smelt the smoke?'

'I suppose so,' said Baines, sheepishly.

'Is there an undertaker in Ravenglass?'

'Yes, sir.'

'Fetch him immediately. The body must be moved.'

'As long as it's here, folk will come to stare.'

When Baines went scurrying off, Colbeck covered the body up again and walked slowly around the wreckage, looking for clues and trying to work out the point at which the fire had first started. He turned to Leeming.

'I know what you're thinking,' he said. 'The victim was killed *before* the carriage was set alight.'

'Yes, Inspector – she was either killed or too drunk to know what was happening. I hope we can identify her before her remains are buried. Her family and friends need to be told what's happened to her.'

'We don't know that she had either. Nobody would sleep in a broken-down old carriage like this if they had a proper home and people who cared about them.'

'That's a fair comment,' said Leeming.

'They only seem to have a stationmaster and a porter here,' noted Colbeck.

'It is a bit off the beaten track, sir.'

'I'll talk to both of them.'

'What about me?'

'Take the luggage and find us a room at a hotel. In a place as small as Ravenglass, there may only be one.'

Leeming looked around and heaved a sigh. 'How can anyone want to live in such an isolated spot?'

'Oh, I could cope with a lot of isolation, Victor. It's infinitely preferable to the hurly-burly of a big city. You have time to think out here,' said Colbeck, inhaling deeply. 'Smell that air – no trace of the London stench.'

'All I can smell is the fire that turned that poor woman into a human cinder.' Leeming gazed down at the figure under the sacking. 'Who *is* she?'

Sam Gazey, the porter, was a short, stout, pot-bellied man in his thirties with a wispy beard that seemed constantly in need of a scratch. Colbeck found him slow-witted and unhelpful. Gazey could remember no woman arriving recently at the station on her own. Nor did he have any idea that the carriage had been occupied at night. Len Hipwell, by contrast, could not stop speculating on the victim's identity. Tucked away in the stream of conjectures he unleashed on Colbeck was some useful information. Hipwell was a self-important man in his forties with a flabby red face and piggy eyes. When holding forth, he hooked his thumbs in his waistcoat.

'If you want my opinion,' he said, 'it's Maggie Hobday.'

'What makes you think that?'

'I get to hear things in my job, Inspector.'

'Are you referring to proven fact or idle gossip?'

'Rumours that reach me tend to have some truth in them.'

'And what were you told about this particular lady?'

Hipwell chortled. 'Oh, Maggie were no lady, sir. She made a living by giving comfort to lonely men – or married ones, if their wives were not looking. Everyone knew about Maggie.'

'Did you actually *see* her in Ravenglass?' asked Colbeck.

'No – but she were spotted in Egremont a week or so ago.'

'What could bring her here?'

'She were always on the move,' said Hipwell, knowledgeably. 'Women like that don't stop in one place for long. They either run out of customers or get chased away by angry wives. Over the years, she's had more than her share of trouble. Maggie was once dumped in a horse trough in Whitehaven.'

'That would be preferable to being set alight in a railway carriage.'

'Mark my words, Inspector. That's her corpse over there. As soon as I knew a woman had slept in that carriage, I said it was Maggie.'

'You must have known her well to be so certain about it.'

Hipwell spluttered. 'That's not true at all,' he said,

indignantly. 'I'm a married man and glad of it when . . . females like her are sniffing around. It's just that, being a stationmaster, you develop a sixth sense about people.'

Colbeck had already developed the sense that the garrulous stationmaster was of no practical help. It was clear that Hipwell lived in a world of tittle-tattle and that made his judgement unreliable. Colbeck had only one more question to ask him.

'When is the station left unmanned?'

'The place is closed at eleven o'clock at night, Inspector. I open it up again in time to meet the milk train at six.'

'So there's nobody here in the small hours.'

'No,' replied Hipwell with a nod towards the siding. 'Unless you count Maggie Hobday, that is.'

Having arranged accommodation at the King's Arms, Victor Leeming stood at the window of his room and looked out. Ravenglass was a pretty town with ample remains of Roman occupation at an earlier point in its history. It was neat, compact and well built. Situated on the estuary fed by three rivers – the Esk, the Mite and the Irt – it had a pleasant feel to it. Leeming could see oyster-fishermen mending nets and repairing boats in the harbour. He could also see groups of people in urgent conversation and could guess what they were talking about.

There had been a trap for hire at the station but, since he had no luggage to carry, Colbeck had elected to walk. When the sergeant saw him coming towards the hotel, he went downstairs to meet him. They adjourned to the lounge so that they could talk in private.

'I waited until the undertaker arrived to take away the body,' said Colbeck.

'Yes, I saw him driving up the street.'

'What have you found out, Victor?'

'Well, I may have the name of the deceased,' said Leeming. 'According to the manager here, it's someone called Joan Metcalf.'

'That's not what I heard. The stationmaster said it was Maggie Hobday.'

'Ah, yes, that name came up as well but the manager said it couldn't possibly be her. He claimed she was up in Bowness.'

'Tell me about Joan Metcalf.'

'She lives wild, sir,' explained Leeming. 'It's a sad case. The husband she loved devotedly was killed at sea but she's never accepted that he was dead. She walks up and down the coast in the hope that he'll come back to her one day. Someone saw her near Selker Bay earlier in the week. I don't know where that is but the manager says that it's not far south of here.'

'When did her husband die?'

'It was all of twenty years ago. Her faith that he's still alive must be very strong to keep her going that long. She begs for food and will do odd jobs to earn a penny. She'll sleep wherever she can. People in Ravenglass are kind to her.'

'Then she's very different to Maggie Hobday. The women here are more likely to drive *her* away because she sells favours to the men. Which one is it,' asked Colbeck, pensively, 'the wife with a broken heart or the lady of easy virtue?'

'We may never know, sir.'

'We *have* to know, Victor. Only when we've identified the

victim can we start looking for people who might have a motive to kill her.' He stood back to appraise Leeming. 'I think that it's time you had a haircut.'

'Do you?' asked the other in surprise.

'I passed the barber's shop on my way here. It's still open.'

'Why should I have a haircut, sir?'

'Because it's the ideal way to get information without appearing to be doing so,' said Colbeck. 'There can't be more than four hundred souls in a place like this. A barber will know almost everyone and have a lot of customers among the men.'

'So?'

'If he realises you're a detective, he may not be so forthcoming. If you tell him that you're a visitor to the area, however, he'll talk more freely. Find out all you can about Ravenglass and the men who live here.'

Leeming ran a hand over his head. 'I don't really *need* a haircut, you know.'

'Pretend that you do. It's in a good cause.'

'Where will you be, sir?'

'Oh, I'll be here, doing something of great importance.'

'What's that?'

'I'll be studying the dinner menu.'

Most of the barber's customers were fishermen or local tradesmen so the sight of a frock coat and top hat caused Ned Wyatt, the barber, to look up. An elderly man was having what little remained of his hair trimmed by Wyatt. They had been chatting happily until the newcomer stepped into the little shop. The conversation trailed off. Removing his hat, Leeming took a seat and waited. When his turn came, he replaced the other customer in the chair and had a white cloth put around him.

'What can I do for you, sir?' asked Wyatt.

'Just . . . make my hair look a little tidier, please.'

'It doesn't need much taking off.'

'You're the barber. I rely on your judgement.'

He could see Wyatt in the mirror. The barber was a tall, thin, sour-faced individual in his fifties but his pronounced hunch took several inches off his height. Beside the mirror was a small framed portrait of a man in a black cloak and white bands. He looked vaguely familiar to Leeming.

'Who's that?' he asked.

'John Wesley.'

'Ah, I see. You're a Methodist.'

'Wesley often came to Cumberland. He preached in Whitehaven twenty-five times. Listening to him must have been an inspiration.'

'I sometimes fall asleep during our vicar's sermons,' said Leeming.

'What brings you to Ravenglass?' asked Wyatt, starting to snip away.

'Friends of mine had a holiday here once and told me what a pleasant spot it was. Since I was travelling north by train, I thought I'd make a small diversion and see what it was that they liked so much.'

'I hope you're not disappointed.'

'Not at all – it's very . . .' He groped for the right word. 'It's very quaint.'

'It's a nice place to live, sir.'

'So I should imagine,' said Leeming, starting to relax into his role. 'But there seems to be some commotion here. I saw some of the remains of a carriage at the station and overheard the manager of the King's Arms talking about a tragic death.'

'That's right.'

'What exactly happened?'

'Nobody can say with any certainty, sir. Everyone who comes in here has a different view. Bert Longmuir, who just left, reckons as how someone wanted to kill theirselves by setting fire to that carriage.' He gave an expressive shrug. 'I'm not sure that I believe that.'

'Oh – what do *you* think happened?'

As his scissors clicked away, Wyatt gave him a range of theories about the crime and told him the names of the people who held those opinions. What he was careful not to do was to commit himself to a point of view. Leeming tried to prod him into voicing his own opinion.

'You must have thought some of those comments ridiculous.'

'I'm in business, sir. I never argue with customers.'

'Has anything like this ever happened in Ravenglass before?'

Wyatt was crisp. '*Never*, sir – and we don't want it to happen again. It leaves a bad feeling in the town. People start to suspect each other and arguments break out. That's not good for us. It could well be that nobody from Ravenglass is involved.'

'No, that's right. He might have come from somewhere else.'

'And *he* might be a she, sir.'

Leeming was startled. 'What's that?'

'Women know how to light a fire.'

Wyatt finished cutting the hair and looked at Leeming from both sides before he was satisfied that his work was done. He removed the white cloak and used a brush on his customer's shoulders. After examining his haircut, Leeming got up, thanked him and paid the barber.

'I'll be on my way then,' he said.

'You'll notice that the barman at the King's Arms has also had a haircut,' said Wyatt, impassively. 'He were talking to manager when you went in to book rooms. Then he came in here and told me who you were.'

'Oh,' said Leeming, uneasily. 'I see.'

'I hope you enjoy your stay, Sergeant Leeming. They're decent people in Ravenglass. They like honesty.' He held the door open. 'So do I, sir. Goodbye.'

After a visit to the undertaker, Colbeck returned to the crime scene. He borrowed a rake from the stationmaster and used it to sift through the debris, taking excessive care not to soil his well-polished shoes. Nothing had survived the fire intact. What few possessions the victim had owned had been eaten up by the flames. He was still raking through the embers when Victor Leeming came towards him.

'They told me at the hotel that you'd be here, sir.'

'Yes,' said Colbeck, 'now that the body has been removed, I wanted a closer look at the scene.' He appraised the sergeant. 'Take your hat off.'

'Why?'

'I want to see what the barber did.'

'He almost turned my cheeks crimson,' admitted Leeming.

'There was I, talking as if I was on holiday there, and he knew all the time that I was lying. The barman from the hotel had seen me arrive and told him who I was.'

'Then I owe you an apology, Victor. But I'd still like to see his handiwork.' When Leeming removed his hat, Colbeck had to hide a smile. 'I'm not sure that I altogether approve,' he said, tactfully. 'To tell you the truth, it looked better before.'

'I know,' said Leeming, putting the hat back on again. 'But I did get what you sent me to get, including another possible name for the victim. Everyone who went into the shop has been talking about the murder. Mr Wyatt saved us a lot of wasted time knocking on doors.'

'Did he suggest who the killer might be?'

'*He* didn't, sir, but other people did. Unlike the manager, most of them are convinced that it was Maggie Hobday in that carriage. I've got the names of three people from Ravenglass we ought to take a close look at and one from a hamlet called Holmrook.'

'Well done, Victor. Your visit to the barber was fruitful.'

'It was very embarrassing.'

'You gleaned useful information and had a memorable haircut.'

'What about you, sir?' asked Leeming, looking at the wreckage. 'Have you found anything of interest?'

'I found nothing here,' said Colbeck, 'but I learnt two things when I called in on the undertaker. First, our instincts were sound. The victim was murdered before the carriage was set alight. On closer inspection than we were able to give, the undertaker discovered that her throat had been cut from ear to ear.'

'If she was dead, why did the killer need to burn the body?'

'He wanted to destroy any evidence of her identity and thus make our task much more difficult. But there was something that was not completely destroyed,' Colbeck went on, taking a handkerchief from his pocket. 'I said that I learnt two things from the undertaker. This is the second discovery.'

Unfolding the handkerchief, he revealed a tiny, twisted, nickel object that glinted in the evening sun. Leeming peered closely at it then shook his head.

'What is it, sir?'

'It used to be a wedding ring, Victor. It was clutched in the woman's hand.'

'Then the body must be that of Joan Metcalf,' said Leeming with conviction. 'It was probably the only souvenir of her husband that she had.'

'Let's not be too hasty. It may well be that Maggie Hobday was married as well. She wouldn't be the only widow to turn to prostitution. Think of the ladies of the night you've arrested in London,' said Colbeck. 'Even if they're spinsters, some of them wear a wedding ring during the day because it bestows a measure of respectability.' He wrapped the wedding ring up again and put it in his pocket. 'It may have belonged to neither, of course. You mentioned that another name for the victim had surfaced. That will give us three potential victims to discuss over dinner.'

Colbeck returned the rake to Hipwell who locked it away in the shed with the other implements used to tend the flower beds at the station. The detectives walked back towards the town.

Leeming was worried. 'Will you give me an honest opinion, sir?'

'I like to think that I always do, Victor.'

'What do you think Estelle will say when she sees my hair?'

Colbeck's face was motionless. 'I think that your wife will say that it makes you look rather . . . different.'

Sam Gazey was sweeping the platform when the stationmaster strolled over to him.

'They won't listen, you know,' said Hipwell.

'Who are you talking about, Len?'

'It's them two detectives from London. I tried to help but they ignored me. It were Maggie Hobday in that carriage – I'd wager my pocket watch on it. They didn't believe me. It's their own fault if they run round in circles.'

'How long will they be here?'

'One day is long enough. I don't like policemen.'

'Cliff Baines is no trouble.'

'That's because Cliff is one of us. Inspector Colbeck and that ugly sergeant of his don't belong here. They'll never solve the crime in a month of Sundays.' Hearing the distant approach of a train, he pulled out his watch and clicked his tongue when he saw the time. 'It's late again.'

Gazey put his broom aside and stood ready to assist anyone with heavy luggage. Thumbs hooked in his waistcoat, Hipwell watched as the locomotive surged towards them, belching out smoke. When they rolled past him, the stationmaster exchanged greetings with the driver and fireman then chided them for being well behind schedule. The train juddered to a halt and a handful of passengers got out. Nobody needed help from Gazey so he picked up his broom again. A woman strode purposefully towards Hipwell.

He touched his hat. 'Good morning to you, madam.'

'You don't know who I am, do you?'

'I'm afraid that I don't.' He looked at her more closely then stepped back in alarm. 'What are *you* doing here, Maggie?'

'I've come to see why everyone in Ravenglass thinks I'm dead. There was a gentleman I met in Barrow last night who happened to call here yesterday and he told me that I'd been burnt to death in a railway carriage.' She caught sight of the wreckage in the siding. 'Is *that* where it happened?' She prodded Hipwell. 'Who decided that I were the victim when – as you can see – I'm very much alive?'

Maggie Hobday was a buxom woman in her late thirties with handsome features ravaged by the life she'd led. In a smart coat and with a hat pulled down over her face, she was unrecognisable from the powdered harlot known throughout the county. Hipwell was agitated.

'You can't stay here,' he pleaded. 'Catch the next train out of Ravenglass.'

'I'm not leaving until I get to the bottom of this.'

'Just go, Maggie – I'll pay the fare, if you like.'

'I'm staying, Len. I want to know who's spreading stories about me.'

'There's a murder investigation going on. Detectives have come all the way from London. You don't want to get involved with them.'

'I want to know the truth of what happened,' she insisted. 'How would you like it if someone told you they'd heard you

228

were burnt to a frazzle? It upset me, it really did – well, it would upset anyone. Where will I find these detectives?'

He blocked her path. 'You don't need to talk to them.'

'Yes, I do.'

'Why not just go away and forget all about it?'

'Get out of my way, Len.'

'I can't let you do this,' he said, grabbing her arm.

Maggie spoke in a whisper. 'It costs money to touch me, Len,' she said, 'or have you forgotten?' He released her as if her arm were red hot. 'That's better.'

She brushed past him and walked towards the station exit. All that Hipwell could do was to run his tongue over dry lips and watch her go. Gazey had heard enough to rouse his interest. He sidled across to Hipwell.

'Maggie Hobday is still alive,' he said with a smirk. 'You bet your pocket watch that she was dead.' He extended a palm. 'Hand it over, Len.'

After enjoying a hearty breakfast, Colbeck and Leeming were just about to get up from the table when they heard sounds of an altercation. The manager was shouting but it was the piercing voice of a woman that they heard most clearly.

'I demand to see the detectives!' she yelled. 'They need to be told that I'm still alive and mean to stay like that.'

'You've been warned before, Miss Hobday,' said the manager. 'You're not welcome at the King's Arms.'

'The King's Arms might not want me but there are plenty of other arms in this town that have welcomed me.'

'Please keep your voice down.'

'Then stop bellowing at me!'

Colbeck and Leeming came swiftly into the hallway to part the combatants. The inspector introduced himself and Leeming to the visitor then assured the manager that – since she might provide evidence vital to their investigation – Maggie Hobday should be permitted to stay for a while.

'I take full responsibility for the lady's presence,' he said, suavely. 'Her stay here will not be of long duration.'

After giving his reluctant agreement, the manager withdrew sulkily. Colbeck invited Maggie into the lounge where she sat down opposite the detectives.

'You've made our job much easier,' said Leeming. 'We were told that you were the person trapped inside that burning carriage. The stationmaster was adamant that it had to be you.'

'Len Hipwell should have known better,' she said.

'You were seen in the area.'

'This is where I work, Sergeant. I'm bound to be noticed from time to time.'

'What do you know about Joan Metcalf?'

'Oh,' said Maggie, face clouding. 'Everyone knows Joan's story. Whenever I think of her, I want to cry with pity. At the same time,' she continued, adopting a sharper tone, 'that sort of thing would never happen to me. If I lost a husband, I wouldn't spend the rest of my life weeping over him. I'd find another.' She grinned. 'I've found quite a few in my time. They just happen to be married to someone else.' She suddenly reeled from the shock of realisation. 'Are you telling me that . . . ?'

'I'm afraid so,' said Colbeck. 'The victim, in all likelihood, was Mrs Metcalf.'

'How could anyone want to hurt her, Inspector? Joan was as harmless as a fly. Only a monster would set fire to someone like her.'

'I suspect that mistaken identity may have been involved, Miss Hobday.' He tried to be diplomatic. 'I understand that, in the course of your visits here, you may have made one or two enemies in this town.'

She cackled. 'Well, I'm never going to be popular with women, am I?'

'Have you received threats?' asked Leeming.

'I get those wherever I go, Sergeant,' she said with a shrug. 'Ravenglass is no worse than anywhere else.'

'It looks as if it could be. The person who burnt that carriage to the ground might have thought that you were inside it.'

'Then he deserves to hang as high as you can string him up!' she declared.

'We need your help to find the killer,' said Colbeck.

'What can I do?'

'For a start, you can tell us who made those threats against you. We are not ruling out the possibility that another woman is the culprit. Thinking it was you in that carriage, the killer first cut Mrs Metcalf's throat.'

Maggie's hand went to her own throat. 'Thank goodness I wasn't here!'

'Can you think of anyone who hated you enough to do that?'

'No,' she said, unsettled by the news. 'When people make threats, they very rarely carry them out. They just want to scare me away.'

'There must be *someone* you can suggest,' said Leeming.

Maggie Hobday brooded in silence for a couple of minutes. Having met hostility wherever she went, it was difficult to disentangle one battery of threats from another. She eventually spoke.

'There is someone in particular,' she said.

'Go on.'

'He called me a witch. He said that I cast spells and ought to be driven away. He said that witchcraft were evil, Inspector, and he meant it.'

'We know what they used to do to witches,' said Colbeck with a meaningful glance at Leeming. 'They burnt them at the stake.'

When he heard the news that Maggie Hobday had been seen in the town, Ned Wyatt was in the act of shaving a customer. His hand jerked involuntarily and he sliced open the man's cheek. Mouthing apologies and thrusting a towel at him, the barber went quickly into the storeroom and locked the door behind him. With his back against it, he considered the implications of what he'd just heard. The woman whose throat he'd cut in the darkness was not the witch he had detested for so long, after all. He had instead murdered an innocuous creature who roamed the coast in the futile hope of seeing her dead husband. Wyatt felt utterly mortified. Driven by blind hatred, he'd killed someone he actually liked. It was a terrifying revelation and he knew at once that he could never live with the horror of what he'd done.

The razor was still in his hand. He put it to his throat and, with full force, he inflicted a deep, deadly, searing slit. When the detectives found him, the barber of Ravenglass was beyond help.

By the time that Colbeck and Leeming finally left Cumberland, the burnt-out carriage had been cleared away from the siding and the sleepy little town had, to some extent, been cleansed of its hideous crime. The barber's suicide was both a confession of guilt and a self-administered punishment. Inquests would be held into both unnatural deaths but the detectives were spared the ordeal of a long murder trial. Anxious to see his wife and family again, Leeming had been disturbed by facts that had emerged about Ned Wyatt.

'Could he really hate Maggie Hobday that much?' he asked.

'As the father of two sons, you should be able to answer that question. If you felt that David or Albert had been abused in some way, wouldn't you have the urge to strike back at the abuser?'

'Well, yes – but I wouldn't go to those lengths.'

'When the barber's wife died,' said Colbeck, 'she left the upbringing of their only child to him. It appears that Wyatt worshipped his son and did everything that was expected of a father. They lived together contentedly. And then . . .'

'Maggie Hobday came on the scene.'

'She wasn't entirely to blame, Victor. It was the lad's friends who put him up to it. They got him drunk, clubbed together then handed him over to a prostitute. He was barely seventeen. I doubt if he even knew what was happening.'

'I can see why the barber was furious.'

'He was a strict Methodist and one of the tenets of Methodism is the avoidance of evil. Maggie Hobday embodied evil to him. She cast a spell on his son and led him astray. The lad couldn't cope with the shame of it all,' said Colbeck. 'That's why he took his own life, it seems. You can see why anger festered inside Wyatt. When he heard the rumour that Maggie was in that carriage, his lust for revenge took over.'

'It was pointless, sir. Killing her wouldn't bring his son back.'

'He felt that he'd rid the world of a witch. That was his justification.'

'Religion can affect people in strange ways, sir.'

'His mind was warped by what happened to his son.'

'I condemn what he did,' said Leeming, 'but as a father, I'm bound to feel some pity for him. It's made me resolve to bring my boys up properly.'

'You have nothing to reproach yourself with, Victor. They're good lads.'

'It's a valuable lesson for me to take away from Ravenglass. A father can never relax his vigilance.'

'Perhaps there's a second lesson to take away,' suggested Colbeck, looking at the sergeant's hair with frank amusement. 'Choose your barber with the utmost care.'

PUFFING BILLY

Though her career as an artist had reached a point where she derived an income from it, Madeleine Colbeck never forgot the debt she owed to the two most important people in her life. Her father, Caleb Andrews, had spent the best part of fifty years as a railwayman and brought her up to appreciate the engineering skills involved in steam locomotion. Whenever she tried to put a locomotive on paper or canvas, he was always ready to give advice and – in many cases – criticism. But it was her husband, Robert, who first realised that she had a flair for painting and who encouraged her to develop her gifts to the full. He urged her to attend art classes and to master the necessary techniques. It served to give her confidence a tremendous boost. Madeleine loved to spend her days working in her studio on her latest project. But there would soon be a pleasing break in her routine.

A holiday was a rare event in the life of a detective inspector. Colbeck was so committed to his job that he sometimes deliberately chose not to take time off owed to him. Under pressure from Madeleine, however, he did agree to have a free weekend and he put himself completely at her disposal.

'Where would you like to go?' he asked.

'That depends on how far you're prepared to take me, Robert.'

'I'd take you to the ends of the earth – provided that I can be back at work on Monday morning, that is. Give me a destination and the matter's settled.'

'Very well,' she said, decisively. 'I want to go to Northumberland.'

He was astonished. '*Northumberland?*'

'I even took the trouble to look at the train timetables.'

'But why on earth do you want to go there, Madeleine?'

'I'd like to make sketches of *Puffing Billy*.'

'Ah, I see – it's a working holiday.'

'Father has been badgering me to paint locomotives from earlier days to show how far they've evolved. For some reason, I have a yearning to see *Puffing Billy*. It would take us back over forty years.'

'I know,' he said, 'but it's a working engine at Wylam Colliery and there are other versions of the original design now in operation there. We can't just barge into a coalfield and expect them to let you sit there and draw.'

'That's why I took the liberty of writing to the mine manager, Robert. I didn't want to go all that distance in order to be turned back. Mr Hooper's letter arrived this morning. He's more than ready to let me do some drawings of *Puffing Billy*.'

'In that case, Wylam it shall be,' he said, impressed by his

236

wife's initiative. 'It will be so restful to travel incognito, so to speak, and to go on a train journey as just another passenger. That will be a luxury.'

'I'm afraid not,' she said, apologetically. 'The manager recognised the name of Colbeck. That was why he was so keen to give me free access.'

He was flattered. 'Has my fame spread *that* far?'

'Not exactly, Robert.'

'But you just said that the manager recognised my name.'

'I said that he recognised the name of Colbeck, but not because you happen to be the Railway Detective. He's probably never heard of you. It wasn't *your* name that he knew – it was mine.'

'Oh!' Colbeck was taken aback.

'Apparently, he has a friend in Newcastle who bought one of my very first paintings – the *Lord of the Isles*. The manager liked it so much that he remembered the name of Madeleine Colbeck. So you'll get your wish, after all,' she said, beaming. 'You can travel anonymously because nobody in Northumberland will have a clue as to who you are.'

Colbeck was unsure whether to be annoyed or gratified. For once in his life, he would have to take second place to Madeleine. His momentary irritation vanished. Loving his wife too much to begrudge her any fame, he burst out laughing and enfolded her in his arms.

Most people would have been daunted by the prospect of a journey north of almost three hundred miles but they were relishing it. Setting off from London on a Friday, they would have three whole days alone together, returning late on Sunday evening. They climbed aboard the train with anticipatory delight. Colbeck loved rail travel because there was always something of interest to see out of the window. He was sufficient of a romantic to bemoan the encroachment of industry on the countryside and sufficient of a realist to accept the need for progress. Critics argued that the advent of railways ruined some of the most beautiful landscape in England but Colbeck believed that the advantages outweighed the disadvantages. Those who toiled in factories, forges, mines and mills had hitherto been imprisoned throughout the whole year in their grim, unforgiving, smoke-filled environments. Thanks to the railway system, they could now catch a train to take them into the country or off to the seaside. Their horizons had been widened in every way.

There were several stops on the way, enabling Colbeck and Madeleine to get out and stretch their legs on the platform. Each new section of the journey provided fresh delights. As they sped through Hertfordshire, Huntingdonshire, Lincoln and Yorkshire, they were reminded that – for all its aggressive industrialisation – England was still very much a place of rural splendour.

'We are going to the capital of the coal industry,' said Colbeck.

'Do you have any objection to that?'

'Not if it's what you want, Madeleine – though I expect to spend a lot of time brushing dust off my clothing. I think that there are fifty coalfields in the vicinity of Newcastle.'

'I hope we have time to explore the city itself,' she said. 'It isn't just an industrial centre. There are some wonderful sights, apparently.'

'I know,' he said, grinning. 'I'm sitting opposite one of them.'

It was early evening by the time they finally reached Newcastle. After booking a room at the Railway Hotel, they set off to explore the city. Nestling around the River Tyne, it had a great deal to offer to visitors. Intriguing remains of Roman occupation were cheek by jowl with more recent buildings, many of them built of granite. It was well laid out and able to accommodate over a hundred thousand inhabitants. The bracing walk was an ideal antidote to the hours spent on the train. They were particularly impressed by the Exchange, with its three Corinthian porticoes, and by the Post Office, Market, Hall of Incorporated Trades and Theatre Royal. Here was a vibrant city that bristled with civic pride.

Dinner at the hotel was surprisingly good and they ate heartily, savouring the pleasure of being on holiday and wishing that they could spend more time together. After a comfortable night, they had an early breakfast then caught a train on the Newcastle and Carlisle Railway. It chuffed along happily for ten miles or so then deposited them at Wylam, a village known to both of them as the birthplace of George Stephenson, one of the greatest pioneers of rail travel. What had once been a little farming community was now a sprawling coalfield with all the attendant grime and clamour. A trap took them to the colliery offices where they met Seth Hooper, a strapping man in his fifties with a craggy face whose dominant feature was a large, square chin. When introductions were made, he was distantly polite to Colbeck, reserving his interest for Madeleine.

'I couldn't believe that a woman had painted the *Lord of the Isles*,' he said.

'My wife has painted several locomotives,' said Colbeck, proudly.

'And she's done so with great skill, sir. I know that we have female artists of undoubted ability but how many of them find inspiration in the railway system?'

'Madeleine is unique in every way.'

'Any more of this undeserved praise,' said Madeleine, 'and you'll have me blushing. I don't see myself solely as an artist. I'm also a recording angel of the rail network. Even in the short time I've been at my easel, there have been radical changes and improvements.'

'*Puffing Billy* will certainly take you back in time,' said Hooper.

'That was its appeal.'

'It's a pity that William Hedley is no longer alive. He'd have been thrilled to discover that the locomotive he designed has attracted the interest of a celebrated artist from London.'

Madeleine laughed. 'I'm not that celebrated, Mr Hooper,' she said, modestly. 'In some ways, I'm still very much a beginner.'

'It's a privilege to welcome you, Mrs Colbeck, that's all I know.' He gestured towards the engine shed. 'Let me take you to meet *Puffing Billy*.'

Wylam Railway had started as a wooden line on which coal wagons were dragged by heavy horses. It had been rebuilt in the second decade of the present century as a five-foot gauge plateway. Over a period of two years, William Hedley, the mechanical inspector at Wylam, had experimented with a locomotive that used some of the elements in engines built by Trevithick and Blenkinsop, adding refinements that improved speed and adhesion. The original *Puffing Billy* had four wheels but was soon altered to run on eight because the axle loading was too much for the cast-iron plate rails. Later versions of the locomotive reverted to four wheels but it was the old eight-wheeler to which Hooper took his guests. It was a curious contraption, small, misshapen and primitive compared to engines now in use on major railways.

Colbeck and Madeleine were fascinated to see it waiting for them in the engine shed. Other locomotives chugged by, pulling wagons piled high with coal, but none had the same place in history as *Puffing Billy*. Madeleine got to work immediately, sketching it from all angles. Colbeck, meanwhile, was taken on a brief tour of the mine so that the artist could work undisturbed. It was a productive day for husband and wife. Colbeck learnt a great deal about the early days of steam locomotion while Madeleine was drawing a prime exhibit. The manager provided them with a midday meal then she worked on into the afternoon.

On the train journey back to Newcastle, she was brimming with gratitude.

'Thank you so much, Robert.'

'I enjoyed it. There's kudos in being the husband of a celebrated artist.'

'Stop teasing.'

'I'm serious, Madeleine. You were the centre of attention and I liked that. I was able to bask in your shadow, if that's not a contradiction in terms.'

'When I started work, I remembered what you once told me about Stubbs.'

He laughed. '*Puffing Billy* may be an iron horse but I don't think you can compare him with those sublime horses that Stubbs created.'

'In order to paint horses in such convincing detail,' she said, 'he actually had a dead one in his studio with the skin stripped off so that he could see every bone and sinew. It's what I tried to do today – look carefully at how the engine worked so that I could paint it from the inside, as it were.'

'Your father taught you how a steam engine worked.'

'I owe him so much, Robert – and you, of course. Thank you again for today. It's been an absolute treat for me.'

'The treat for me was to see you so happily immersed in your work,' he said. 'But you don't need to hug your sketchbook like that. It won't fly away.'

Madeleine hadn't realised she was holding the book protectively in both arms.

'I'm sorry,' she said, putting it on the seat beside her. 'These sketches are very precious to me. I'd hate to lose them.'

'Then you must ask a policeman to keep an eye on them for you.'

They returned to their hotel, washed, changed then went down to dinner. Once again the standard of cuisine was high. As they left the restaurant, they overheard a conversation between an elderly lady and the manager. She was complaining bitterly about the loss of a brooch and he was suggesting that it might have gone astray elsewhere. The woman was adamant that she'd brought it to the hotel when she stayed there days earlier. Its disappearance had only just come to light. The manager was patient and emollient. It was only when he offered her compensation for the loss that she was pacified. Colbeck and Madeleine went up to their room.

'That was very generous of the manager,' he said. 'He was replacing a brooch that she may never have had here in the first place.'

'Are you saying that she was a confidence trickster, Robert?'

'Heavens, no – she genuinely believed that she lost the item at the hotel.'

'The manager poured oil on troubled waters very swiftly.'

When Colbeck let her into the room, the first thing she did was to go to the drawer where she'd left her sketchbook. Madeleine was looking forward to viewing the results of a day at Wylam Colliery. But she was disappointed.

'Where is it?' she cried, looking at the empty drawer.

'Are you certain that's where you put it, Madeleine?'

'Yes,' she replied before conducting a frantic search of the room. 'I swear that it was here, Robert. Someone has stolen *Puffing Billy*.'

It was time for Colbeck to emerge from anonymity. He went straight downstairs to confront the manager, Andrew Whitchurch, a tall, angular individual in his forties, wearing an expensive frock coat. Surprised to hear that he had a detective inspector at the hotel, he issued a stream of apologies for the loss of the sketchbook.

'We don't want your apologies,' said Colbeck. 'We simply want it back.'

'I will replace it with a new one, sir.'

'You don't understand. My wife is an artist and she made sketches at Wylam Colliery today that are vital to the project on which she is working. It's impossible for us to go back to the colliery tomorrow because we will be catching a train at noon. As for replacing it, where would you find a shop selling artists' materials on a Sunday?'

'I'll refund the cost, Inspector Colbeck,' volunteered the other. 'In the interests of good customer relations, I'll give you twice the cost of the sketchbook.'

'Twenty times the price would not satisfy my wife. She wants the original one back. It is, literally, irreplaceable.'

Whitchurch cleared his throat. 'I'll see what I can do, sir.'

He was standing behind the reception desk. On the wall behind him were rows of hooks on which keys were dangling. They caught Colbeck's eye.

'How many master keys are there to the rooms?' he asked.

'There are only two, sir. I hold one and the housekeeper has the other. She went off duty at six o'clock this evening.'

'The theft occurred while we were having dinner. That would seem to eliminate the housekeeper – unless she sneaked back here unseen, of course.'

'Mrs Garritty is above reproach, sir. She's been with us for years.'

'Then somebody else gained access to our room. The puzzling

thing is that the intruder chose to take my wife's sketchbook. Why? It's of no use to anyone else. There were far more valuable items in the room yet they are still there.'

'I'll do my very best to trace the missing book, sir.'

'Why didn't you offer to trace the brooch belonging to the lady we overheard complaining to you earlier on?'

'That was a different matter, Inspector.'

'Not necessarily – its disappearance may well be the work of the same thief who took the sketchbook. Have many other things have vanished from rooms here?'

'Two or three,' admitted the manager, uneasily.

'Do you have a hotel detective?'

'We don't, Inspector.'

'Well, you've got one now,' said Colbeck, looking him in the eye, 'and I mean to get to the bottom of this. I'll speak to the housekeeper the moment she arrives tomorrow. In the meantime, I suggest you look closely at every member of your staff to assure yourself that none of them could have been responsible for this spate of thefts. Don't be misled by feelings of loyalty,' he warned. 'There's a thief under this roof and you are paying his wages.'

The manager was clearly shaken. Recovering his composure, he manufactured a soothing smile and spoke with quiet determination.

'Mrs Colbeck will get her sketchbook back,' he said. 'I give you my word on that, Inspector.'

Madeleine was not content to leave the detective work to Colbeck. When he went off to speak to the manager, she explored the building. At the end of the corridor was a servants' staircase with bare stone steps. She descended to the ground floor. Facing her was a door with the word HOUSEKEEPER painted on it in bold capitals. She knocked hard but got no response. When she tried the handle, she found that the door was locked. Madeleine was about to go back up the stairs when a young man in the uniform of a hotel porter came into the passageway. He was very surprised to see her.

'That's the servants' staircase,' he said, deferentially. 'Guests use the main one. Shall I show you the way, madam?'

'I know the way, thank you.' He turned to leave. 'No, wait a moment . . .'

He faced her again. 'Is there anything I can do for you?'

'How long have you worked here?'

'It's almost a year now.'

'It's a very comfortable hotel.'

'For the guests, it is,' he said, ruefully. 'Staff quarters are a little different.'

'Have there ever been reports of theft here?'

'I've never heard of any – unless you count the gentleman whose spectacles vanished. He got very angry about that, by all accounts. The manager said that he was so forgetful that he probably didn't even bring them to the hotel.'

'My husband and I heard a lady complaining about a missing brooch.'

'I don't know anything about that.'

She looked at the steps. 'Who's allowed to use this staircase?'

'The housekeeper and her staff,' he replied. 'Why do you ask?'

'I just wondered.'

'Is there anything else, madam?'

'No, no – thank you for your help.'

After shooting a wistful glance at the staircase, the porter turned on his heel and walked away. Madeleine went slowly back up the steps. When she reached the first floor, she went into the corridor that led to her room. She then heard the tap-tap of feet and turned to see a well-dressed woman going down the steps. It was a momentary encounter because, once she realised she'd been seen, the woman spun round and dashed back upstairs.

Colbeck and Madeleine compared their respective findings and they talked well into the night. He eventually dozed off, wondering why anyone would steal a sketchbook that they could buy fairly cheaply; and she fell asleep, asking herself who the mystery woman had been. Colbeck and Madeleine slept in each other's arms. Neither of them heard something being pushed under their door.

When they awoke next morning, they had a pleasant surprise. The sketchbook had magically reappeared with Madeleine's drawings of *Puffing Billy* intact. She was so determined not to lose it again that she took it down to breakfast and tucked it behind her on the chair. Now that they had it back in their possession, there was no need to talk to the housekeeper. As soon as the meal was over, therefore, Colbeck went to the reception area to challenge the manager.

'Why were you so certain that the sketchbook would be returned?'

'It was just a feeling I had, sir,' said Whitchurch, glibly. 'When the thief realised that he would get next to nothing for it, he decided to give it back.'

'I've spent my career dealing with thieves,' Colbeck told him, 'and I've never met one who would even consider returning stolen property. If it's no use to them, they simply toss it away or destroy it. You *knew*, didn't you?'

Whitchurch feigned bafflement. 'I don't understand, Inspector.'

'You understand me all too well. You knew who took it from our room and you probably knew who took that lady's brooch as well. I believe that a pair of spectacles was also taken. I daresay that the same thief took those.' He locked his gaze on the manager. 'What's his name?'

'I don't know what you're talking about,' said the other, briskly.

'I think you're lying.'

'Why on earth should I do that, sir?'

'That's what I'm trying to find out.' Colbeck remembered something. 'When that other guest complained about the loss of her brooch, you promised to reimburse her. Couldn't you have arranged for that item to be returned as well?'

'I'm very sorry, sir, but I don't follow.'

'Then let me put it more bluntly. I suggest that you are either a conjurer who can pluck things out of the air or you are in league with the thief. How else can you predict the return of a sketchbook?'

Whitchurch squared his shoulders. 'I really don't see what all the fuss is about, Inspector Colbeck. Your wife's property was lost and now it's been returned. I would have thought it was a cause for celebration and not an excuse to accuse me of crimes that I didn't commit.' His smile was icy. 'If you have incontrovertible evidence that I was an accomplice, please arrest me and I will defend myself robustly in court. If, however, you are unable to furnish any proof in support of your insulting allegation, I'll ask you to let me get on with my job.' He brushed an imaginary crumb off his lapel. 'You and Mrs Colbeck are just two of a large number of guests that I have to look after. I apologise for any inconvenience caused but, as far as I'm concerned, the matter is now settled.'

At that moment, an elderly couple came into view. They had come to check out of the hotel and the manager switched his attention to them. Colbeck was irked. Certain that the man was hiding something, he was unable to interrogate him in the presence of others. When more guests converged on the manager, Colbeck decided to postpone his questioning until later.

Madeleine was as eager as her husband to find out what had really happened. While he was talking to the manager, she was ascending the servants' staircase. Instead of leaving it at the first-floor level, however, she carried on to the floor above then walked slowly along the corridor. Madeleine was startled when a door ahead of her suddenly opened and an old woman crept out before closing and locking the door. She was of medium height and wore an elegant dress. Although she looked like a guest, she headed towards the servants' staircase. When she saw Madeleine in front of her, she gave an apologetic giggle and went off to the main staircase at the other end of the corridor. There was an almost childlike glee in the way that she scurried along. Madeleine wondered if it was the same woman that she'd seen on the staircase the night before. The other one had looked younger but, then, the gaslights had shed an uncertain light. Madeleine could have been deceived. The similarity in their build and attire inclined her to decide that it had been the same woman. Why was she so intent on using the wrong staircase?

When she returned to her room and told him what she'd seen, Colbeck provided a possible answer to the question.

'Perhaps the lady you saw is the thief,' he said, thoughtfully. 'It's not the manager who's the accomplice, it's that porter who was about to go up a staircase which was barred to him. If he took luggage up to the guest rooms, he'd be able to advise the woman what she could steal.' He checked himself. 'But why pick on a sketchbook and a pair of spectacles?'

'There was something odd about the woman,' recalled Madeleine. 'She was in what I can only call a state of excitement.'

'That's easily explained,' he said, fondly. 'Whenever I look at you, I'm always in a state of excitement.'

She smiled at the compliment. 'Be serious, Robert.'

He kissed her. 'I *am* serious.'

'I'm going back up there,' she decided.

'Then I'll come with you.'

Once again, Madeleine took the sketchbook with her. There was no way that she was going to part with *Puffing Billy*

250

again. They went up the main staircase to the second floor and found it empty. Halfway along it was an alcove so they were able to conceal themselves from view. It was a long wait and they were tempted to abandon their vigil as an act of folly. Then they heard footsteps coming up the stone steps. A face peered into the corridor. Thinking that it was safe to do so, a young man crept into view and knocked four times in quick succession on a door. It was opened almost immediately and he went inside. After the door was shut, they heard the key turn in the lock.

'It's that porter I met last night,' said Madeleine.

'He's obviously gone to visit the thief to see what her latest haul is.'

'But she didn't come out from *that* room, Robert. She came out of one on the other side of the corridor.'

'Did she lock it afterwards?' he asked.

'Yes, she did.'

'Then she must have a master key. She's posing as a guest at the hotel so that she can let herself into rooms that she knows are unoccupied. That young porter has given the game away,' he said, stepping out of the alcove. 'Thanks to you, we've caught them red-handed.'

He led Madeleine to the room that the porter had entered and rapped on the door with his knuckles. When there was no sound from within, he banged with his fist. A woman's voice called out that she would be there in a moment. In fact, it was over a minute before the door opened a few inches and an attractive face peeped around it. Madeleine knew at once that it was not the old lady she'd seen earlier. This one was much younger and – though they only got a glimpse of it – was wearing a silk dressing gown. Before he could speak, Colbeck felt her grab his arm.

'Do excuse us,' said Madeleine to the woman. 'We've obviously come to the wrong room.' She pulled her husband away. 'I think it must be at the other end of the corridor.'

The woman didn't linger. Closing the door firmly, she locked it behind them.

'What's going on?' asked Colbeck, bemused.

'We were misled, Robert. *That* was the woman I saw on the staircase last night and she wasn't letting an accomplice in.' Madeleine smiled uncomfortably. 'I should have noticed how handsome that young porter was because I fancy that one of the guests certainly did.'

'Oh, so it was an assignation,' he realised. 'When her young friend didn't turn up last night, she came down the servants' staircase looking for him, and fled when she spotted you. Oh dear!' he exclaimed. 'I can't pretend to condone what may be going on in that room but it's no business of ours and I'm embarrassed that we interrupted them.' He scratched his head. 'What do we do now?'

'I'll stay here in case the older lady comes back.'

'Then I'll tackle the manager again. Something very strange is going on in this hotel – and I don't mean the secret liaison that we just stumbled upon. The manager is involved somehow and I intend to discover exactly how.' He glanced at the sketchbook. 'Would you like me to look after *Puffing Billy* for you?'

'No,' replied Madeleine, hugging the sketchbook more tightly. 'I'm not letting go of him until we get safely back home.'

When he got back downstairs, Colbeck saw that the assistant manager was handling enquiries from guests. Andrew Whitchurch had retired to his office. Thinking that the man was deliberately avoiding him, Colbeck went across to the office and bunched his hand to knock. Before he could do so, he heard sounds of a heated argument on the other side of the door. He returned to the assistant manager.

'Mr Whitchurch appears to have company,' he said.

'Yes, sir.'

'Is it yet another guest complaining that something has been stolen?'

'I don't think so, sir.'

'I distinctly heard a woman's voice raised in accusation.'

'That would be Mrs Whitchurch,' said the other. 'It's the manager's wife.'

Hidden in the alcove, Madeleine did not have long to wait this time. The old woman she had seen earlier made a second appearance, creeping stealthily along the corridor. She then let herself into a room and shut the door silently behind her. Madeleine came out of her hiding place at once. The woman had gone into a different room to the one she'd earlier left and her furtive manner confirmed that she had no right to be there. Madeleine had found the thief at last.

It was less than a minute before the woman came out of the room, clutching a pair of slippers. When she saw Madeleine waiting for her, she giggled. Making no attempt to run away, she held up the slippers as if they were some kind of trophy. Madeleine showed her the sketchbook.

'Why did you steal this from our room?' she asked.

'I liked the drawings,' said the woman, grinning inanely.

'But this is my property. You shouldn't have taken it.'

'I didn't mean any harm.'

'It upset me a great deal.'

The woman giggled. 'You've got it back now.'

Madeleine saw that it was futile to attempt a proper conversation with the woman. Her voice was high and childish and she clearly had no idea that what she had done was to commit a crime. Madeleine felt desperately sorry for her. The woman was patently deranged in some way. The next moment, Colbeck came walking along the corridor with the hotel manager. Whitchurch was horrified when he saw what the woman was holding in her hands.

'Oh, Mother!' he cried in despair. 'What have you taken *this* time?'

Madeleine was as good as her word. When they stepped into an empty compartment, she was still clasping *Puffing Billy* to her breast. He would be held close to her heart all the way back to London.

'I think it's safe to say that it was an eventful visit,' remarked Colbeck.

'It was a little *too* eventful for my liking, Robert.'

'You got what you came to get, my love.'

'But I had it stolen for a while,' she recalled. 'That was terrifying. I'd have been far less upset if she'd taken my handbag or one of my dresses.'

'The poor lady simply took the first thing that came to

hand, Madeleine. There was no thought of stealing for gain. Kleptomania is a cruel disease of the mind,' he said, sadly. 'It's an uncontrollable desire to take things from others for the simple pleasure of doing so. Nothing she stole was of any practical use or value to her.'

'All that I could do was to offer her my sympathy.'

'I reserved mine for the manager,' said Colbeck. 'Think how much Mr Whitchurch must have paid out in compensation to angry guests. He did everything in his power to conceal the fact that his mother had somehow acquired a replica of the master key so that she could let herself into any room she chose. His wife tried to keep an eye on her mother-in-law but the older Mrs Whitchurch was far too guileful. Driven by the urge to steal, she always found a means of escape.'

Madeleine shook her head. 'She won't be doing that any more, Robert.'

'No, her spree is over at last. Whitchurch accepted that he and his wife can no longer cope with her antics. He's putting his mother in the care of a cousin who lives in the country. She'll have far less opportunity to steal anything there and will, to some extent, be isolated from temptation. It's not an ideal solution but it avoids the stigma of having his mother committed to a mental asylum. However,' he went on, brightening, 'let's remember the more pleasant aspects of our holiday, shall we? You achieved your objective and we had the luxury of time alone together. In addition, of course, you proved that you were more than a match for me as a detective.'

She laughed. 'I don't know about that, Robert.'

'Take full credit,' he insisted. 'I was tempted to arrest the manager. It was you who discovered the real identity of the thief. In terms of detection, I am merely a *Puffing Billy*, an ancient relic, whereas you are truly a *Lord of the Isles* – or, should I say, a *Lady of the Isles?*'

THE END OF THE LINE

England, 1852

Matthew Proudfoot was a man who insisted on getting value for money. As one of the directors of the Great Western Railway, he had invested heavily in the company and believed that it entitled him to special privileges. When he learnt that an off-duty train was going from London to Swindon that evening, therefore, he effectively commandeered it, and, as its sole passenger, issued strict instructions to the driver. James Barrett was wiping his hands on an oily rag when the portly figure of Proudfoot strode up to the locomotive. Recognising him at once, Barrett straightened his back and gave a deferential smile.

'Good evening, Mr Proudfoot.'

'I need to be at Reading station by eight o'clock,' said the other, curtly. 'I expect the ride to be swift but comfortable.'

'But we're not supposed to stop, sir,' explained Barrett, glancing at his fireman. 'The engine is being taken out of service so that repairs can be made at Swindon.'

'On her way there, she can oblige me.'

'I have to follow orders, Mr Proudfoot.'

'I've just given them. Take me to Reading.'

'But I need permission, sir.'

'You've *got* permission, man,' said Proudfoot, testily. 'I've spoken to your superiors. That's why the first-class carriage was added to the train. It's the only way I'd deign to travel.'

'Yes, sir.'

'Remember that you have a director of the company aboard.'

'Oh, I will,' promised Barrett.

'I'll be keeping an eye on the performance of the train.'

'You'll have no reason for complaint, sir.'

'I hope not,' warned Proudfoot.

And he turned on his heel so that he could stalk off and accost the guard at the rear of the train. Barrett and Neale watched him go. The driver was a wiry man in his thirties with years of service on the Great Western Railway. He took a pride in his job. His fireman, Alfred Neale, short, thin, angular, still in his twenties, was also an experienced railway man. Unlike his workmate, he showed open resentment.

'He shouldn't have spoken to you like that, Jim,' he said.

'I take no notice.'

'But you're one of the best drivers we've got. Mr Proudfoot should have shown you some respect. Who does he think he is – God Bloody Almighty?'

'Forget him, Alf,' suggested Barrett. 'We've got a job to do even if it don't get the recognition it deserves. Is he on board yet?'

'Yes,' replied Neale, sourly, looking back down the platform.

'His Majesty's just climbing into his first-class carriage. Anyone would think that he *owned* the train. Stop at Reading, he tells us! I think we should go all the way to Swindon and to hell with him.'

Barrett gave a weary smile. 'Orders is orders, Alf.'

'I've half a mind to ignore 'em.'

'Well, I haven't,' said the other, consulting a battered watch that he took from his waistcoat pocket. 'Mr Proudfoot wants to be there by eight, does he? Fair enough.' He put the watch away. 'Let's deliver him bang on time.'

Fifteen minutes later, the train steamed out of Paddington.

When he first heard the details of the crime, Robert Colbeck was baffled. As an inspector in the Detective Department at Scotland Yard, he had dealt with many strange cases but none that had made him blink in astonishment before. He rehearsed the facts.

'When the train left London,' he said, 'Matthew Proudfoot was the only passenger in a first-class carriage. The guard was travelling in the brake van, the driver and fireman on the footplate.'

'That's correct,' agreed Edward Tallis.

'None of those three men left his post throughout the entire journey yet, when the train stopped at Reading station, Mr Proudfoot was dead.'

'Stabbed through the heart.'

'By whom?'

'That's for you to find out,' said Tallis, crisply. 'As you know, the Great Western Railway has its own police but their work is largely supervisory. They watch over the track and act as signalmen. A murder investigation is well beyond them. That's why we've been called in.'

Robert Colbeck pondered. Tall, slim and well favoured, he wore a light brown frock coat, with rounded edges and a high neck, dark trousers and an ascot cravat. Though he had the appearance of a dandy, Colbeck was essentially a man of action who never shirked danger. He pressed for more detail.

'What was the average speed of the train?' he asked.

'Thirty-five miles per hour.'

'How do you know that?'

'Because that's the approximate distance between Paddington and Reading, and it took almost exactly an hour to reach the station. So you can rule out the obvious explanation,' said Tallis, briskly. 'Nobody jumped onto the train while it was in motion – not unless he wanted to kill himself, that is. It was going too fast.'

'Too fast to jump *onto*, perhaps,' decided Colbeck. 'But a brave man could jump *off* the train at that speed – especially if he chose the right place and rolled down a grassy embankment. That might be the answer, Superintendent,' he speculated. 'Suppose that Mr Proudfoot was *not* the sole occupant of that carriage. Someone may already have concealed himself in one of the other compartments.'

'That's one of the avenues you'll have to explore.'

Superintendent Edward Tallis was a stout, steely man in his fifties with a military background that had left him with a scar on his cheek. He had a shock of grey hair and a well-trimmed moustache that he was fond of caressing. With a lifetime shaped by the habit of command, he expected obedience from his subordinates and, because Colbeck did not always obey in the way that was required of him, there was a lot of tension between them. Whatever his reservations about the elegant inspector, however, Tallis recognised his abilities and invariably assigned the most difficult cases to him. Colbeck had a habit of getting results.

The two of them were in the superintendent's office in Scotland Yard. It was early in the morning after the murder and the scant information available was on the sheet of paper that Tallis handed to Colbeck. When he studied the paper, the inspector's handsome face puckered with disappointment.

'There's not much to go on, I'm afraid,' said Tallis with a sigh. 'Beyond the fact that Matthew Proudfoot got into a train alive and was dead on arrival at his destination, that is. You have to feel sorry for the company. It's not exactly a good advertisement for passenger travel.'

'Did the train go on to Swindon?'

'No, it's been held at Reading, pending our investigation.'

'Good.'

'The driver, fireman and guard were also detained there overnight. You'll find their names on that sheet of paper.' Rising from his desk, he walked around it to confront Colbeck. 'There's no need for me to tell you how crucial it is that this murder is solved as quickly as possible.'

'No, Superintendent.'

'Mr Proudfoot was a director of the Great Western Railway. That means they are putting immense pressure on me for action.'

'I'll catch the next through-train to Reading.'

'Take Sergeant Leeming with you.'

'No,' said Colbeck, thoughtfully. 'Victor can travel independently. I need the fastest train that I can get, but I want him to stop at every station along the way to make enquiries. This is high summer. There was good light between seven and eight yesterday evening. Someone may have seen something when Mr Proudfoot's train went past.'

'A phantom killer stabbing him to death?'

'I doubt if we'll be that fortunate.'

'Keep me informed.'

'I always do, Superintendent.'

'Only when you are under orders to do so,' Tallis reminded him. 'I want none of your usual eccentric methods, Inspector. I expect you to conduct this investigation properly. Bear one thing in mind at all times. Our reputation is at stake.'

Colbeck smiled. 'Then I'll do nothing to tarnish it, sir.'

There were eight stations between Paddington and Reading and, thanks to his copy of Churton's *Rail Road Book of England*, Robert Colbeck knew the exact distance between each of them. Travelling in the compartment of a first-class carriage with two uniformed Metropolitan policemen, he tried to reconstruct the final journey by Matthew Proudfoot. When, how and why was the man killed? Was it conceivable that the murder victim had, in fact, had a travelling companion who had turned upon him for some reason? If that were the case, was the other person male or female? And at what point did the killer depart from the train? Colbeck had much to occupy his mind.

The first thing he did on arrival at Reading was to visit the undertaker who had taken charge of the body of the deceased. Sylvester Quorn was a small, wizened, unctuous man, dressed entirely in black and given to measuring each word carefully before he released it through his thin lips. Conducting the inspector to the room where the corpse was laid out on a cold slab, he watched over Colbeck's shoulder as the latter drew back the shroud. The naked body of Matthew Proudfoot was large, white and flabby. Colbeck studied the livid red gash over the man's heart. Quorn pointed a skeletal finger.

'We cleaned him up, sir, as you see.'

'Just the single wound?' said Colbeck.

'One fatal thrust, that was all.'

'There must have been a struggle of some sort. What state was his clothing in when he was brought in here?'

'The lapel of his coat was torn,' said the undertaker, indicating some items in a large wooden box, 'and his waistcoat was ripped where the knife went through. It was soaked with blood. So was his shirt.'

'What about his effects?'

'Everything is in here, Inspector.'

Colbeck sifted through the garments in the box and felt in all the pockets. 'I don't find any wallet here,' he said. 'Nor a watch. A man like Mr Proudfoot would certainly have owned a watch.'

'It must have been taken, sir – along with the wallet.'

'Murder for gain,' murmured Colbeck. 'At least we have one possible motive.'

'I have a request to pass on,' said the other with an ingratiating smile. 'You can imagine how shocked his family were by the news. His wife is inconsolable. Mr Proudfoot's brother has asked if the body can be released as soon as possible.'

'He'll have to wait until it's been examined by a doctor.'

'But *I've* done that, Inspector. I've been examining cadavers for almost forty years. There's nothing a doctor can tell you that I can't.'

'The coroner will want a qualified medical opinion at the inquest.'

'Of course.'

'A man in your profession should know that,' said Colbeck, putting him in his place. 'Who informed the family of the tragedy?'

'I did,' said Quorn, mournfully. 'Being acquainted with the Proudfoots, I felt that it was my duty to pass on the bad tidings. The railway police agreed that I should do so, though one of them did accompany me to the house. He was so grateful that I did all the talking. It was no effort for me, of course. I deal with the bereaved on a daily basis. It requires tact.'

Colbeck gazed down at the corpse for a few moments before drawing the shroud back over it again. He looked up at the undertaker.

'How can you be tactful about a murder?' he said.

When he returned to the railway station, the inspector found the three men waiting to be interviewed in the stationmaster's office. They were side by side on a wooden bench. None of them looked as if he had slept much during the night.

James Barrett seemed deeply upset by what had happened but Alfred Neale had a degree of truculence about him, as if resenting the fact that he was being questioned. The person who interested Colbeck most was George Hawley, the guard, a plump man in his fifties with a florid complexion and darting eyes.

'What did you do in the course of the journey?' asked Colbeck.

'I did my job, Inspector,' replied Hawley. 'I kept guard.'

'Yet you saw and heard nothing untoward?'

'Nothing at all, sir.'

'There was a definite struggle. Someone must have called out.'

'I didn't hear him.'

'Are you sure, Mr Hawley?'

'As God's my witness,' said the guard, hand to his heart. 'The engine was making too much noise and the wheels were clanking over the rails. Couldn't hear nothing above that.'

'So you remained in the brake van throughout?'

Hawley shrugged. 'Where else could I go?'

'What about you two?' said Colbeck, turning to the others. 'You spent the entire journey on the footplate?'

'Of course,' retorted Neale.

'We're not allowed to leave it, sir,' added Barrett, quietly. 'Or, for that matter, to have any unauthorised persons travelling beside us.'

'Did the train slow down at any point?' said Colbeck.

'No, Inspector. We kept up a steady speed. The truth is,' he went on, stifling a yawn with the back of his hand, 'we didn't wish to upset our passenger. Mr Proudfoot wanted a smooth journey.'

'You look tired, Mr Barrett. Where did you sleep last night?'

'Here, sir. On this very bench.'

'I was on the floor,' complained Neale.

'So was I,' moaned Hawley. 'At my age, I need a proper bed.'

'Perhaps you should think of the murder victim rather than of yourself, Mr Hawley,' scolded Colbeck. 'I don't believe that Mr Proudfoot deliberately got himself killed so that he could upset your sleeping arrangements.'

'George meant no harm, sir,' said Barrett, defensively. 'He spoke out of turn. This has really upset him – and us, of course. It's a terrible thing to happen. We feel so sorry for Mr Proudfoot.'

'That's right,' said Hawley. 'God rest his soul!'

'I ain't sorry,' affirmed Neale, folding his arms.

'Alf!' exclaimed Barrett.

'I ain't, Jim. No sense in being dishonest about it. I'm like most people who work for this company. I got reason to hate Mr Matthew Proudfoot and you knows why.'

'Oh?' said Colbeck, curiosity aroused. 'Tell me more, Mr Neale.'

'Don't listen to him, Inspector,' advised Barrett, shooting the fireman an admonitory glance. 'Alfred lets his tongue run away with him sometimes. We may not have admired Mr Proudfoot, but we all respected him for the position he held.'

'He gave himself airs and graces,' sneered Neale.

'Only because he was a director.'

'Yes, Jim. He never let us forget that, did he?'

'What do you mean?' said Colbeck.

'Mr Proudfoot was not a nice man,' confided Hawley. 'Before we set off from Paddington, he said some very nasty things to me.'

'You're lucky that's all he did, George,' said Neale, before swinging round to face Colbeck. 'Every time he travelled by rail, Mr Proudfoot had a complaint. He's had two drivers fined and one dismissed. He had the stationmaster at Slough reprimanded and reported any number of people he felt weren't bowing down before Mr High and Mighty.'

'In other words,' concluded Colbeck, 'there are those employed by the GWR who might have a grudge against him.'

'We've *all* got a grudge against him, Inspector.'

'That's not true, Alf,' said Barrett, reproachfully.

'All except you, then. You're too soft, Jim.'

'I never speak ill of the dead.'

Colbeck was interested in the relationship between the three men. As well as being workmates, they were clearly friends. James Barrett was the senior figure, liked and respected by his two colleagues, treating Neale in an almost paternal way. The driver's main concern was to get his engine to Swindon. All that worried Alfred Neale was the fact that he had spent a night apart from his young wife. The railway police had informed her that his return would be delayed but given her no details. It made the fireman restive. George Hawley was a weak man who sided with anyone who seemed to be in the ascendancy during an argument.

Looking from one to the other, Colbeck put a question to them.

'Would any of you object to being searched?' he asked.

'No,' replied Barrett, calmly. 'I wouldn't, Inspector, though I don't really see the purpose of it.'

'Certain items were taken from Mr Proudfoot by the killer.'

The driver stiffened with indignation. 'You surely don't think that *we* had anything to do with it?'

'No,' said Colbeck, 'I don't. But I want to be absolutely sure.'

'You've no right to search me,' declared Neale, angrily.

'That's why I'm asking you to turn out your pockets yourself.' He pointed to the burly Metropolitan policeman who stood in the doorway. 'If you find that too much of an imposition, Mr Neale, I could ask Constable Reynolds to help you.'

Neale was on his feet. 'Keep him away from me!'

'Then do as I request. Put your belongings on that table.'

'Come on, Alf,' counselled Barrett, resignedly. 'Do as the inspector says. That goes for you, too, George.'

'I'm no thief,' protested Hawley.

Nevertheless, he emptied his pockets and put his few possessions on the table. Barrett followed suit and, after some cajoling, so did Neale. They even submitted to being patted down by Constable Reynolds as he searched for items concealed about their persons. None were found.

'Thank you, gentlemen,' said Colbeck. 'I think that it's safe to say that you've been eliminated as possible suspects.'

'Does that mean we're released, sir?' said Barrett.

'Not exactly.'

'But we have to deliver the train to Swindon.'

'I need to inspect it first, Mr Barrett. After all, it's the scene of the crime. I want all three of you there with me, please.'

'Why?' asked Hawley, collecting his meagre possessions.

'Because I want you to show me exactly where you were at the time when – in all probability – Mr Proudfoot was murdered.'

When the crime had been discovered the previous evening, the train had been backed into a siding. It comprised a locomotive, a six-wheeled tender, second-class carriage, first-class carriage and brake van. The train was guarded by two uniformed railway policemen, who stood to attention when they saw the inspector coming. As they approached, Robert Colbeck ran an admiring eye over the steam engine, glinting in the morning sunshine. It had a tall chimney, a sleek, compact boiler and a large domed firebox. Its two driving wheels were 84 inches in diameter and its name – *Castor* – was etched in large brass letters.

'What's wrong with her, Mr Barrett?' he enquired.

'Old age,' said Barrett, sadly. '*Castor*'s over ten years old now and she's starting to look it. There's a problem with her valve gear that needs to be put right and her boiler piping has to be overhauled. She's part of the *Firefly* class, designed by Mr Gooch.'

'Yes,' added Neale, proudly. '*Castor* hauled the first train between London and Bristol when the line was opened in 1841. The fireman that day was a certain Jim Barrett.'

Barrett smiled fondly. 'It was an honour.'

'Why did you have a second-class carriage in tow?' asked Colbeck.

'Due for repair at Swindon, sir,' said Barrett. 'It was damaged in a collision. It was Mr Proudfoot who had the first-class carriage attached and, of course, we needed a brake van.'

'Let's start there.'

Reaching the van, Colbeck took hold of the iron handrail and pulled himself up. The driver and fireman remained on the ground but the guard followed him. The brake van was little more than a wooden hut on wheels. Colbeck noted that few concessions had been made to comfort. On a stormy day, wind and rain could blow in through the open windows. He glanced at Hawley.

'Where were you when the train was in transit?'

'Sitting in that corner,' said the guard, pointing to the bench that ran along the rear of the van. 'Never moved from there, Inspector.'

'I think I can see why.' Colbeck bent down to retrieve a large stone jar from under the bench. He sniffed it. 'Beer,' he announced. 'Do you always drink on duty, Mr Hawley?'

'No, no, sir. I hardly ever touch it.'

'Then why have you got a gallon jar of the stuff on board?'

'It must have been left there by someone else,' said Hawley.

But they both knew that he was lying.

After fixing him with a sceptical glare, Colbeck jumped down to the track and moved along to the first-class carriage that was coupled to the brake van. He hauled himself up to examine the scene of the crime. The carriage comprised three compartments, each capable of accommodating eight passengers. The seats were upholstered and great care had been taken with the interior decoration, but all that Colbeck was interested in was the blood on the floor of the central compartment. It told him the exact place where Matthew Proudfoot had been murdered.

Colbeck stayed in there a long time, trying to envisage how the killer had struck the fatal blow, and how he had got in and out of the carriage. When he eventually dropped down to the ground again, his curiosity shifted to the second-class carriage.

'No point in going in there,' said Barrett. 'Doors are locked.'

'Were they locked throughout the journey?' asked Colbeck.

'Yes, Inspector.'

'Who has the key?'

'I do,' said Hawley.

'I'd like to borrow it.'

Taking the key from the guard, Colbeck clambered up and unlocked the doors of the second-class carriage. Going into each compartment in turn, he searched them for signs of recent occupation but found nothing beyond a newspaper that was two days old. Colbeck put his head through the window to look back at the first-class carriage. Those below beside the track were amazed when Colbeck, having taken off his top hat, suddenly emerged through the window and made his way around the back of the carriage before flinging himself across the gap to grab the handles on the adjacent first-class carriage.

Hawley snorted. 'You'd never do that when the train was going fast,' he observed, grimly. 'Not unless you was feeling suicidal.'

'That reminds me, George,' said Barrett, 'you did check that second class was empty before we left Paddington, didn't you?'

'Yes, Jim.' A long pause. 'I think so, anyway.'

'Someone could have been hiding in there.'

'I'd have seen him.'

'That depends on how much drink you'd had beforehand,' said Colbeck, swinging back athletically to the second-class carriage to retrieve his hat. 'No wonder you heard no sounds of a struggle when the train was in motion, Mr Hawley. I suspect that you may have been fast asleep.'

'I never sleeps on duty,' denied the guard, hotly. 'It ain't allowed.'

'Nor is drinking a gallon of beer.'

Hawley bit back a reply and turned away, shamefaced.

It only remained for Colbeck to look at the locomotive and tender. James Barrett was an informative guide, standing on the footplate with the inspector and explaining how everything worked. His deep love of *Castor* was obvious. She had been one of the finest steam locomotives that he had ever driven. Alfred Neale waited until the two men descended from the footplate before he turned detective.

'That's how it must have happened,' he said, brow furrowed in thought. 'The villain was hiding in second class when we set off. Some time during the journey, he climbed into Mr Proudfoot's carriage and stabbed him. It's the only explanation, Inspector.'

'You may well be right, Mr Neale,' said Colbeck, pretending to agree with him, 'though it does raise the question of how the killer knew that Matthew Proudfoot would be travelling on what is, after all, an unscheduled train.'

'He must have followed his victim to Paddington.'

'Possibly.'

'Then slipped into the carriage when nobody was looking.'

'He weren't there when I checked,' said Hawley, officiously.

'And I'm sure that I did. When there's no conductor on board, it's my job.'

'There is another way he might have got into that carriage,' said Barrett, stroking his chin reflectively. 'We moved quite slow out of Paddington. He could have jumped on the train then.'

'That would mean he was a railwayman,' noted Colbeck. 'Someone who knew his way around the station and the goods yard. Someone agile enough to leap onto a moving train.' He distributed a polite smile among the three of them. 'Thank you,' he went on. 'You've been most helpful.'

'Can we can take her on to Swindon now, Inspector?' asked Barrett, hopefully. 'We're already half a day behind on delivery.'

Colbeck shook his head. 'I'm sorry, Mr Barrett,' he said, 'but I'd like you and the train to stay here a little longer. Sergeant Leeming will be here soon. I want him to take a look at the scene of the crime. A second pair of eyes is always valuable.'

'I need to get back to my wife,' said Neale, irritably.

Hawley tapped his chest. 'So do I. Liza will miss me.'

'I got no wife myself,' said Barrett, 'but I'd still like to be on my way. There's mechanics waiting for us at Swindon.'

'You can't hold us here against our will,' insisted Neale.

'This is a murder investigation,' Colbeck told them, 'and that takes precedence over everything else. Now, why don't you all join me for luncheon? I've a lot more questions to put to you yet.'

Sergeant Victor Leeming arrived early that afternoon. He was a stocky man in his thirties with the sort of unfortunate features that even his greatest admirers could only describe as pleasantly ugly. Though he was relatively smart, he looked almost unkempt beside the immaculate inspector. Leeming was carrying a well-thumbed copy of *Bradshaw's Guide*, the comprehensive volume of public railway timetables that was issued monthly. Colbeck took him aside to hear his report.

'What did you discover, Victor?' he asked.

'That Matthew Proudfoot is well known on this stretch of line,' replied Leeming. 'He lived in Reading and travelled up and down to London all the time. He wasn't a popular man – always trying to find fault with the way that trains were run and stations manned. I wouldn't like to repeat what a porter at Slough called him.'

'Did anyone see him as the train passed by yesterday evening?'

'Oh, yes.'

'Who?'

Leeming took out his notebook. 'Here we are,' he said, flipping to the right page. 'He was seen going through Hanwell station, West Drayton, Langley and Maidenhead.'

'By whom?'

'Railway policemen, in the first three cases.'

'And at Maidenhead?'

'The stationmaster, Mr Elrich.'

'Are they sure that it was Matthew Proudfoot?'

'Completely sure, Inspector. By all accounts, he was a very distinctive man. All four witnesses swear that he was sitting in the window of the first-class carriage as *Castor* went past.' He tapped his notebook. 'I even have the approximate times written down. Do you want them?'

'No thank you, Victor,' said Colbeck, holding up a hand. 'You've told me the one thing I needed to know. Mr Proudfoot was alive when the train left Maidenhead. I had a feeling that he would be.'

'Why is that?'

'Because the longest stretch between stations on that line is the one that runs from Maidenhead to Twyford. It's just over eight miles. Given the speed at which they were travelling, that would allow the killer the maximum time – well over a quarter of an hour – in which to strike.'

'That's true,' agreed Leeming. 'It's only two miles between Hanwell and Ealing – even less between there and Southall station. He must have waited for open country before he attacked.'

'Biding his time.'

Leeming put his notebook away. 'Have you made any progress at this end, Inspector?'

'A great deal.'

'Do we have any clues?'

'Several, Victor,' said Colbeck. 'When a little more evidence has been gathered, we'll be in a position to make an arrest. Meanwhile, I want the stretch of line between Maidenhead and Twyford to be searched.'

Leeming gaped. 'All of it?'

'They can start at Twyford station and work their way back. My guess is that it will be nearer that end of the track.'

'What will?'

'The murder weapon. It was thrown from the train.'

'How do you know?'

'Would you hang on to a bloodstained knife?' asked Colbeck. 'But that isn't the only item I want to locate. Close by, they should also find the wallet and watch that were stolen from Matthew Proudfoot.'

'You sound as if you already have the name of the murderer.'

'Let's say that I've narrowed it down to two people.'

'Accomplices?'

'No, I don't think so somehow.'

'Who are these men?'

'I'll introduce them to you in a moment,' said Colbeck. 'First of all, let me tell you what I've been up to while you were busy elsewhere.'

Driver Barrett was relieved when he was told that he had permission to take the train on to Swindon. What neither he nor Fireman Neale could understand, however, was why Robert Colbeck insisted on travelling on the footplate with them. They were also mystified to hear that Victor Leeming would be sitting in the first-class carriage. George Hawley was even less pleased with the arrangement. Deprived of a supply of beer, he sat alone in the brake van and moped.

Swindon was over forty miles down the line and they had to time their departure so that they did not interfere with any of the down-trains from London. An able fireman, Neale had gotten up a good head of steam as *Castor* finally pulled out of Reading station. Colbeck had never been on a moving locomotive before and he was glad that he had given his top hat to Leeming for safekeeping. There was no real protection from the elements on the footplate and, the faster they went, the greater the strength of the wind. Colbeck's hat would have been blown off his head.

There were other problems he had not anticipated. Dust got into his eyes, noisome fumes troubled his nostrils and he had to brush the occasional hot cinder from his sleeve. The ear-splitting noise meant that speech had to be conducted in raised voices. Nevertheless, Colbeck was impressed by the remarkable running quality of *Castor*, given greater stability on the broad gauge track.

'What speed are we doing now?' he asked.

'Almost thirty miles an hour,' said Barrett, who had an instinctive feel for the pace of the train. 'She can go much faster, Inspector.'

'Take her up to thirty-five – the speed you were doing yesterday.'

'Very well, sir.'

Colbeck stood back so that the two men could do their work. He felt a sudden rush of heat as the door of the firebox was opened so that Neale could shovel in more coke. The door was slammed shut again. Smoke was billowing out of the chimney and forming clouds in their wake. Steam was hissing and the locomotive rattled and swayed. Colbeck found it an exhilarating experience but he was not there to enjoy it. As soon as he had got used to the rocking motion of the train, he checked his watch before slipping it back into his waistcoat pocket. Then he stepped back onto the tender and worked his way slowly along its side.

'What, in God's name, is he doing?' cried Neale.

'Leave him be,' said Barrett.

'Where does he think he's going?'

Colbeck heard him but gave no reply. He needed every ounce of concentration for the task in hand. The second-class carriage was coupled to the tender but it was shaking crazily from side to side. Not daring to look down, Colbeck reached across the void, got a grip on the roof of the carriage and, with a supreme effort, heaved himself up onto it. He needed time to grow accustomed to the roll of the carriage. Getting up off his hands and knees, he remained in a crouching position in the middle of the roof until he felt sufficiently confident to stand up properly. He then made his way gingerly towards the first-class carriage.

Victor Leeming was leafing through his copy of *Bradshaw's* when his colleague swung unexpectedly in through the window. The sergeant's jaw dropped in wonder.

'What are you *doing*, Inspector?' he gasped.

'I'm coming to kill you, Victor.'

'Why?'

'Because you're Matthew Proudfoot. Now – resist me!'

Drawing an imaginary knife, he mimed an attack on his companion. Leeming caught his wrist but Colbeck was too quick and too strong for him. Tripping up his victim, he pulled his wrist clear then straddled him on the floor before stabbing him in the heart. Colbeck let out a laugh of triumph. When he had pulled Leeming to his feet again, he looked at his watch.

'Less than four minutes,' he said, contentedly, 'and that was my first attempt. A man who is used to walking along the roofs of the train would do it in half the time.'

'Why would anyone be stupid enough to do that, Inspector?'

'To get to the brake van to drink beer with the guard. Mr

Hawley obviously has a thirst, but even he would need some help to shift a whole gallon. Yesterday,' Colbeck went on, 'the person who came along the roofs of the carriages stopped off here to commit murder.'

'That young fireman,' decided Leeming, snapping his fingers. 'It must have been Alfred Neale. I thought he had a wild look about him.'

'That was caused by deprivation, Victor.'

'Deprivation?'

'Mr Neale was only married a couple of months ago,' said Colbeck with wry amusement. 'I daresay that he was feeling deprived of the joys of wedlock. With a loving wife to care for, I don't believe that he'd take chances on the roof of a moving train. As for Mr Hawley, our guard,' he pointed out, 'he's too old and fat to climb up there – particularly when he's been drinking.'

'That only leaves the driver.'

'James Barrett has to be our man.'

'What was his motive?'

'I don't know,' admitted Colbeck. 'I'll go and ask him.'

Without another word, he climbed back out through the window.

The speed of the train had increased perceptibly, making for more noise and a greater roll. When Colbeck hauled himself back up onto the roof, he had some difficulty steadying himself. He was not helped when a passenger train raced past in the opposite direction, deafening him with the sound of its whistle and momentarily doubling the amount of thick black smoke with which he had to contend. As he rose to his feet, the smoke began to clear, only to reveal a new hazard. Walking towards him along the roof of the second-class carriage was James Barrett with a fire shovel in his hand. The driver was moving with practised ease.

'You're too clever for your own safety, Inspector,' he said.

'Put that shovel down, Mr Barrett.'

'Not until it's sent you to kingdom come.'

'There's no escape, man.'

'Yes, there is,' argued Barrett. 'You signed your own death warrant by travelling on my train. When I've got rid of you, I'll see to that Sergeant Leeming as well. By the time the alarm is raised, I'll be a long way away from here.'

'With the money you stole from Matthew Proudfoot no doubt.'

'Yes, I know exactly where to find it.'

'That's why you were so ready to let me search you,' recalled Colbeck, taking a step backwards. 'Because there was no chance I'd find anything incriminating, was there?' Barrett leapt onto the first-class carriage. 'Just tell me this – what drove you to kill him?'

'Revenge.'

'For what?'

'All the things he did to the people employed by this railway,' said Barrett, curling his lip. 'Mr Proudfoot was ruthless. He went looking for reasons to have drivers fined or reprimanded. Dan Armitage, my closest friend, was dismissed because of him – Dan hasn't worked since. And I could name you dozens more who fell foul of Matthew Proudfoot. We give blood for this railway, Inspector. We work long hours in all weathers yet we never got a word of thanks or a touch of respect from Mr Proudfoot. You should have heard the way he talked to me at Paddington. He treated me like dirt. That's why he deserved to die.'

'Not that way,' said Colbeck, keeping one eye on the shovel as his adversary inched his way towards him. 'You must've known that you'd never get away with it.'

'But I have, Inspector. Nobody will ever arrest me.'

'Do you want two more deaths on your conscience?'

'What conscience?'

'You'll be hounded for the rest of your life, Mr Barrett.'

'I'll take that chance.'

Lunging forward, he swung the shovel hard in an attempt to dislodge Colbeck but the inspector managed to duck under the blow. Barrett was about to strike again when a voice rang out behind him.

'Stop it, Jim!' yelled Neale, standing on the tender.

'Mind the engine!' called Barrett over his shoulder.

'Are you going to kill *him* as well?' taunted Colbeck. 'He knows the truth about you now. I'll wager that you told him you were going to have a drink in the brake van yesterday evening, didn't you? Mr Neale trusted you. When you swore that you didn't commit the murder, he believed you. So did Mr Hawley.'

'Be quiet!' snarled Barrett.

'Come back here,' pleaded Neale.

'And *you* can shut up as well.'

'What's got into you, Jim?' asked the fireman in dismay.

Barrett turned round. 'Just drive the train!'

Colbeck did not hesitate. Alfred Neale had provided a

timely distraction. Taking advantage of it, the inspector stepped forward to grab the shovel and tried to wrest it from the driver's grasp. There was a fierce battle as both men pushed and pulled, barely maintaining their balance on the roof. Alfred Neale was yelling from the tender and Victor Leeming, hearing the pounding noise on the roof above his head, put his head out of the window even though he could not see what was happening. *Castor* steamed on as if in some kind of race.

Holding on to the shovel, each man struggled desperately to shake off the other and gain control of the weapon. Barrett was a powerful man with a murderous impulse but Colbeck was more guileful. As the driver heaved on the shovel with all his might, the inspector simply let go and Barrett was suddenly at the mercy of his own momentum. Staggering backwards along the roof, he lost his footing and slipped to the edge before being thrown violently from the train. He hit the ground with such force that his neck was snapped like a twig. Yet, at the moment of death, he did not relinquish his hold on the shovel.

Frock coat flapping in the wind, Colbeck knelt down to get his breath back. Alfred Neale was horrified by what he had seen. Since he was now in charge of the train, he applied the brakes and put the engine into reverse, bringing the locomotive to a screeching halt a long distance down the line. When Colbeck got to him, the fireman was in tears.

'Jim Barrett, a killer?' he whimpered. 'I don't believe it.'

'He told me that he wanted revenge.'

'We all did, Inspector, but none of us would have gone that far.'

'Mr Barrett did,' said Colbeck. 'There was too much anger penned up inside him, and too much injured pride. It was like steam building up inside an engine – when it was released, it had frightening power.'

A full report of the investigation was submitted to Superintendent Edward Tallis. After studying it with interest, he summoned Robert Colbeck and Victor Leeming to his office in Scotland Yard.

'Congratulations are in order,' said Tallis, stroking his moustache.

'Thank you, Superintendent,' said Leeming, modestly, 'but I can't take much credit. It was the inspector who identified the killer.'

'Unfortunately, he was unable to take the man alive. It's a great pity. Had the fellow been caught and convicted, we would have enjoyed some good publicity in the newspapers for a change.' His eyes flicked to Colbeck. 'Try to remember that next time.'

'Arrest was not an option, sir,' explained Colbeck. 'I couldn't put handcuffs on a man who was armed with a fire shovel on the roof of a moving train.'

'You shouldn't have got involved in such heroics.'

'With respect, Superintendent,' said Leeming, loyally, 'I think that the inspector deserves profound gratitude. He risked his life in the course of doing his duty. I wouldn't have dared to climb up there.'

'The risk was unnecessary.'

'It didn't seem so at the time,' argued Colbeck.

'Perhaps not.'

'I had to find out *how* it was done before I could accuse James Barrett of the murder. When he realised that I'd found him out, he chose to resist arrest.'

'Resist arrest?' echoed Leeming with a hollow laugh. 'He tried to knock you off the top of that train with a fire shovel. He tried to *murder* you. That's rather more than resisting arrest, Inspector.'

'It was, Victor. I can vouch for that.'

'The main thing,' said Tallis, waving the report in the air, 'is that the murder was solved swiftly by my officers. The Great Western Railway is delighted with the speedy resolution – though shocked to learn that one of its own drivers was responsible for the crime.' He put the report back on his desk. 'The search that you instituted has also borne fruit. The wallet and watch stolen from Matthew Proudfoot were found on an embankment about a mile away from Twyford station. They were wrapped in a silk handkerchief taken from the victim. The watch, I am told, is still in working order.'

'What about the murder weapon?' asked Colbeck.

'That, too, was recovered nearby.'

'As I anticipated.'

'Well,' said Tallis, complacently, 'I think we're entitled to feel rather pleased with ourselves. This case is well and truly closed. It gives me great satisfaction to know that I assigned the right detectives to the investigation.' He gave one of his rare smiles. 'Thank you, gentlemen. The Great Western Railway is in your debt.'

'I can't say that I enjoyed the work,' confessed Leeming, loosening his collar with a stubby finger. 'The simple truth is that I hate trains. I never feel entirely safe in them.'

'You should try travelling on the roof of a carriage,' said Colbeck with a grin. 'You get the most wonderful view of the countryside up there and there's always the possibility that – like James Barrett – you'll reach the end of the line far sooner than you imagined was possible.'

If you liked *Inspector Colbeck's Casebook*,
try Edward Marston's other series . . .

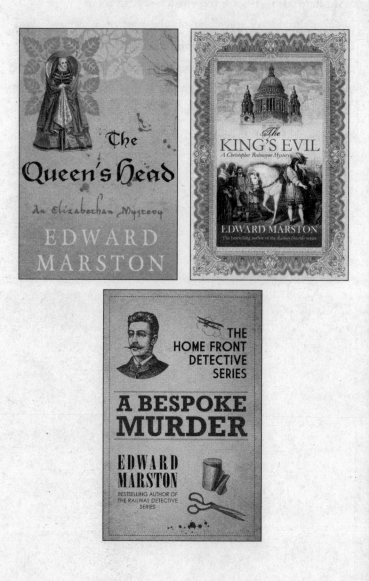

THE
Queen's head
An Elizabethan Mystery
EDWARD
MARSTON

The
KING'S EVIL
A Christopher Redmayne Mystery
EDWARD MARSTON
The bestselling author of the Railway Detective series

THE
HOME FRONT
DETECTIVE
SERIES
A BESPOKE
MURDER
EDWARD
MARSTON
BESTSELLING AUTHOR OF
THE RAILWAY DETECTIVE
SERIES